inside
daisy
clover

inside daisy clover

by gavin lambert

MIDNIGHT
CLASSICS

LONDON / NEW YORK

First published in 1963 by The Viking Press Inc, New York

This edition first published in 1996 by Serpent's Tail,
4 Blackstock Mews, London N4, and
180 Varick Street, 10th floor, New York, NY 10014

Cover design by Rex Ray
Printed in Great Britain by Cox & Wyman Ltd, Reading,
Berkshire

ACKNOWLEDGMENTS

Acknowledgment is made with thanks for permission to
quote from copyrighted material to:

A-M Music Corp.: "I Wonder What Became of Me" by Johnny
Mercer. Copyright © 1946 by A-M Music Corp., New York,
N.Y.

Chappell & Co., Inc.: "Young and Foolish." Copyright © 1954
by Chappell & Co., Inc., New York, N.Y.

Duchess Music Corp.: "The End of a Love Affair" by Edward
C. Redding. © Copyright MCML by Duchess Music Corporation, New York, N.Y. All rights reserved.

Lu-Mel Music, Inc.: "Solitaire" by Luther Henderson and
Charles Burr. Copyright © 1961 by Lu-Mel Music, Inc.

Music Publishers Holding Corp.: "Love is Sweeping the
Country," Copyright 1931 by New World Music Corporation, Copyright Renewed; "Indian Love Call," Copyright 1924 by Harms, Inc., Copyright Renewed.

Pickwick Music Corp.: "Nobody Knows You When You're
Down and Out" by Jimmie Cox. © Copyright MCMXXII,
MCMXXIX by Pickwick Music Corp., © Copyright renewed
MCML, MCMLVI and assigned to Pickwick Music Corp.,
New York, N.Y. All rights reserved.

TO SALKA VIERTEL

inside daisy clover

1

Talking to yourself is something you're not supposed to do, especially in public places such as buses, sidewalks, hot-dog stands, and church. So today—it's the 12th of February, 1951, and it was supposed to rain but didn't, and it's Lincoln's birthday, which in my opinion is a bore, because a particular booth on the pier (of which more later) is closed—I bought this 10½ by 7½ thing called Theme Book. It has a shiny yellow cover and wide marginal ruled pages and cost 25 cents, which anyone will tell you is quite a lot of money these days.

This Theme Book is the sole and private property of Daisy Clover, daughter of Mrs. Lucile Clover, a grass widow otherwise known as The Dealer. It will contain thoughts, secrets, outbursts, and confessions. If I were rich I wouldn't be starting it on ruled pages at all, but on the wall of the biggest john in the world, *which I would build*. See how I am. Anyway, in the years to come—if there *are* any, as The Dealer likes to say—it may be a small thrill to look back on. But I don't suppose anyone will ever read it right through, unless they're morbidly interested in how long little girls can go on pissing for.

Dot, dot, dot. I can smell refried beans and garlic sausage and maybe an old potato, so dinner's ready. It certainly ought to be. The Dealer put all that Mexican junk on the stove hours ago. I'm sitting outside on the steps and the fumes are practically knocking me out, so I don't care to imagine what it's like *inside* our trailer. All the windows have been stuck closed for months.

I should explain why Mother is called The Dealer. It's because she's always playing cards, solitaires, any card game for one person. You name it, she plays it. She has a dozen sets going at the same time, you can hardly move around for the unfinished solitaires. She'll take days over a difficult game, move over to an easier one to calm her nerves, then wait till I've gone out to move back to the difficult one and cheat. She doesn't care to go out much, except to the Mexican delicatessen and the lounge of the Sea Breeze Hotel. This lounge has got TV, and The Dealer sneaks in whenever there's a Bridge Contest showing, but gets thrown out again when the old people, who've fallen asleep in front of the set, wake and find that an intruder has switched channels on them.

The Dealer is quite a small woman, with wild, gray, untidy hair and not much chin. I don't mean this unkindly, but sometimes she reminds me of a pigeon in a fright wig.

I should explain also about this trailer. It's in a park with twenty others, and we live in it. Just The Dealer and me. The Dealer has a husband—which means, if you're smart at figuring out family relationships, that I have a father. Somewhere. Around three years ago he *said* he was going to Seattle to meet a man who had some kind of invention, and they'd be partners. When he gets back, we're supposed to move out of this darned place, but you and I and The Dealer know that he *won't* be back. Ever. Nor will my sister Gloria. Frankly, I used to think that my sister Gloria was a horse's ass. But last month she wrote me quite a nice letter, and said if there's *real* trouble—like The Dealer just can't *connect* any more—I must let her know.

Gloria married this man Harry who's in real estate. The Dealer hated him the first time he ever came around to the trailer. He offered to find us a little house somewhere, but The Dealer told him to lay off the soft soap.

Oh. Let me describe where this trailer is. It overlooks the Pacific Ocean, which in my opinion is a dump. And it's in a kind of town called Playa del Rey, California. That name is the only Spanish thing about it, unless you count the delicatessen where The Dealer buys her refried beans and stuff. The only way I can describe Playa del Rey is that it's a lot of people sitting it out in a cockeyed dump between two other cockeyed dumps called Hermosa Beach and Venice. The beach has oil derricks on it, and there's a huge sewage-disposal plant within sniffing distance.

✳

2nd of March. First Day of Lent.

People might think—on account of where we live, and my being cooped up in this trailer with The Dealer and her solitaires —that I don't have a normal and happy childhood. Well, if they think that, they lack imagination, that's all. Even though I'm adolescent—pushing fourteen, and two buds pushing up like pears on a tree—I am an extremely *happy, adjusted, polite young lady*. It's true I'm quite sophisticated for my age, but that's only skin-deep, and underneath the veneer I'll bet my simple healthy instincts against yours any day. I am also obedient without being sickening, and can shoulder responsibilities (like The Dealer) with a smile. For a few days after Gloria went off I admit I wasn't the life and soul of the party, and I wrote "My sister Gloria is the Pope's nose" on the wall of the girls' john at school —but that was just expressing a rage of the moment. Now I've adjusted. I wrote Gloria a nice long letter, telling her I think she was quite right to go off the way she did. God knows, this trailer was getting crowded with the three of us, anyway.

✳

Here are some things I like to do. I don't include school— which'll be over at the end of this month—or work, which is baby-sitting jobs I get through the Playa del Rey Young People's Association. That just helps to pay the rent, as they say, and means that I sit in somebody else's trailer while they're at the movies and enjoy a cigarette or two. But here's a real kick. Around three o'clock in the morning, when The Dealer's in a deep sleep and I'm alone with the night and the stinking rotten air, *I like to take off my pajamas and look at myself*. I pick my way across the solitaires on the floor and shine a flashlight at the mirror reflecting my body, and I can see those buds are really pushing and I have good legs, etc. Then I say to myself, "Daisy Clover, your beauty will never launch a thousand ships but I don't think the boys will exactly ignore you." Then—if it's sum-

[3]

mer—I go out and sit on the steps for a while, just as I came into the world. So far, I have been totally ignored. The conformity around here is depressing.

I quite like my hair, which is wavy and short and cereal-colored, and I'm mad about my eyes, which are sensational. Great big dark *liquid* eyes. Gloria always said they looked *starved*, and reminded her of those poor little orphans on posters asking you to adopt foreign refugees. "Maria is only six and has never seen a Cadillac. Won't you help?" That kind of stuff. However, Gloria has a weight problem.

Now let's cut this out before it gets embarrassing, and I'll describe what I like best. I like going down to the old pier at Venice, which is a rotting dump like every other place in this whole area, but has this booth for recording your voice. You're supposed to use it for sending messages to loved ones overseas, but I pay my twenty-five cents—saved up from baby-sitting wages—and I go inside and face this old man with a nervous twitch who works the machine, and I SING!

There's no orchestra or anything, of course, and sometimes it feels like a hopeless battle against the surf and people screaming on the Big Wheel and the old man's twitching left eye—but I can sing songs I like and then go home and put the disk in my Oriental casket, which I paid a dollar for because it has a key and I prefer to lock these songs up.

So far I have recorded: "I've Got Five Dollars"—"Isn't It Romantic?"—"They Can't Take That Away from Me"—"Let's Do It"—and "Love Is Sweeping the Country." The only trouble is, I can hardly ever play them afterwards. We don't have a phonograph. However, occasionally I baby-sit in a trailer with a phonograph—and then I get to play them very softly, without waking Baby. Also, I don't want anybody to know about this whole thing. I can't explain why, except that a person is entitled to privacy, and sometimes you just can't let people in on a thing without them trying to take over.

The songs I sing are ones that I really and truly like. They make my palms sweat. I can't explain why I like them, either—except that even if, as The Dealer says, this world is a shithouse and we're just the flies it attracts, there's a moment or two when

[4]

you can sniff another kind of perfume. Dot, dot, dot. I'm an optimist, you see.

For a month now The Dealer has been extremely moody. Yesterday (Mothers' Day—there's a laugh) I found her sitting quite still on the floor like someone in a trance. She was staring at a card in her hand. "This Joker," she said, holding it out to me, "who does he remind you of?"

I said, nobody I knew. "Now come on, you know he's exactly like your father!" The Dealer said. "He's got the same shifty eyes and he's turned up just when I've no use for him."

"Oh, well, that's certainly like him." I decided to make a joke of it, you see, and then I decided to go out and catch a bus to the pier and record "You Are My Sunshine," which I'm ready for. But The Dealer got up and put a hand on my arm.

"Daisy honey, don't go yet, I'll make some coffee." She gave me a long look—which is unusual, because The Dealer hardly ever looks at me. And for some reason she was suddenly like a very old lady. I think she's pushing forty-seven anyway, but right now she was like that lady in *Lost Horizon* when she left Shangri-La and turned into a hundred before you could say James Hilton. It was The Dealer's eyes that had all this age in them. They were staring and fixed as if it was very important to concentrate and cling very hard to the sight of me. All I could do was smile and think, *This is how a raft would feel if it could, a raft in the ocean that sees a drowning face gazing up at it.* Wouldn't a raft in this situation feel *absolutely terrible*—because all the strength it has is used up in keeping itself afloat!

Finally The Dealer patted my hand and said my name quietly a couple of times. Then—"Oh, the coffee!" she said and went to the stove.

I tried to open one of the stuck windows, but it was hopeless.

"You've left school now, haven't you?" The Dealer said.

I nodded.

She didn't answer, but looked pleased. Then: "Tell me, Daisy honey, do you have a good memory?"

"Hell, I don't know. Try me."

"Did you say hell?"

"Yes, I think so."

"It's a terrible word. I should slap you. But can you remember, for instance, when a lot of things around here were considerably *different?*"

"You mean when we had that nice little shack in Hermosa Beach?"

"Well, yes." Her voice sounded doubtful. "That kind of thing."

"Oh, sure, I can remember that."

"What else?"

"What else do you have in mind?"

The Dealer frowned. "Honestly, honey, it's all so confusing."

I guessed what she really meant was, she hadn't always been as crazy as this. (Well, I should hope not.) I said, "Oh no, it's all quite clear! Really."

She gave me that look again, then her eyes wandered. She peered in turn at each solitaire lying around. One set of cards seemed to interest her particularly. Her eyes had a gleam in them as she went over to this solitaire and smartly turned up the jack of diamonds. "*That's* come out, anyway!" she said. The water on the stove was boiling but she took no notice. She was dealing again.

✳

This next bit comes under the heading of Extremely Private and Confidential. Two weeks ago—the day after The Dealer almost made me a cup of coffee—I was on the pier and heading for the booth to record "You Are My Sunshine" when a boy came up and spoke to me. He said his name was Milton, and he'd seen me around. "Around what?" I asked him, and he said, "This old pier." And then he told me that before long this pier was going to be pulled down. "*Dee*-molished!" Milton said with a sweep of his hand. And I thought he was quite nice-looking, he had muscles and butch hair and good teeth, but also a slight weight problem. "Well, that's *dee*-pressing!" I said, and Milton agreed. Then I said, "Considering this whole area is just a rotting slum, why pick on the pier?" Milton told me they have a mania in this country for pulling down old things, there's a cult of newness. He went on to explain that certain old things, such as this

[6]

pier, had charm. And I must say it suddenly seemed very nice and appealing to me, with the loudspeaker shaking and crackling out music, and the bright fading colors on the booths, and the dime-store prizes and sticks of pink salt-water taffy, and the pinball machines nearly all "Out of Order." I got highly indignant that anyone should want to pull this thing down. Most of all, I wondered where I should be able to go and SING, but I didn't mention this to Milton, of course.

Anyway, our mutual affection for this pier led, as you might say, to mutual interest in each other. Instead of recording "You Are My Sunshine"—and possibly "This Can't Be Love," which would have depended on my mood—I spent the afternoon wandering around with Milton. We looked into some very boring old flicker machine which showed two people in old-fashioned costume going to make love. The woman unwound at least thirty feet of hair piled on top of her head, and took off a gown and some petticoats, but still looked more bundled-up than an Eskimo. The man only took off a ring. Finally I said, "Milton, I just don't see how they'll ever make it," and we went off to gamble and lose a bit on the track machine. Then I weighed myself and got a fortune card which said "Plan Your Investments Wisely," and Milton shot a few clay pigeons and won a green ashtray with a nude woman on it, her legs sticking out and "Hit the Spot" written right across her pussy.

On the beach, around seven o'clock, we said good night. I let Milton roll his tongue around my mouth for a bit, which was fine, but he's also a great Ass-Tweaker, which in my opinion is monotonous. He didn't want me to leave, and said the beach was perfectly all right for it—and we were certainly surrounded by people who thought so too, there was enough heavy breathing in the twilight to drown out the surf—but I told him enough is as good as a feast, and I'd see him tomorrow. When I got home, The Dealer was already eating her beans—but extremely moody, and didn't ask why I was late.

I've seen Milton almost every day since. We've been to the movies twice, but the rest of the time—except for the beach at twilight—we can't think of any better place to go than the pier. We've played every machine in the place and put a couple out of order. The pier is really becoming a fixation, like French kisses with Milton. I haven't recorded a song since I met him. And last night, after a siege that should go down in history as Daisy Clover's personal Alamo, the author of these crazy lines had her first experience. *Not* on the beach, but in Milton's father's used-furniture store, on an old brass bedstead without a mattress, priced at $25 and marked VERY NICE. Dot, dot, dot, *dot*.

I may be in love with Milton, and I'll explain why. We were on the pier and out of a clear blue sky I decided to tell him about my recordings. He said, "Well, I never heard of anybody doing that before." Three hours later he mentioned he had a phonograph. After thinking it over and taking my time, I offered to let him play "They Can't Take That Away from Me" and "Love Is Sweeping the Country." While he listened, Milton just chewed gum with a blank expression—his face is often quite blank unless he's feeling sexy—and then he asked, "What's the matter with you, Daisy? You want to be a singer or something?"

Now the point of this story is not that Milton's a pumpkin-head, which is obvious, but *my* reaction. Trying to be cool and not reveal that I was hurt, I asked, "And what's the matter with wanting to be a singer—or something? Don't *you* want to be anything?" Milton only laughed and said, "I'm a bum at heart" —so calmly I wanted to hit him. Then my lover remarked that attractive young studs like himself could be kept by rich older women, and this was really his ideal.

I felt doubly insulted, as a woman and a singer. I burst into tears and swore I'd never speak to him again. The next moment I was permitting him to kiss me, and for a while after that I couldn't speak—but when I could, I heard myself *actually promising* Milton that if I ever got rich I'd keep him!

Since this event, I've been singing "Love can be a sweet endeavor and a dirty shame" under my breath quite often. I suppose Milton must be both.

✻

When I got home today—the 25th of July—there was a police car parked outside the trailer. I went inside and found The

Dealer talking to this cop. She was telling him how her husband started off for Seattle to see a man with an invention, and had disappeared. When the cop asked for details, like the date on which she last saw Mr. Clover, The Dealer said, "Oh, it's too long ago to remember." He looked puzzled, and she said, "Well, it's more than three years."

The cop looked at me. "How about some coffee?" I suggested. He shook his head and asked The Dealer why she'd taken all this time to report her husband's disappearance. "I only started to miss him this morning," The Dealer said. When the cop asked for a description of Mr. Clover, she got up to rummage for something. He was expecting a photograph, but I silently laid 100-1 odds that The Dealer would bring out that darned Joker. Which is exactly what she did. And the cop got sore and accused her of making fun of him, and The Dealer got sore because the cop wouldn't understand that the Joker was a better likeness of Mr. Clover than any photograph.

Finally the cop turned to me and said, "This is ridiculous. Come outside, please." And when we were alone: "How long has your mother been like this?" I honestly couldn't remember when it first hit me that The Dealer was loco, so I said, "Well, she was in pretty good shape when we lived at Hermosa Beach. Then she found out Mr. Clover was carrying on with a cute little widow who lived next door. She turned the garden hose on them both and there was one hell of a scene. She said Mr. Clover beat her up, and I wouldn't be surprised. Anyway, she went on a crying jag for days, then she refused to speak to anybody, and we seemed to be losing her."

The cop seemed quite shaken, so I said, "Don't worry. My sister Gloria has given me instructions to write or phone if there's real trouble." He only sighed. "Is your mother's story about the disappearance of Mr. Clover," he asked, "is that story true?" "Of course it's true," I said. "The Dealer may be loco but she's no liar. My father definitely left for Seattle, or somewhere, and furthermore the widow got out of town a week later."

The cop still looked shaken. He said, "I'd better figure out what sort of report to make." Then he asked how The Dealer and I managed to live. I explained that Mr. Clover had left her some Government bonds when he disappeared. Also, by mistake, his gold cuff-links and tie-pin.

The Dealer came out on the steps now and said, "It's no good asking Daisy. She doesn't remember as well as I do."

When that cop drove off, I felt it was unlikely we'd ever see him again. Let alone my father.

Sometimes, I must admit, The Dealer is too much. She came back today from the delicatessen with three cardboard boxes and started packing furiously. "What the hell do you think you're doing?" I asked, and she explained we had to move, because that stupid cop might find her husband and she didn't want him back. "Last week you said you missed him after all," I reminded her, but she only shook her head and went on stuffing junk into a box. "Listen, let's talk this thing over," I said. "I think we should call up this cop and find out whether he's really got the bloodhounds going."

She wouldn't listen. "Get this, Daisy. *I certainly do not want that Joker around.*" And she insisted I start packing too, because now it was *our* turn to disappear without trace.

I think it's time to call Gloria.

2

Last day of August. New home, new Theme Book. Some low cloud in early morning.

If you happen to walk along the ocean front from Santa Monica pier you'll pass an old mottled pink building with store fronts on the ground floor and towels, brassières, and underpants hanging from the window upstairs. The first store has a sign, UMBRELLAS AND BACK RESTS FOR RENT. Next to it there's a minty café which serves Home-made Chili all day. If you look very closely—which most people don't—you'll see a narrow doorway between the umbrella and back-rest store and the chili all-day café. This doorway leads to a very steep, dark flight of stairs, and these stairs lead to the Paradise Hotel and Apartments. Turn right along the narrow corridor, past the sign NO PETS, and follow it to the end. Behind the last two doors you'll find The Dealer and me.

How The Dealer ran this weird old dump to earth I'll never know. My hunch is, it had something to do with the smell of beans. Anyway here we are, each in a room—mine's the size of a lousy closet—overlooking Muscle Beach, where body builders work out all day. You might describe the neighborhood as slightly run-down, but Milton says it has charm. (I guess if you're brought up in a used-furniture store, you have a different perspective.) Personally, if I was in charge of demolishing the whole area, I'd start with this particular block.

From our rooms we can hear everybody's radio and, when the wind blows in the right direction, music from the carousel on Santa Monica pier. The pier's not much good, except for fishing, but there's a little wooden tram with a canopy that runs all the

[11]

way from here along the ocean front to the pier at Venice, and it certainly saves my life, it's more frequent than the darned buses. Outside the Paradise Hotel and Apartments, on the other side of the boardwalk, is a row of redwood tables where old men sit spitting and playing chess. I'd say they average six expectorations and one move every half-hour. Muscle men wander around in briefs, and winos slump all over the benches. And a few young fellows, all tattooed, just *loaf in doorways* wearing nothing but a pair of Levis. There's one who waits outside the entrance to our hotel, which I've christened the Stairway to Paradise. The Dealer doesn't like him, she always shakes her head and clicks her teeth at him, while *he* always manages to save up a fart for her. This has been going on for weeks.

Our landlord, Mr. Elmer O. Sweeney, is pushing seventy and directed movies when they didn't talk and only ran twenty minutes. He says Sound drove him out of the business and into real estate, which is a flattering description of this hotel, and the seashell and postcard store he owns farther up the block. Three other people room here, all old ladies. Mrs. Angela Schmeldt is pushing eighty, and 200 lbs. as well. She looks like Teddy Roosevelt in female costume, if you can imagine, and can hardly walk but insists on trying. She holds on to a stick and breathes very hard and often she doesn't really seem to be moving in any direction at all, but somehow she makes it. Every day she gasps and rumbles down to Muscle Beach, sits on a bench, and watches the body builders. In the afternoon she calls a cab and visits a friend in the hospital. I call that a strange way to end up—but then, I heard *her* say to Mr. Sweeney that she thought there was something peculiar about The Dealer and me.

The top floor of the hotel is called the Suite, and it's been rented for years by two sisters who tell fortunes on Santa Monica pier. Their booth says CONSULT MARA AND CYNARA, but The Dealer—who's gotten quite friendly with them—calls them Nellie and Minnie. They're on the small side, four feet two maybe without their high heels, they wear high straw hats like upside-down ice-cream cones, and bright colors, mainly heliotrope. Their speciality is a Tarot reading, and since the

Tarot is a pack of cards, The Dealer's getting extremely interested. Sometimes they let her hide out behind a tacky bead curtain in their booth during consultations. I'd say The Dealer is definitely moving toward the Occult now.

It's not the most encouraging environment, but I tell myself all I can do is sit it out. I've recorded "I've Got Plenty of Nothing," which suited my mood somehow, and "It All Depends on You," which I gave to Milton.

Here's something I forgot to mention. My sister Gloria has proved herself to be, beyond any reasonable doubt, Garbage. The Dealer yanked us out of the trailer in such a hurry, it wasn't until the day after a Yellow Cab had brought us smoothly to our destination, that I was able to call Gloria up and say, "Listen, I think The Dealer's flipped her lid." I went through the whole story of her reporting Father's disappearance, and then changing her mind and moving us to the Paradise Hotel and Apartments, but Gloria only said in a very cool superior voice, "That doesn't sound so crazy to me, dear." "Maybe you don't hear so good," I suggested, which made her more grand than ever, and she pointed out that a hotel is more like a home than a trailer, and even the wrong end of Santa Monica is better than Playa del Rey, which has no right end. Then she gave me a lot of stuff about how as long as The Dealer could go on *connecting*—she meant, taking showers, getting her sleep, eating her beans, etc.—there was no reason to worry. "So don't bother me, dear," Gloria said, "unless there's *real* trouble."

"You're a hog's turd."

She hung up on me. I was pretty mad for a while, and seriously thought of sending her quite a lot of unpleasant stuff through the mail.

22nd of September. Yom Kippur. It's raining. Mrs. Angela Schmeldt is fasting, and has stayed in her room all day. Boardwalk's empty. The Dealer's behind that bead curtain on the pier. And I've got an attack of the blues. Mood Indigo in spades, to put it mildly. Milton's father suddenly sold that store, you see, and they left for San Francisco this morning. I know I'll never see him again.

Tick, tock.

Aren't I taking this whole thing about Milton too seriously? It wasn't L-O-V-E that kept us together, it was just S-E-X.

Tick, tock, tick, tock.

So what's wrong with S-E-X keeping two people together? Tick, tock.

And there's more fish in the sea than ever came out of it. TICK, TOCK.

Oh God, it's still raining!

Tick, tock, tick, tock, tick, tock.

Pull yourself together, you little fool! Isn't there a world waiting for you outside? Get up and go into it, or at least open the window and take a look! See? *It's stopped raining!* The darling old people are coming out, like lizards from caves. And who's that weird old girl heading this way? Why, it's the dear old Dealer, of course. Maybe I can persuade her to go out on the town tonight, eat fishburgers on the pier or something.

Well. I've recorded "Shakin' the Blues Away" (jes like dose darkies do). And I guess Milton's not much more than a small ache now.

The Dealer called me into her room this morning. She's sitting up in bed, her hair untidy and a ratty old shawl around her shoulders. The wind's blowing music from the carousel this way. The Dealer holds a card in her hand and stares. It's the Ace of Spades.

"Daisy honey," she says, matter-of-fact and almost pleased, "it seems to have turned up."

I know of course the Ace of Spades means you're going to kick the bucket, but I'm not letting on. Besides, I've no time for this occult junk. "So who does this one remind you of?" I ask.

She shakes her head. "He's always a stranger." And she lies back quite suddenly and closes her eyes.

"What the hell are you doing?"

One eye opens. "Did you say hell?"

"Yes. I say it quite often."

"Well, cut it out." Eye closes. She lies still, breathing quietly. "I'm preparing myself!" This out of the corner of her mouth. "Light me a cigarette, honey."

The Dealer is smoking too much.

She sits in bed all day, puffing through this long ivory holder that's all stained and yellow, and getting ready to meet what she calls The Dealer in the Sky. Minnie and Nellie are quite excited and keep bringing her books about conditions in the Happy Land. I've kept my vow about not bothering Gloria, but I got Mrs. Schmeldt's doctor to come in and cast his stethoscope over The Dealer. He gave her a clean bill of health and said Nellie and Minnie are a couple of idiots. The Dealer only turned her face to the wall and murmured in a pitying voice, "There are more things in heaven and earth . . ."

One thing really worries her. She's made up her mind that Father's dead and she hates the idea of bumping into him in the Happy Land. Her reason for thinking him dead is that she read a newspaper story about a man who had a car wreck at night up on Coldwater Canyon. His body wasn't discovered for a week, and it was half eaten away by wild creatures, birds and maybe some lion that came down from the mountains. There's a hopeful glint in The Dealer's eye when she says she's sure something like this happened to Father. Only, the wild creatures will have been eating *him*, of course, for three years and eight months.

3rd of October. Daisy Clover's birthday. And just wait till I describe it.

She woke up at 8 a.m., not particularly interested in being fourteen. (I mean, she felt so much older, she wondered if The Dealer hadn't got her birth date wrong, along with everything else. It would figure.) She washed her face and dressed, putting on a white sweater and a pair of blue jeans. Outside the window, acres of fog and the surf extremely loud. She heard The Dealer knock over a pile of books next door, went into her bedroom and picked them up. If The Dealer had any idea it was her daughter's birthday, she certainly wasn't letting on. Daisy went to the chili-all-day café, had coffee and an old doughnut. She wondered whether the mail might bring anything from Gloria, and it didn't. There was no reason to expect Milton to write—even if he still cared—because she'd never told him when her birthday was.

It seemed very clear now that the only person in the whole world who knew this was Daisy Clover's fourteenth birthday was—dot, dot, dot—the young lady herself. Depressing? Oh, I wouldn't say that. Typical, maybe. She started thinking about Milton. *If you go on like this, sister, look out for the blues.* So what do people do on their birthdays, I mean when the possibility of celebration is slightly less than nil? Hang around your room and it'll be like the day Milton left, you'll start counting the pink roses on the fading wallpaper, or the pieces of furniture —one Hollywood bed with brown chenille spread, one early Early American rocker, one mahogany commode with (cracked) marble top, two stains on the ceiling, etc.—and then you'll *know* you've got the blues. Didn't someone say, "Work is the Great Healer"? And aren't there times in your life when it's advisable to take stock? Then for Christ's sake let's have some action.

Daisy unlocked her casket, took out Theme Books 1 and 2, went downstairs again, boarded the little tram, and paid her dime for Venice. This time in the morning, the pier was quite empty. There was fog all over the sky, no music yet, an old bum waiting for the track machine to start, and gulls swooping down from the clouds, mewing at the world and taking off again. Daisy was afraid her booth mightn't be open yet, then she saw Twitcher waiting, went inside and recorded "I've Got the World on a String." Pretty good, if she says so herself. The moment she came out she felt so dizzy with hunger she nearly fainted. A hot dog hit the spot. Her palms were sweaty, she wiped them with a paper napkin and noticed this man staring at her. He was thin, long legs and arms, dressed all in black corduroy with a cap, and pushing thirty-five. He stood resting one elbow on an

Out of Order pinball machine and one hand on his crotch. Humdrum? O.K., but she suddenly noticed he had small pale, angry, *hypnotic* eyes, real gimlets, and it came to her in a flash he was a sex maniac.

Extremely casual, she turned away, hummed "Shall We Dance?" and walked slowly down to the beach. He followed, keeping the distance they do in the movies. She could tell without looking that he never took his eyes off her. The beach was all gray sand and silence like a desert on the edge of the ocean, no one in sight, rows of empty lifeguards' towers stretching away, a bad smell of fog, tar, and seaweed. She was alone with the elements and a maniac, and it was her birthday, but she felt surprisingly relaxed and calm. She took off her sneakers and paddled in the water. Chilly, not too clean, but she acted as if it was a beautiful summer's day. She turned her face to the sky, making believe there was sun instead of fog and cloud, she waved her Theme Books and skipped a little. The man just watched. After a while her feet felt as if they'd turned blue, she came out of the water and bent down to put on her sneakers. When she looked up, the man was standing over her. He didn't smile or anything, but asked quietly what her name was. Because she was feeling in a special kind of mood, she said Gloria. Then she asked if he had any candy. The man shook his head and asked what kind she liked. Peanut Brittle, she told him. He offered to buy her some. She said she had to go now but maybe they could meet later. She gave him Gloria's phone number and suggested he call around five o'clock. He wanted her to stay, naturally, and promised her a ride on the Big Wheel and a movie and almost anything she could name, but Daisy said she was very sorry but she'd get into trouble if she didn't go home right now. She touched the maniac's hand, it was hard as a shell, then she winked, said to be *sure* and call Gloria's number around five o'clock—and beat it. She tore up the beach and didn't look back until she reached the little tram. He was still near the shore, black and strange like a person just arrived from the sea.

The tram back to Santa Monica was full of old people not talking, and fog was spilling over everything like a stain. Only the chess players were out, and a dog and two women with rods and baskets, going to the pier to fish. Daisy walked up to Palisades Park, the really elegant section with trees and beds of flowers laid out, and a path along the edge of the cliff. There was no one around except an old lady painting. She saw Daisy, sniffed the fog, and called out in a very British accent, "Lovely day!" Daisy didn't answer but walked on and sat down under a palm tree. She had no idea what to do. She flicked through her Theme Books and thought, What's the use of taking stock when you have a ledger as crazy as this? She was certainly right in the middle of the rottenest birthday anyone ever had. If the sky opened now and a voice said you can have one wish, it would be to wipe out every single thing she could remember or see, start all over again asleep and bulging in some foreign woman's belly and come out feet first thousands of miles away. In Tahiti, maybe.

It was much too silent, only a faint traffic thud from the highway down below and a funny little sound like a gasp from the palms above her head. She felt something had to be done right now, before this panic in the air really took over. She put her hand over her mouth and hollered a couple of times like an Indian. It didn't do much, only startled the old lady. "Home, James?" she said next, putting on a British accent. Then, still sitting there and leaning back against the tree, she started humming "You Are My Sunshine." After a few bars she was singing, and by the last verse fairly belting it out to the fog. The old lady stared up from her painting, not liking this at all. Suddenly, for no reason except she needed a good laugh, Daisy imagined the sex maniac calling up Gloria for a date at five o'clock. It was funny all right, but the laughter turned into crying and made the old lady put down her brush and run over in a state of alarm. Well, that was the last thing Daisy wanted, so she got up very calmly and said, "Hey, my ass is damp, watch out that doesn't happen to yours," and walked away leaving the old goose speechless.

Here comes the pay-off. She'd walked maybe a dozen steps when a terrific whoop of sirens seemed to come from every direction at once. A fire engine rushed past, then a police car. Daisy looked toward the pier and saw the fog was darker over there. She began to run, and when she got nearer she saw a crowd of people on the ocean front, all pushing each other and gawking. Flames roared out of the Paradise Hotel and Apartments. As Daisy pushed her way through the crowd someone let out a Bronx cheer. They were all craning their necks, so Daisy craned hers too, and there was The Dealer! being hoisted out of a second-floor window and sent careering down the fire escape in her nightgown and ratty old shawl. She never looked weirder. It made quite a group when she joined Mrs. Schmeldt, who must have worn a wig all along because now she was in her usual black but completely bald, and the Tarot sisters, who'd skipped over from their booth in Oriental hand-me-downs.

The rest is too sickening to describe, and I'm afraid I can't get a laugh out of it. It's Daisy, you see, being told she can't go up and rescue those records in the casket under her bed. Just having to stand there and wait while part of the roof and most of her hopes fall in. And finally—after what seemed like a year and a day but was maybe half an hour—staring like an idiot at the Paradise Hotel, which is now a complete mess with a little pile of melted wax somewhere inside it.

The smoke clears and the crowd drifts away, except for a few people who hang around and snigger while a cop questions The Dealer. Elmer O. Sweeney had suddenly turned on her, in a great rage and with a smudge on his face, and said, "*You* started it!" It turns out he only spoke the truth. While getting ready for the Happy Land, and reading some mystic trash with a cigarette burning away in that holder, The Dealer dropped off to sleep and woke up in flames. So we reluctantly say farewell to Daisy Clover on her fourteenth birthday, standing on the boardwalk in a pair of old jeans and her dreariest sweater, holding in one hand "I've Got the World on a String" and in the other the story of her life.

3

~~~~~~~~~~~~~~~~~~~~~~~~~~~~~~~~~~~~~

The book is another book and the year is another year and I'm more than an inch taller and I've let my hair grow too. It's practically shoulder length and has a Bang in front. I copied the style from *Mademoiselle*, it's supposed to make you look more feminine. In my case I'm wondering if it hasn't turned me into a slob. This morning I looked in the mirror and thought, What the hell, I'll give it a run. Too late to change it now, anyway, because the Limousine had drawn up and caused a small sensation, and a couple of stupid kids were following this old driver across the courtyard—

Let's try and get some kind of order into this thing. The date is 14th of April, 1952. You'll notice the piss has been running dry for a few months. That's because this has been the Winter of My Discontent, and if I hadn't refused to give up the ship—

For Christ's sake, you're making no more sense than The Dealer! And reading *Mrs. Parkington* by Louis Bromfield seems to have ruined your style! Count up to ten, will you, and then take it *step by step*.

1 2 3 4 5 6 7 8 9 10! O.K. Before we get to the Big News, let's clear up a couple of minor items. The sex maniac never called Gloria—at least, she's still alive. I wrote Milton at Christmas and got no answer. This disgusted me. I decided not to get involved again for a while. If you saw the neighborhood kids, you'd realize there wasn't much temptation, anyway. There's a couple of them I let take me to the movies, but they'll never make first base. I've got a reputation for being prissy with boys, which is quite a laugh.

After the fire, The Dealer and I moved to the top floor of an old house on the waterfront near Venice. It's a Spanish joint and must have been pretty fancy once. Inside, there's an open courtyard with balconies running all the way around each floor. We go up two flights of iron steps and past lines of washing to reach our apartment, which is one big room with three alcoves—not bad for $35 a month. The alcoves are screened off with bead curtains. Behind the first one there's a kitchen, behind the second a bath and a john, and behind the third there's me. I wouldn't call it inspirational, but somehow it's got more style than the Paradise Hotel.

The Dealer doesn't stay in bed any more, since that Ace of Spades was obviously a bum steer and she still has a while to go. She thinks it might have been a sign about Father. Meanwhile, the burns are healed, and it's back to the solitaires.

Soon after we moved in, I got this idea of cadging or stealing old copies of high-class magazines like *Reader's Digest* and *Coronet*, and selling them to people in markets for a dime. I found that, especially when old ladies are peeking at magazines on newsstands in the markets, wondering whether to part with a quarter or more, I could nip in and tempt them with a slashing reduction on a five-year-old *Reader's Digest*. "Don't waste your money on that flashy new stuff," I told them. "The old ones are still the best. Everything I've got is just packed with good reading. And you'll be helping to send a poor kid to summer camp next year."

This little racket earned me a dollar a week. I got banned from two markets for soliciting, which meant I had to take the little tram and extend my operations farther up the coast, but it was worth the extra overhead because after three months I'd made new records of all my best numbers on the pier. Just in time, by the way, because shortly after I'd completed the set with "Let's Do It" Twitcher had a stroke and went out of business.

I'll explain why having my little recordings again was so important—apart from the psychological boost, I mean. If I hadn't made them, I could never have entered the Talent Contest sponsored by the Bay Area Markets in Association with Magnagram Studios, and Mr. Raymond Swan would never have cried when he heard my rendition of "Love Is Sweeping the Country," and sent this limousine for me, so big it could hardly get down the alley. It looked pretty funny, you can imagine, parked outside this run-down Spanish joint on the waterfront. A lady ran out very excited from the Twilight Convalarium next door, to ask the driver what mortuary he was from and whose body he'd come to collect.

The body in question had been spending a nervous two hours wondering what the hell to wear to the studio. Most of my clothes are slacks and sweaters and casual stuff like that. The kind of life I lead, why buy anything formal? I settled on something The Dealer picked out for me a couple of years ago as a party dress. It's a sickening little white number with too many flounces—I told The Dealer at the time it would have been all right if I'd still been pushing eight—but it was the only clean thing I had with a skirt.

When I came down the iron steps wearing this skimpy Alice in Wonderland outfit, too tight under the arms and only just reaching my knees, the old driver certainly gave me a stare. I played it cool, waited for him to open the door of the limousine for me, and told him I'd like to stop on the way for a Coke. He said we'd be late, but I gave him this line—which I'd read in some article about a big Norwegian soprano—about having to lubricate my vocal cords. He fell for it.

In Beverly Hills it started to rain, and I felt pretty grand rolling by in this luxurious automobile and for once not being part of the bus-shelter crowd. I suppose I ought to have been concentrating on the impression I was going to make on Mr. Swan and all that, but the whole thing somehow didn't feel real yet, and my mind wandered all over the place. I thought about myself getting rich and keeping Milton. (If he'd answered my Christmas letter, he might have stood a chance.) I thought of all the stuff, like a gift-wrapped baby cobra, I might have sent Gloria through the mail. I even wondered if my father and that little widow were making out somewhere under false names, and imagined the story in the newspapers when they were unmasked. In those stories a neighbor always says, "They were such a quiet, friendly couple." All these idiot ideas reeled through my brain

[22]

as we drove, and suddenly there was a big sign saying MAGNA-
GRAM and a cop was peering in at me through the window.

We'd reached the entrance to some large ordinary dump. I
looked around and saw high wire fences and rows of gray buildings without windows. What with the cop standing there, it felt
for a moment like we were waiting outside a jail. I should explain that I've never been movie-struck, I always go to Cary
Grant pictures and I admire Myrna Loy for her poise, but the
idea of getting in the movies and hobnobbing with all that
crowd never meant much. I want to sing, but that's different.
So I wasn't disappointed that Cary and Myrna and Clark and
Ingrid weren't lined up at the gates to welcome me. Anyway,
the cop grinned and said, "Good luck, Daisy!" and we moved
on again, through various alleys with these barns on each side
saying Stage 23, etc., and a few trailers parked outside. It's a
funny thing, but I can't look at a trailer these days without
being almost overcome by an imaginary smell of beans. Fortunately, sitting on the steps of one of them, I saw a nun in
bright orange make-up, smoking a cigarette, and this jolted me
back to reality, as you might say. The doors to one of the stages
were wide open, and I also noticed some kind of backcloth
with purple mountains, a ring of spotlights, and horses looking
patient but sad. Finally we came to some office blocks with a
bit of lawn in front, and stopped. The driver opened the door
and as I stepped out—*wham!* The panic hit me. I felt ridiculous
and sick and looked about wildly for a hole in the ground.
Somehow I followed the driver into the gray building, past another cop and a cigarette machine with a mirror—I saw someone in this mirror and didn't recognize her, then we connected, and I started up a flight of stairs like I'd been shot out
of a cannon. The driver turned along a wide green corridor. We
passed a couple of businessmen-types with very white shirts and
a tall girl carrying a coffee percolator. They all stared at me.
Finally the driver started to open a green door marked PRI-
VATE.

"JUST A MINUTE!" I said, so loudly I startled him.

"What's the matter?"

"Nothing. But just a minute!"

[23]

I'd sidestepped to the wall and stood leaning my back against it. When I closed my eyes I saw pink and yellow dots. When I opened them, I *thought* I saw Myrna coming down the corridor. But it wasn't, and for some reason this did the trick.

"I can make it now," I said.

It's only the outer office, of course, with a desk and a typewriter and a vase of flowers and a secretary. She's a cheerful auntie, wired for sound.

"So this is Daisy!" Looks me up and down several times and doesn't seem to bat an eye. "My, what a pretty dress!"

If she means it, she's out of her mind, and if she doesn't, then it must be so awful she's trying to reassure me. Either way I'm nervous. We smile at each other for a few centuries, then her machine crackles and she wonders why I didn't bring my mother.

I look so startled, it alarms her. "Oh, no!" My voice comes out an octave too high. "She's feeling under the weather today. It's probably the twenty-four-hour flu. There's a lot of that flu deal around and it's better not to fool with it. Stay in bed, I mean!"

Something tells me I overplayed that hand. She bats an eye now, you can see it, and her voice has that tone which means I'm changing the subject. "Well, I guess this is the most exciting day of your life, Daisy?"

"Well, I guess you've guessed right." I'm disgusted with myself for even *thinking* I could get away with a line like that, and I feel like diving under the desk—but she surprises me by laughing. She twinkles. I feel I'm recovering lost ground.

Then she does a strange thing. She frames her eyes by holding up her hands at right angles to her cheekbones, and peers out at me like a horse between blinders. I think my mouth starts to drop open. Anyway—

"I'm just trying to imagine how you'd photograph," she explains.

"Like a horse's—" I stop myself just in time. "Honestly, I've never had a picture taken that I like."

Wrong move, but it doesn't matter. There's a weird buzzing noise, a door opens automatically, and Mr. Swan—it has to be Mr. Swan—stands looking at me. I suppose because of his name

I expected someone tall and slim with a long neck, but he turns out to be a broad-shouldered fellow with a weight problem, and the most beautifully manicured shining nails I've ever seen. He doesn't smile or anything, but as automatically as the door opened I'm looking *up* at him—way, way *up*—as if he's on the top of a mountain, *his* mountain, which I've started climbing by mistake. He reminds me of that old King Stag in *Bambi*, although I'd say he's only just pushed fifty.

After a moment he says, "Daisy Clover, come on in." He has a voice you wouldn't expect, very soft and quiet but not friendly. It seems to come from far away. Then he holds out his hand, which you also wouldn't expect. I mean, he does it in such a way—like the Pope in a newsreel—that for an insane moment I feel I'm supposed to kiss it. It's a thick dark square hand with freckles, and those nails almost like mother-of-pearl. No ring, though. I go over, he takes my wrist, and we start to walk, the door gives out that buzz and closes itself behind us. I'm standing on a gorgeous Oriental rug and staring at an antique clock in a glass case. You can see the pendulum swinging. This clock's on a black desk the size of a grand piano, next to it there's telephones and stuff and a photograph of a lovely woman who looks like she ought to be a movie star. Maybe it's the combination of the way everything's arranged and the whiff of Mr. Swan's perfume that I'm getting, so cool and *expensive* I want to shut my eyes—but I feel I'm looking at an altar in a church, and I wouldn't be surprised if an organ started to play.

Mr. Swan leads me to an enormous old chair with a high back and I sit there. Then he goes around to his desk, but doesn't sit. We're like twenty feet apart. Behind him on the wall there's a bright splotchy painting. The room feels extremely quiet. I guess it must be soundproofed. When Mr. Swan opens a drawer in his desk there's a kind of rumbling echo. He takes out an envelope and stares at it. Not looking at me, he snaps out suddenly in a very hard businesslike voice—

"All right, Daisy. I've got fifteen minutes. What do you want to see me about?"

Naturally I'm taken aback and stammer out something about thinking *he* wanted to see *me*.

"Why should I be interested in seeing you, Daisy?"

"You've got me there," I tell him, recovering my poise now and thinking that Mr. Swan is a man who likes to play games. "But if you go to the trouble of sending a limousine all the way to Venice, I'd say you must have something on your mind."

He looks at me now, and for the first time he almost smiles. "Maybe it's this," he says. And he opens the envelope and takes out my record of "Love Is Sweeping the Country."

I feel I'm getting wise to Mr. Swan's character, so I go poker-faced and ask him what he's holding in his hand. He reacts as if he didn't hear this. "I'm not ashamed," he tells me, very slow and serious, "I'm not ashamed to say it made me cry."

This is flattering, of course, but somehow I can't imagine Mr. Swan crying. "That's an upbeat song, you know. It's supposed to make you feel good."

"It did, Daisy. It made me feel very good."

"Well, I've got some more. I've done 'Isn't It Romantic?' and 'They Can't Take That Away from Me' and—"

"Why do you tell me that?" he interrupts, back on the snapping tack. "What do you expect I'm going to do for you, Daisy? Give you a contract to sign and make you a little movie star?"

I don't say anything.

"You're certainly dressed up for something," he goes on. "Is that your best dress?"

I tell him it's a matter of opinion.

"It's a matter of *my* opinion that it makes you look like a fool," he says, really cutting me down to size. "But I'm glad you're wearing it, Daisy. It shows you've some innocence left."

"Don't be too sure." (I'm going to give it to him now.) "And if you've only got five minutes, maybe you should get to the point!"

"There's no point." He pauses to light a cigarette. I could kill him. "I like your recording, Daisy. That's all. You can go now."

Well, it's obvious that Mr. Raymond Swan is a deeply disturbed human being, not to say a nut, but I refuse to get mad because that's what he wants. From now on he can whistle for free kicks from me. I walk over to the door, extremely cool, turn the handle—and can't get the darned automatic thing

[26]

open. I pull at it and hit it, nothing happens, I'm really furious and a bit scared and I'll never forgive myself if I start to cry and I don't want to look at Mr. Swan because I know he's laughing. So I take a leap at his desk and start flipping every switch and pressing every button, thinking that one of them's got to spring me. *Nothing happens!* I have to look at the old gadget-fiend now, tears brim over, and I decide I like him less than anybody in the world.

"Daisy," he says, "I like you very much. You've got a sense of humor."

"Oh," I manage to come back, wiping my eyes. "I didn't know it showed. Just open that door, will you, and I'll get the hell out of here."

He shakes his head. "Sit down. I don't want you to leave yet."

"Okay." I obey, and flash him a smile. "I was hoping you'd say that, Mr. Swan. I'm having such a good time."

Something buzzes on his desk, he flips a switch, and the secretary's voice comes over one of the thingamadoodles. "Mrs. Swan is here, Mr. Swan." He doesn't answer, but flips back the switch, presses a jigger *under* the desk, and the door opens.

It's the lady of the photograph. She's very tall and lovely, but she couldn't be a movie star because her hair's gray. She wears a stunning outfit, bright red, and huge chunky bracelets.

"Melora," Mr. Swan murmurs, she smiles at him, then comes straight over to my chair and without any kind of preliminary looks absolutely *through* me, the tip of her tongue just sticking out between her marvelous teeth, like a cat remembering cream. I'd say Mrs. Swan has what they call Drive.

"Not pretty," she says finally, "but my God those eyes."

I can take anything now. "Do they remind you of foreign orphans on posters?"

She's surprised, but she laughs. "Well, I could certainly adopt you for them." They exchange glances, obviously thinking I'm a character.

"It was my sister Gloria's idea," I explain, and Mrs. Swan suddenly runs her hand through my hair. She says, "Tell me about your family, dear."

"It's small. I have this sister Gloria who married a man in real estate, and my mother who's got the twenty-four-hour flu."

"What about your father?"

"Vamoosed, four years ago."

They exchange glances again. Then Mrs. Swan gives Mr. Swan a funny kind of nod. And he says, "Well, if that's how you feel, we could use Julie's bedroom set and shoot her there this afternoon."

I'm not saying a word, naturally, but my mind's working fast. Isn't this whole Talent Contest just a front for a cannibal organization headed by the Swans? The Bay Area Markets must be in it too. They lure young and tender human flesh to the studio, take it to one of those barns and kill it, then ship it out in a truck with MAGNAGRAM painted on the side to put people off the scent. They can cover up as much as they like, giving me this line about how we're going to get some lunch in the commissary first, then send me to Wardrobe and Make-Up, then put me on a set and make me sing—but you can bet your bottom dollar they'll slip me a drugged Coke on the way.

So I'm not saying a word, though I've got news for Mr. Swan. Bluebeard's Eighth Wife is sitting right in this chair!

A few telephone calls later—it seemed to me that Mr. Swan was calling up everyone in the studio and snapping out orders—we're sitting around this table in a small room. There's a main restaurant where most people eat, but we're important—I can see no one here is more important than Mr. Swan—so we go straight into this adjoining place where the paint's fresher and the windows have fancy shutters. It's empty except for us.

Mr. Swan's extremely charming, he doesn't try and put me down at all, but passes the menu and asks if I see anything I like. Of course I realize this is part of the fattening-up routine, but I'm not saying a word, and order Chicken Gregory Peck. Mrs. Swan only nibbles cottage cheese and fruit because she's on a diet, but Mr. Swan has his special, a big rare steak with french fries—1500 calories worth, I'd say. They ask me a lot of questions—all about movies, they don't seem to talk about anything else—and want to know my favorite pictures of all time. I explain I'm not really a fan at all, but *Mrs. Parkington* hit the spot and I liked the book too. Also, anything with Cary Grant or Myrna I'm liable to see twice around. Mrs. Swan says that's a very sophisticated list, and I tell her I've been called that word before, but it's only skin-deep. This makes her laugh, and she says to call her Melora. Mr. Swan doesn't ask me to call him Ray.

Over the raspberry sherbet, though, he does ask me if I've heard of Mary Pickford. I tell him yes, but that's about as far as it goes. "Is she in the commissary or something?" He shakes his head, and explains that he's going to make a musical picture called *Little Annie Rooney*, and it was once a movie with Mary Pickford, in the silent days. "If it was silent, I guess it wasn't a musical then?" I ask him, and he says, "That's right, Daisy." It's not easy to get with all of this, but I suppose he knows what he's doing. Then, without finishing his sherbet, Mr. Swan suddenly jumps up, looks irritable, and asks why the hell Wardrobe didn't call him back, and we'd better go. I gulp down the rest of my dessert, and wouldn't you know that the first movie star of the day comes up just as I'm wiping a pink dollop off my chin?

She's wearing a kind of green housecoat that trails to the ground, and make-up as bright as that nun's outside the trailer. It's Julie Forbes! I remember when we lived at Hermosa Beach and The Dealer was in better shape, she used to say Julie Forbes was the greatest. You'd certainly know at once she was a star, just like you know the Swans are millionaires. Everything about her's so *bright*, the green of her housecoat thing and the red of her nails and the blonde of her hair. FANTABULOUS is the only word. But behind her there's a real spook, a woman with a white butch haircut and shoulders as broad as Mr. Swan's. She's dressed like a cowboy, Levis and an old denim shirt, and her name is Carmen.

Julie Forbes kisses Melora and Mr. Swan, Carmen kisses Melora and shakes Mr. Swan's hand, and then I'm introduced. Miss Forbes impresses me as an extremely gracious lady. She tells Mr. Swan what an attractive kid I am, then gives me a big smile. "I'd like you to meet my Timmy. He's a great kid, too."

"He's only six and a half," Carmen says.

"Timmy's very advanced for his age," Miss Forbes points out. "They'll get along fine. They can swim in the pool."

Melora asks how her picture's going, and Miss Forbes says, "Great. It's going to be just great." They go into a lot of details I don't understand, except it seems some director was giving Miss Forbes trouble, but she's fixed him now. Also, they don't have a title for the picture yet. The book was called *All Men Are Ghosts*, but you can't use it. Mr. Swan agrees, then looks suddenly irritable again and says we have to go over to Wardrobe.

Right where I'm standing now it's very bright—but beyond all this light, everything looks very dark. Somewhere, people I *can't* see are hammering. Anybody I *can* see is a shadow. There used to be a machine on the old pier at Venice—it went Out of Order about a year ago—which showed you figures dancing and bobbing up and down in silhouette. This is what it looks like now. Way up above, on a platform, there's an old man grinning and pointing a spotlight at me. Suddenly there's a flash and a *pop!* People yell "Look out!" and little pieces of something start coming down like hot red rain. The lady from Wardrobe explains that a bulb exploded and it happens occasionally.

I've been made up, just like the nun and Julie Forbes, and put into some kind of old-fashioned costume that makes me feel like the kid sister in *Little Women*. The lady from Wardrobe keeps on saying she isn't entirely satisfied. She brings me different ribbons and things to try on, but frowns and shakes her head when she sees the result. If she pulls this act once more, I'll get snippy. Mr. Swan and Melora are talking to this fellow in a check shirt and baseball cap, standing beside a camera. Mr. Swan says there's something wrong with the background. And in front of my eyes two men start wheeling away this backcloth with trees and stuff painted on it. I should explain that where it's very bright there's a big brass bedstead, against which I'm presently leaning. It's newer than the one in Milton's father's used-furniture store, but otherwise *exactly* the same, and it brings back memories. There's also an Early American chair that reminds me of the Paradise Hotel and Apartments, and a window looking out on this backcloth they've just removed. Mr. Swan was certainly right, because if I looked out the window I could see only the very tops of the trees, which made me feel much too high up—almost in the clouds, as you might say, except there weren't any. Now they wheel in some new deal with a few shrubs and geraniums in pots and I guess a bird bath. "That's better!" says Mr. Swan.

Here's something else. A piano coming from nowhere. They leave it on the edge of the darkness, a man strums a few chords, then comes over and tells me we should run through my number. I tell him I've got ten thousand frogs in my throat. He goes over to Melora, who comes over to me and says, "Honey, would you like a Coke or something?" I admit I could use a crate of the stuff, and she calls to someone, "Miss Clover wants a Coke!" Then the Wardrobe lady's back saying, "Try *this*, honey," and clamps some chain with a locket around my neck. I look at her, narrowing my eyes and *daring* her not to like it. She seems to get the message, because she mutters, "Cute!" and goes off again. Now some man brings me a Coke, but it's warm and leaves me slightly nauseated.

"How's the voice now?" The piano player's back again. I let out a note which sounds like wild geese calling to me, but he smiles and says it seems to be all there. So we move over to the piano and I go straight into—

> *"Love is sweeping the country,*
> *Waves are hugging the shore.*
> *All the sexes*
> *From Maine to Texas*
> *Have never known such love before—"*

and he's just about caught up with me by the time I leave off. "Don't worry, my friend," I tell him, "I keep a good strong steady beat going in this one, and all you've got to do is follow it." Then I turn away quickly so he can't see my face, because I'm thinking *And what the hell chance has this caper got? I've never had an accompanist in my life before, all I know is that booth on the pier and poor old Twitcher, so keep clear of this eager piano player, in fact don't let anybody in on anything or they'll take over, wait for 1-2-3-Go! and shoot the works as if—*

Dot, dot, dot.

Would you believe it?

I passed out! I fainted! I actually swooned! Started to keel over, they told me afterward, and it was lucky the lady from Wardrobe happened to be coming after me with another ribbon or something, because she caught me in her arms and stopped my fall. When I came around and blinked my eyes open, I was lying on the big bed under all the blazing lights, and Mr. Swan and Melora and the piano player and the whole gang were staring down at me. For a moment I couldn't think who they were. Then I said, "I'm okay. I'm just not used to those hot lights." So Mr. Swan orders them to be turned off, and then I'm lying almost in darkness and people are shadows. The sensation is so refreshing that although I'm feeling fine again I close my eyes for a few seconds, and imagine this is a magic bed, and it's starting to float—way, way up to the roof of this dump, which opens, and we're in the sky, it's night, the moon's simply gorgeous and Milton's waiting on it. I'm really reluctant to come down to earth again, but all kinds of whispers are breaking through now, so I look up at Melora and say, "It's the first time this has ever happened!" "Of course, honey, you must be under a strain," she answers. "I don't mean this test or whatever you call it," I tell her. "I mean it's the first time I ever actually fainted!"

I start to get off the bed, but Mr. Swan puts his hand on my arm and says, "Lie still, Daisy, till the doctor gets here." I tell him I'm fine, but he insists I'm not to move till the studio doctor's looked me over. So I lie back again, think of something, and burst out laughing. Melora asks what's so funny, and before I can stop myself I say, "Of course that warm Coke was drugged, that's what did it!" and let out another hoot. They look at me like I'm out of my mind, and I can't explain this whole joke, obviously, so I say I must have been dreaming, and the Wardrobe lady whispers, "Is she hysterical?" Then the doctor arrives and takes my pulse and listens to my heart and I stick out my tongue at him, etc. He murmurs something about a rush of adrenalin to Mr. Swan, and thinks it's absolutely all right for me to start singing. The man in the baseball cap says *he's* ready, the Wardrobe lady and the make-up man and the hairdresser start tugging and patting and combing me all at once, a man comes up and holds a tape measure under my nose, Mr. Swan asks if I remember about the chalk marks, and I do, then from all around there's a *tsssss!* and a crackle and all the lights come up. The whole place seems suddenly very bright, I can hardly see anything in the darkness now, just figures moving about and one person in green—a strong sharp green you can't miss. It's Julie Forbes come over to watch.

Am I nervous? Frankly, now that the chips are down, I'm as surprisingly relaxed as I was that day I skipped in the ocean and hummed "Shall We Dance?" in front of the sex maniac. So, if they want to stick me in this bedroom wearing this heavy old skirt and a ribbon in my hair, and sing "Love Is Sweeping the Country" looking out the window at this backcloth with geraniums and a bird bath—Okle-dokle, that's all I can say, it's Okle-dokle with me!

Just before we start, I hear Julie Forbes whisper to Melora, "You can tell that kid's a trouper." Then they're calling "Quiet, please!" etc., and Mr. Swan says in his quietest, coldest, farthest-away voice, "Daisy," the piano player rattles out a few chords, and we're off to the races. As far as I'm concerned, this whole enormous barn shrivels right up and I'm back in that booth and can just hear the sound of the ocean. And it all seems to be over before it started—until Mr. Swan says, "Uh-huh, Daisy, now let's do it over again," and the camera starts forward like it's out to get me. This happens three more times, and by the end I'm practically nonchalant and the piano player gives no trouble at all. My voice cracked a bit the last time around on "There never was so much Love," but otherwise they could have signed me up on the spot for Carnegie Hall. Melora comes over and kisses me—lightly, though, on the forehead—and Mr. Swan says, "You did pretty well, Daisy, considering everything," which I guess is a big hand from *him*, and even Julie Forbes tells me she knows talent when she sees it! They turn off the lights, and someone slides back the wide door at the other end of the barn. Outside, it's dusk and raining again.

I can just hear the rain, hissing down beyond the cables and the scaffolding and all the different scenery, and I look at the shadows moving around, and suddenly I'd like to say—Listen, if you let me out of this costume and stuff, and lean me against the piano or something, I'll give you "Let's Do It," and you'd get much more for your money. But then I think, Maybe they wouldn't agree.

Obviously I'm confused. And my head aches, and my throat's hoarse, and right now the only way you could keep my eyes open would be to prop up the lids with matchsticks. Good night.

4

~~~~~~~~~~~~~~~~~~~~~~~~~~~~~~~~~~~~~~~

Good morning.

I woke up and saw The Dealer sitting very thoughtful at the end of my bed. She looked at me, which as I've said before is unusual and means she has something on her mind. I should explain that when I got home from the studio last night, she was deep in at least two solitaires and hardly noticed me. I went straight through my bead curtain, wrote in my Theme Book, and hit the sack.

She watched me yawn. Then she said, "Daisy honey."

I yawned again.

"Shall I make some coffee?"

I knew she wouldn't so I said, "Fine, go ahead."

"I will," she said, and didn't move.

I waited for whatever was coming.

Finally The Dealer said, "It's nine o'clock. Why don't you get up?"

"I'm moving toward it."

She sighed. "And what took you so long yesterday?" Before I could answer, she went on: "I hear you went off in somebody's car. You shouldn't accept rides from strangers."

"It was nothing," I told her. "Just some people who came to put me in the movies."

"You mean, cops?"

"Will you try and concentrate?" I said. "It's nothing to do with the cops. It's the MOVIES!"

She looked extremely at sea.

"I've never told you this before," I said, "but I can sing."

Now she was thrown for a loop.

"I open my mouth," I explained, "and a song comes out."

She put her head on one side and gave me a suspicious look. "Show me!"

After yesterday I felt like resting up, but it was a situation that had to be made clear, so I took a deep breath and launched into a few bars of "Let's Do It." The Dealer listened very carefully. I could see her thinking it over and her face wrinkling in a deep frown. "Now that's pretty dirty stuff, you know," she said finally.

"Okay, here's something clean." I gave her the first verse of "Isn't It Romantic?" She seemed to enjoy it, and asked what else I knew.

"Quite a bit," I told her, "but I'm not going through my whole repertoire now. Not before I've had coffee, anyway."

"I'll make it," she said. Didn't budge, of course. So I yawned, lay down again, and asked if she felt I'd put her in the picture now.

"You're getting fresher every day," she came back at me, rather unexpected. "I should slap you. I'm always in the picture."

"That's fine. So if I go off again, it's to be put in the movies. It may never happen, because yesterday was only a test. But I think they liked me." I was talking more to myself now.

The Dealer nodded and went back to her cards. I got up and made coffee.

Mr. Swan had said, "We'll call you tomorrow, Daisy." Now I still don't care about being in the movies, of course, and—wait a moment, what the hell, scratch, that's the most solid lie I ever told. Like a sail needs wind I want to get in the movies! Now I'm really awake and have swallowed some coffee, it's just hitting me that yesterday the test was really another test, because in spite of everything *I still meant what I sang*. It's hard to make sense when you're waiting for an extremely important telephone call, but that's what I've suddenly discovered and I know it's why I'm feeling so good!

Later. Feeling so discouraged I can't write out anything properly. Here's the log—

9:45 a.m. Went out for a walk but kept it short in case phone rang.

9:48. Returned. Drank more coffee, ate doughnut.

10:00. Tried to read *Leave Her to Heaven*, couldn't concentrate.

11:00. Still trying.

11:30. Decided to keep busy, dusted a bit, made own and Dealer's bed, etc.

12:00. Dealer got up from cards and made lunch. (Beans.) Felt nauseated. Dealer said I should go out. Went behind bead curtain and tried to sleep.

Couldn't.

Tried *Leave Her to Heaven* again.

Couldn't.

All afternoon, sat looking out of window. Saw—ocean. Some clouds. Sun in and out. One boat, freighter I think, passed on horizon. Kids playing, old couples walking, some dogs, one crazy swimmer.

5:00. Big white moon moving up, sun on way down. Obviously Mr. Swan isn't going to call now.

But he might.

Coffee.

He won't.

I *despise* him!

6:15. Snuck out with tail between legs. Bought hamburger and took bus to movie theater. Didn't care what's playing, wanted to see movie. It was *Don't Bother to Knock*, about lovely blond insane baby-sitter, she finished off a few before they got her.

Home, James! Dealer still at cards. Through bead curtain to sack.

∗

The phone rang at ten o'clock next morning.

I picked it up but didn't say anything until I heard a woman's voice—"Hello? Hello?" I recognized Mr. Swan's secretary.

"Clover residence!" I said in a haughty, disguised, slightly (I think) French voice. The secretary asked if Daisy was there. "I'll see," I said, still playing the French maid, "*Mees* Daisy may still be asleep." I waited a moment, then gave an enormous yawn right into the phone, and announced myself.

"Mr. Raymond Swan on the line." The secretary sounded a bit puzzled. "Hold on, please."

"Good morning, Daisy!" He came on after a lot of flipping and buzzing. "How are you?"

I yawned again. "Oh, pretty good. How are you bearing up?"

It stopped him for a moment. Then he asked rather stiffly, "Will you be home this afternoon?"

"I was planning to have luncheon with Cary and Myrna," I told him, "but they didn't ask me. So I guess I'll stick around the house."

"You'd better!" His voice sounded quite sharp now. "I'll be there at three o'clock." And he hung up.

Well. I was only paying him back for yesterday, of course, and maybe it sounded pretty silly to him, but I enjoyed it. Besides, people should have a sense of humor about these things. I figured the deal was in the bag, anyway—I mean, would Mr. Swan come out all this way, to a slum in Venice, if he wasn't extremely interested? "I guess they liked my test," I told The Dealer. "They're coming out this afternoon."

"If they try and make you sing dirty stuff," The Dealer said, "don't let them."

That was the only reaction I could get out of her. In fact, she fell asleep in her chair two minutes later, and went into some happy dream—that all her solitaires were coming out at last, I'd say, because she smiled and once or twice gave a little excited squeak like a puppy dreaming of rabbits. I went out and took a walk on the beach. It was marvelously clean, with hardly a footprint. Near the shore I found a beautiful little shell, some kind of conch maybe. The outside was rough and scraggly, but the inside, which was like the entrance to a tiny cave, was smooth and polished, white as a bone with streaks of orange and purple. I put the shell to my ear, and although the cave inside was only three inches long, I was listening to an ocean three thousand miles away. It was the longest, quietest, most distant echo I ever heard, and it came out of this funny little shell.

Here's the strangest thing of all. The ocean echo went on sounding after I'd taken the shell away from my ear. It was very faint, like the echo of an echo, and not nearly as loud as the real ocean just a few feet away, yet I went on hearing it. Quite clearly. Then it stopped, and I looked at the waves coming in, and each time they broke I seemed to hear them break a moment later *on the other side of the world*—Australia, Tahiti, anywhere. And I could put this shell to my ear again, and take it away again, and the same thing happened. The waves were always breaking somewhere else as well.

It was certainly a kick, and I took the shell home and put it on the window ledge in my alcove. Then I got busy cleaning up the joint, and after lunch I used a whole can of Spring Bouquet, spraying it everywhere to kill the smell of beans. At 2:53 the doorbell rang. For Mr. Swan to be early, I thought, *after* I'd sassed him a bit, he must really be falling over himself. Maybe this was the way to handle him, like those crusty old millionaires in movies who say, "I like you, young man, how about becoming vice-president?" after they've been called selfish, mean, boring, etc. So I opened the door humming a nonchalant bar or two, and got stopped dead in my tracks because there was—my sister Gloria, in the sleaziest sheath-type dress in the world, puce and shiny, with a matching turban and a week's supply of make-up plastered over her face! She gave me a smile so big I thought the sides of her mouth would meet at the back of her head, then hugged me, stepped back still holding me by the shoulders, and sang out, "Hey there, you with the stars in your eyes!"

I was so stunned I couldn't speak. Finally I asked what the hell she was doing here. She smiled again, in that sickening way people do when they know something they shouldn't, and said, "I had a telephone call last night!"

"Who from?"

"Can't you guess?"

"I'd rather not."

"S as in Sister," Gloria said, so pleased with herself I wanted to strangle her, "W as in Wonderful—"

"A as in Asshole," I cut in, "and N as in Nuisance. Okay, but that's impossible! I never gave him your number or anything."

"People like that," Gloria gave me her cool superior tone, "can always find out anything they want. *People like that can open locked doors.*" She looked around the room, wrinkled her nose, and spotted The Dealer, who was totally ignoring the scene and sitting with her back to us reading an old Sears Roebuck catalogue. "How are you, Mother?" she called. "Isn't this exciting?"

The Dealer turned around and gave Gloria a long disapproving look. "I should slap you," she said.

"Daisy, you dark horse," Gloria cried, deciding to concentrate on me. "Nobody had any idea you could *sing!* Why did you keep it a secret so long?"

"I'm only sorry it's out now," I said. "Did Mr. Swan ask you to come here?"

"Well, of course he did." She looked important and mysterious. "We'll have things to discuss." Then, whispering, with a nod in The Dealer's direction: "She's *much* worse!"

"I seem to remember telling you that on the phone a few months ago," I said quietly, "and you gave me the brush-off."

Gloria shook her head. "You didn't make yourself clear. Really!" She looked around the room again. "I'm quite shocked," she announced, and sat down on The Dealer's bed.

"Gloria, you be careful now!" This from The Dealer, looking up suddenly from her catalogue.

"Careful of what, Mother?"

"Careful of what, Mother!" The Dealer squeaked, imitating her. (Quite funny.) Then she went back to her catalogue. Gloria rolled her eyes at me but I gave her no encouragement. To tell the truth, I had a real hate on for her. She looked like a stupid doll in that puce sheath thing, and it annoyed me the way she'd painted an enormous mouth on herself. In real life she has a very thin pair of lips. Most of all I wondered why she was getting into the act, and I knew that whatever reason she had couldn't be a good one. I must have been sending out *silent waves of hostility*, because her eyes went beady now and she almost snapped at me, "How about offering your sister a cup of coffee?" I was about to tell her to get her ass off The Dealer's bed and make it herself when the doorbell rang.

"I'll get it!" And Gloria nipped over to the door before I could stop her. Melora was standing there with Mr. Swan. She looked straight out of *Vogue,* her hands deep in the pockets of a very swanky spotted white coat exactly like a Dalmatian dog's, which I suppose must have been some extremely expensive fake because I don't think they actually strip Dalmatians for ladies' wear—at least, not yet. Mr. Swan looked elegant too, in a blue silk suit with gold buttons.

I thought Gloria was going to curtsy, she started to sink to her knees, then she gave her smile and said a little nervously, "I'm Gloria Goslett, Daisy's sister, a real pleasure to meet you!" The Swans were disappointingly polite, they said they were delighted to meet *her,* then Melora came in the room first, sniffing the air and raising her eyebrows for a moment. She walked over to me, didn't say anything, but ran her hand through my hair. Mr. Swan said, "Well, Daisy." Since Gloria didn't seem about to introduce The Dealer, I performed the honors myself. The Dealer nodded, really very nice and friendly, and Melora said, "Mrs. Clover, I hear you play a lot of cards!" "I like to keep a game or two going," The Dealer answered, and Melora went to the window and stood looking out at the ocean.

There was quite a pause, during which I wondered what kind of rundown on The Dealer my sister Gloria had given the Swans. They had something going between them, I could feel it. "How about some coffee?" was Gloria's way of breaking the ice, and Melora shook her head as if the idea was amusing but impossible, while Mr. Swan said maybe he'd have some later. The Dealer didn't seem interested in any of this, and was frowning and quietly tut-tutting to herself over an unfinished solitaire. Then Mr. Swan said, "Well, Daisy," again—and then, not sounding very enthusiastic, "you did a great test and we think you're the girl for *Little Annie Rooney.* How does that appeal to you?"

He took my arm as he spoke and walked me to the other end of the room. By the window Melora was deep in something with my sister, but they talked so quietly I couldn't hear. I knew I should be saying "How can I ever thank you?" and "This is the happiest day of my life!" to Mr. Swan, but I could only nod and smile like an idiot and sneak glances all the while at those two

[41]

by the window. It was strange to see them talking like old friends, Melora so elegant and Gloria so cheesy. Anyway, Mr. Swan went on to explain all the things I'd have to do, like being in the movies might *sound* glamorous but was really the hardest work in the world, much harder than school, and I said "Sure" and "Anything you want," etc., and he seemed satisfied but a little puzzled. Finally there was a pause and I *did* hear from Gloria across the room, "Oh, I can sign the papers," and Melora gave a nod and they both came over to us.

"Here's the calmest little movie star you ever saw," said Mr. Swan. "Oh, Daisy's got a head on her shoulders," said Melora. "She was always independent, a very independent little kid, weren't you, baby!" Gloria said, not going to be left out of this. They all stood looking down at me, very satisfied, and Gloria remarked it was a pity we didn't have any champagne. I still couldn't concentrate on anything except my suspicions, and while they all went on congratulating me and each other, and Melora said something about my being one of the Family now, and to regard her and Mr. Swan as friends, not to say parents, I noticed The Dealer walk slowly over to her bed and, without a word, lie down on it. She lay stiff on her back, staring at the ceiling, almost like a person in a coffin. I ran across and asked her if anything was the matter. She said No, she felt fine, maybe a little tired.

When I looked up, the others were watching me but turned away quickly and pretended they weren't.

After talking some more with Gloria about my contract, and getting the Court to approve it, and hoping I could report to the Studio two weeks from now, etc., the Swans went away. But not Gloria. She launched into some nervous small talk about the weather—my, the air was good and fresh down here! and gosh, the sun had come out! and would you believe it, she hadn't even *seen* the ocean in months?—all of which built up to: "Daisy, why don't you and I take a walk along the beach?" I didn't like the idea at all and nearly told her so, but Unfinished Business was written all over her silly face, and it made me nervous too, and I wanted to clear it up right away. The Dealer had dropped off to sleep, so I said to Gloria I could face maybe a short stroll with her, and we went down the iron steps and across the courtyard, her high heels clinking away in time to some funky sounds coming from a downstairs radio.

It certainly was a pretty afternoon now, with the sky very blue and clear, a sparkle on the ocean, gulls riding the waves, people walking and lying on the sand, you could feel summer on the way. Personally I thought Gloria looked ridiculous, mincing along the beach in her sheath thing and turban—and judging from the looks she got, so did a few others—but I didn't make any cracks. I decided to try and be nice to her because I didn't plan on seeing her again for a very long while. She took off her shoes and stockings and walked barefoot, which was weird but practical. She said she bet the ocean was cold, and I said that was the safest bet anyone could make, and we just managed to get a laugh out of it. Then her eyes went shifty and she asked, "I guess you're wondering why the Swans called me on this whole thing?"

"Gloria," I told her, "that's the understatement of the year."

"Well, baby, you see, it's a marvelous wonderful Thing that's happening to you, and I'm so proud and excited, and I don't want to scare you, because I *know* everything'll come all right," I wondered why she was suddenly talking to me as if I were a six-year-old and why her voice sounded so anxious, "but there are problems as well, Daisy, and we've got to face them!"

"There's tar on this sand," I said after a moment, "and you just stepped on some." She gasped, and turned up the sole of her foot. It was black and sticky. "There's a lot of that stuff around," I said, "and it's hell to clean off. Watch out for it, Gloria."

"Yes," she said. "Maybe we're walking too close to the water."

I shook my head. "Doesn't make any difference, that tar is everywhere. Just watch out for it."

"Yes," she said. "I certainly will. *Now*, honey, here's the first problem. The Studio's in the Valley and that's almost thirty miles from here. It'll be a ridiculous long trip for you every day."

"You think we should move?" She nodded. "Well, that's fine with me."

"I'm glad you understand that," Gloria said.

"It's not very difficult. What's the next problem?"

She turned up her foot again and frowned at it. Then: "Wherever you live, Daisy, even though it'll be nearer the Studio than here, someone's got to drive you there."

"Unless there's a bus."

She gave me a rather pitying look. "That's no good. Someone's got to drive you there," she repeated.

"Well, the Studio's got limousines. I've been in one."

"That's true," Gloria said, "but it doesn't solve the problem of where you're going to live."

I felt we were going around in circles. "There's a motel right across the street from the Studio," I told her. "Maybe The Dealer and I could shack up there and kill two birds with one stone, as you might say."

"That's not practical, baby."

"I'm afraid you just stepped on some more tar," I said. "No, the other foot this time."

Gloria looked annoyed. "Can't you tell me *before* I step on it?"

"I'll try."

"Anyway," Gloria said, "I told the Swans I could drive you to the Studio, and they thought it was a wonderful idea."

I stared at her. "That's extremely kind of you, Gloria, but think how much time it would take up. I mean, when you'd driven me there, would you stay until it was time for me to go home? Or would you go away and come back? Either way, it would take up a lot of time. It's not practical!"

She didn't answer this, only said, "If you lived with Harry and me, it would be simple."

I'm not stupid, but the proposition took me entirely by surprise. "You really want The Dealer and me to move in with Harry and you?"

There was a pause. "Not exactly." And another pause. "Just you, Daisy."

I stopped in my tracks. "I think I'm losing you. Honestly."

"Our Mother's very sick, you know!" Gloria was speaking very fast now, her voice high. "She needs medical attention!"

[44]

"The last doctor who saw her said she was strong as a horse."

"I mean," Gloria said more quietly, "she's sick in the head."

"Oh, sure." I really couldn't see what she was driving at. "But I'm used to it. The Dealer's no trouble."

Gloria put her hands on my shoulders and swung me around to face her. "You're so used to it, baby," she said, solemn as a judge, "that you don't realize how *abnormal* it is."

"The Dealer's no trouble," I said again, and tried to pull away.

Gloria hung on. "Do you realize," she asked me, "do you realize what an unnatural, *dangerous* life you've been leading? I blame myself, of course! I should have had more *imagination*. I should have realized our Mother was much sicker than you told me on the phone, but it's only now that I *see* it and thank God no *lasting harm* has been done!"

For a moment I couldn't think of anything to say. Then I found some words. "Turn blue. You're a horse's ass." I pulled away from her, feeling suddenly weak and sick. We were standing near an empty lifeguard's tower. I went and sat on the steps.

Gloria watched, then came over slowly. She put her shoes and stockings on the steps, then said, "Listen, baby. Our Mother set fire to the Paradise Hotel and Apartments."

"For Christ's sake, it was an accident."

"She's fed you for years on a terrible unhealthy diet, refried beans and garlic sausage."

"Can you guess where I'd like to put all that stuff now?" I said. "And from the look of it, there's plenty of room. Anyway, I could always go out and buy a hot dog or lettuce sandwich when I felt like it."

"She plays cards all day, Daisy! She gets hung up on cranky spook ideas."

"She's through with the spooks and there's nothing wrong with cards, for Christ's sake."

"She is not a responsible Parent!" Gloria's voice went up again. It sounded like somebody else's phrase she was repeating. "She's no Mother for an unusual talented adolescent girl! She leaves you to take care of yourself in sordid notorious neighborhoods!"

"And I *do* take care of myself," I said. "I made all my recordings. I won a talent contest. They're going to put me in the movies. How's that for a start?"

Gloria gave me an impatient look. "If you won't try and understand," she sounded cutting and disagreeable now, "I'll have to lay it on the line. You're coming to live with Harry and me, and we're going to commit Mother."

I swear I'm not stupid, but there are some things that just never occur to me. I just gaped at my sister and asked, "Commit her to what?"

"She needs attention." Gloria picked up her shoes and tapped the heels together. "She'll be better off in a place where they specialize in making that kind of person happy."

"You can't do it," I said feebly after a moment. "You can't send The Dealer to an institution!" I wanted to seize one of Gloria's shoes and wipe off her artificial mouth with the heel, but I couldn't move. I could hardly speak or listen. I heard Gloria say something about a strong case, and consent of a relative, and not to use the word institution *or* asylum because The Dealer was going to a home for people who need looking after.

"Whose idea was this?" I said at last.

Gloria didn't answer, only repeated that The Dealer would be much happier. "And if she could make sense, I'm sure she'd *ask* to go there!"

And now I don't remember exactly what I said. I must have fallen back on a lot of old names, and they must have heard them in Alaska. I think I screamed. I know I bit Gloria's hand, and *she* screamed. I started running along the beach. Gloria followed. I picked up a pebble and threw it, only missing that turban by a couple of inches. She called my name again and again. I threw another pebble, to make sure she was getting my message. Somebody's dog got excited and made circles around her, snapping and barking. Then I went on running, very close to the shore, until my energy gave out and I flopped down on the wet sand and closed my eyes for a while.

Later. I'm sitting on the parapet of this old bridge which leads from nowhere to nowhere, across a dry canal. It's supposed to be exactly like a bridge in Venice Italy, there's quite a few of them around here because once upon a time some millionaire who must have been nuttier than The Dealer, though I never heard they committed him, started building a complete imitation Venice Italy right where I'm sitting. I guess it didn't catch on, because he never finished it, and they struck oil, so today it's the creepiest, most beautiful ruin you ever did see. When you're depressed anyway, you could hardly choose a more depressing dump in the world in which to go and sit than this old bridge in the middle of an oilfield, but it suits my mood. The sun's going down and I can't see a human being anywhere. There's a notice stuck on an old pump, it says CHRIST DIED FOR YOU.

I have to figure out what to do. No good trying to explain the situation to The Dealer, she'll never understand why I want her to make tracks and go into hiding with me. And I can't think of anyone who'd appreciate my point of view, which is that sometimes crazy people make more sense than people who are supposed to be in their right minds, for instance I'd commit Gloria to an institution any day, also the Swans if they had anything to do with this, and I'm fairly sure they did, also the people who want to pull down the old pier. I could sit on this bridge till tomorrow morning, making a list of people I'd commit, but the old pier reminds me of Milton, and he seems the only person I know who might possibly help. They say it's better to light a new fire than try to get an old one going again, but I say what about Auld Lang Syne? And, all tumbles apart, Milton with his background and everything certainly ought to appreciate my point of view.

I convince myself anyway, and go into a market to phone, thinking if I go home that Gloria might be there. Luck seems to be on my side, because Long Distance tells me Milton's father is listed in San Francisco, and when I don't have enough money to pay for the call and ask the operator to ask Milton if he'll speak to Daisy Clover *collect*, she says he will. A moment later he's on the line, saying in a surprised voice, older than the one I knew, "Well, Daisy, what is it?"

"MILTON!" I go straight into it. "This is an Emergency! I'm

[47]

phoning you *collect* from a market because I'm in trouble and I don't know what to do!"

"All right, now take it easy," Milton says. "What's the trouble?"

"They're going to put me in the movies, and—"

"If you're kidding," Milton interrupts, "don't expect me to pay for this call. I'm hanging up."

"Every word I'm saying is God's truth, Milton, I swear to you on your father's old brass bedstead, remember? I won a talent contest, and they're going to put me in the movies and let me sing!"

"Then what's the trouble?" Milton asks again.

"They want me to go and live with my sister, and—"

"Who's going to put you in the movies?" Milton cuts in. "Some studio? Who is it?"

"It's Magnagram. They want me to go and live—"

"Well, I'll be darned!" I hear him actually *laughing*. "You mean they liked those crazy recordings?"

"Yes, Milton, it was my rendition of 'Love Is Sweeping the Country' that won the talent contest. But please listen! They want—"

"Well, I'll be darned!"

"Milton!"

"Honestly, I just can't get over it."

"FOR THE LOVE OF GOD!"

"What is it, Daisy?"

"WHAT IS IT? They want to send The Dealer away to an institution, that's *what is it!*"

"Well," after a pause, "she's pretty crazy, you know."

"I know, but she's no trouble. And she has a pretty good time the way she is. And there's no reason to shut her up in one of those places, she'll be more confused than ever. But my sister Gloria's going to sign the papers, and—"

"Then there's nothing you can do." He sounds bored. "Besides, she may be happier there."

It's my turn to pause. And even the old words stick in my throat. "What the hell," I say finally. "It's a rotten connection."

Then I hang up and go out to the street. After all that exercise

I'm hungry, so I buy a hot dog. I wander along the boardwalk, sniffling a bit. It is simply not to be believed that Milton Hopwood Jr. was my first love, and we whiled away three long summer months together, and even after he went away and didn't answer my Christmas greeting, I care enough to be disgusted.

Another CHRIST DIED FOR YOU poster hits me now, stuck on the window of a closed-up Bingo parlor. Some religious jerk must have had a busy day in this area. Well, I've got news for him. Maybe Christ died for somebody, but it wasn't for my sister Gloria. Where that gets me, I don't know. But it's certainly a thought.

5

They say in this business, when you work together you get to know each other, and it's not true. I've seen a great deal of Mr. Raymond Swan for more than six months now, but his behavior on Christmas Eve certainly surprised me.

I was sitting in the office, in Mr. Swan's own swivel chair, with that photograph of Melora and the glass clock right in front of me on the desk. About fifty people were milling around, drinking Scotch out of Dixie Cups. Belle, the old secretary, told me this happened every Christmas Eve. There was a phonograph on the desk in her office, it played Bing Crosby singing "Silent Night, Holy Night." That hateful automatic door was propped open, because the bar was in Belle's office too, and when the party started Mr. Swan told everyone to help themselves and get as drunk as they pleased. As usual, people did what Mr. Swan said. He told me I was the guest of honor, and to sit in his chair, and he stood behind me drinking Scotch out of a real tall glass. It was a different Scotch; he'd open a desk drawer from time to time and pour himself a snifter of his own brand from a bottle with a gold stopper.

Guest of honor or not, I was feeling pretty bored, when Mr. Swan suddenly swung me around a couple of times in the chair. I was going to say What the hell? or something, then decided to shrug it off, because in the department of four-letter words I must hand it to Mr. Swan; he's my only serious rival, and when we start on each other it makes him laugh, which annoys me. He stopped the chair by putting his hand on my shoulder and pressing his thumb quite hard against my neck. Then he called to Belle to turn off the phonograph, and went into a speech about what a great picture *Little Annie Rooney* had turned out to be, and what a great star it was going to make Little Daisy Clover, and how you can't beat pure instinctive talent that comes from the heart of a child, etc. I wriggled a bit but his thumb pressed harder, so I decided to concentrate on the pendulum swinging inside the glass clock, and mentally I put warts on Melora's face in the photograph, then took them off because in spite of the terrible thing she did with The Dealer I can't help liking her. At last Mr. Swan finished and everyone clapped, and my embarrassment was completed by someone putting my first record album on the phonograph. They're launching it next month, just before the movie comes out, and it's called *Four-Leaf Clover*, which in my opinion is a bore.

Mr. Swan, who still hasn't asked me to call him Ray, poured himself another Scotch, raised his glass to me, and said quietly, "Merry Christmas, Daisy."

"Oh, Merry Christmas," I gave him back, and tried to get up, but his thumb wouldn't budge from my collarbone.

"I've got a present for you." He handed me a package, very small but beautifully wrapped. "Thank you!" I said, but he told me to hold back my expressions of gratitude (I quote) until I knew what it was. This took a little while, the package was done up in so many curlicues of scarlet ribbon, but I finally wrenched the thing open and took out a tiny marvelous wristwatch in a diamond setting.

"My God!" I said loudly, and then, remembering that Mr. Swan didn't like me being profane in public, "Hot-diggity-dog! It's beautiful! It really is! I feel terrible! I didn't get anything for you or Melora, you see, in fact I wasn't really expecting this whole party deal at all."

"It's unimportant," Mr. Swan said rather stiffly, then took my wrist and slipped on the watch. "Hold it up, let them see it," he said.

I felt embarrassed again holding up my wrist with this watch on it, but everyone crowded around and applauded and counted the diamonds, then went back to their drinking.

"I *did* send you a Christmas card," I told Mr. Swan. "I hope you got that all right."

"I'm sure we did." He put his mouth close to my ear. "And

now, Daisy, since I'm so pleased with you, and so proud of you, and so fond of you, and it's Christmas—I'm going to give you another present!"

"Oh Christ," I said. "I mean, you know what I mean. I feel terrible."

He almost smiled. "This one's very special," he whispered. "I'm going to swivel you around in this chair, Daisy, and while I do that, you're going to have to think very hard."

"I'd think better if you'd let me sit still."

He shook his head. "Do it while I swivel you." His thumb pressed harder. "And when I stop—you'll tell me who in this office, in this room, you'd like me to fire!"

"These people who work for you?" I stared at him. "Now that's not a very nice thing to do at Christmas, Mr. Swan."

"It's funny," he said, though he was far from smiling now. "Don't you think so? Don't you like the idea of anyone in this room being able to lose his job through the whim of a child? You could fire the most valuable person in my studio, Daisy—if you knew who he was."

"Oh, I do," I said. "It's you."

"I'm not included." He sounded annoyed. "Now pick on someone else." And he swung me around. The people in the office had no idea what was happening, they were all laughing and getting drunk. I closed my eyes. The chair stopped turning and Mr. Swan took his hand off my shoulder. I took a slug of Coke and looked up at him.

"I'll tell you," I said. "This is the season of good will and all, and I just love everybody here. I love them all so much there's nobody I could stand to see you fire!"

I could see he was extremely disappointed. His voice went hard and dry. "How nice for you to love everybody." Then he added, "I wouldn't have gone through with it, of course. It was only a game. You should have played it."

"Well, Merry Christmas," I said. "And thanks again for the watch."

Melora came into the office, wearing her Dalmatian coat. Mr. Swan went over and kissed her, then joined some other people. I was dying for a cigarette, but that was also forbidden in public, of course, so I flipped the intercom switch on Mr. Swan's desk—I can work all those gadgets in my sleep now—and heard Belle's voice come through anxiously from the outer office: "Yes, Mr. Swan?"

"It's me. Tell Mr. Swan to bring me another Coke."

"Naughty," Belle said, and switched off.

Melora was standing over me now. "Honey, I've got a present for you," and I had to repeat the whole performance, thanking her and apologizing and getting tangled up in a mile of ribbon. "*Jesus!*" I said when I got to first base. "This is too darned much!" and held up my *first diamond bracelet*—actually some kind of silver bangle with three whoppers mounted on it. Melora laughed, kissed me, and said she had to find a drink. I slipped the bracelet on my other wrist, held out my hands, and couldn't believe they were my own. Then, since nobody came and talked to me, I decided to order my limousine and make tracks. Not that I was dying to get back to Gloria and Harry, but I felt ridiculous sitting at this desk covered in diamonds while people were drinking away and getting to the blue-joke stage. So I flipped the switch again and said, "Belle, it's me, and this time I mean it, I'm tired and I want my car." As I started to leave, a squat little fellow in a pin-stripe suit and thick glasses came up and asked how was his favorite actress. It was Alex Conrad, who directed my picture.

"Anyone slip you a bottle of Scotch yet?" he went on. Alex loved to kid. I once overheard him explain to Mr. Swan that it was the basis of our relationship. I liked him pretty well, he thought I was funny, and whenever I fluffed a take he'd say, "Clover, what's the matter with you, you been drinking again?" We had this running joke, you see, that I was a child-star alcoholic.

"No," I said. "All I've collected is a few diamonds."

"I'll fix that." He started to turn away. "What's your favorite brand these days?"

"Alex!" I called after him, "maybe you're kidding, but I'm not. I'd give my life for a quart of the stuff."

"There's a stack of bottles in the other office. If that's how you feel, slip one under your coat on the way out."

[53]

"I think I will," I said, and he didn't realize I was serious. It suddenly struck me as a wild idea, going up to my bedroom and hitting the booze while Gloria and Harry worked themselves into a holiday-season mood below. I certainly couldn't think of anything kickier to do. When I started work at the studio I hoped to get out and meet new people, but they weren't in my age group, of course, they were all extremely friendly but not friends. Only the actor who played my father took what you might call a strong personal interest in me. (I should explain that Little Annie Rooney was the daughter of an Irish policeman and secretly headed a gang of juvenile delinquents, and he finds out in the end—but as it's a musical comedy we never did anything really bad.) Anyway, this actor made a terrific pass at me in his dressing room on the second day of shooting. I told him I was desperately in love with a boy who lived in San Francisco and just couldn't give myself to another man right now, however attractive. He fell for it, promised to keep my secret, and we got along fine. There was another child star on the lot, a prissy little thing with red hair done up in ringlets like frankfurters. I used to go up to her from behind, lift a frankfurter and whisper Bullshit, etc., but that wasn't exactly friendship either.

Julie Forbes, who certainly knows the ropes, warned me anyway that when you're working on a picture you don't have time for social life, except week ends. It interferes with dedication. I finally went up to swim in the pool at her house, and the atmosphere spooked me. Her son Timmy is bright but really hates everyone, his mother most of all, and so much spying goes on it makes you nervous. I mean, Timmy and I splashed around while Carmen Lynch peered at us from an upstairs window in a cowboy hat, and then Timmy wanted me to watch his mother with some man who was a week-end guest. I couldn't honestly enjoy it.

Dot, dot, dot. I went into Belle's office looking extremely casual and waited for a good moment to heist that bottle of Scotch. I'd definitely made up my mind, and when no one was looking I grabbed a quart of Old Heather. Just as I put it under my coat I heard somebody roaring with laughter, turned guiltily around—and a man with very dark and glittering and slightly bloodshot eyes was staring at me as if I was the greatest joke in the world.

I decided immediately that in a situation like this attack was the only defense, so I said, "Excuse me, as long as you think it's a joke that's fine. But if you tell on me, the joke is certainly over."

"Your secret couldn't be in safer hands," he said, quite amused, then introduced himself. "I'm Wade Lewis."

"I know." He was a rising star, pushing thirty, handsome in an offbeat way, cheekbones like a Russian, not particularly suntanned and only medium height. I think you'd say wiry. He had a lot of untidy black hair. His eyes went on slanting at me, I could tell he found me hilarious.

"I'm Daisy Clover." I held on tightly to the bulge under my coat.

"I know that," he said.

"Oh," I said. "How are you?"

It was hardly surprising he didn't answer this stupid question, in fact he went on smiling as if he hadn't heard it. And then, would you believe it, I saw a tear come into the corner of each eye. He frowned at the floor and muttered that his father was very ill. We were suddenly alone. For some reason everybody had gone into Mr. Swan's office. The phonograph played a gorgeous arrangement of the Tara theme from *Gone with the Wind*. It didn't seem right, and I turned the sound down. Then I said, "You mean he might die?"

Wade Lewis nodded.

"That's really awful. And at Christmas."

I was embarrassed, not just from having to hold on to the bottle of Scotch under my coat, but because I felt *immensely concerned*, and—I can't explain this at all but I'm going to try— Wade Lewis had convinced me that he was the most unhappy and helpless person in the world, and it seemed unfair, because —okay, I give up. I just thought he was terribly attractive.

"And at Christmas!" he repeated, looking up at me again. There were no tears now. "Dear heart, you'd better get out of here," he said, laughing, "before they catch you with that stolen liquor under your belt."

I told him I'd already ordered my Limousine.

"You'd look ridiculous in a Limousine. I'll drive you home—unless you live way out at the beach."

"Not any more. I live at 7215 Arcadia Drive in Hollywood."

He looked quickly around the room, which was still empty, picked up a bottle of vodka, and put it under *his* coat, then grabbed my hand and pulled me into the corridor. I thought I saw Mr. Swan come to the doorway of his office and disapprove.

Wade Lewis and I had nothing more to say to each other until we reached his car. For one thing, I was completely out of breath. He made me run after him along empty corridors, through an alley, and across two parking lots, as if our lives depended on it. Most of the way he was laughing quite wildly, and though the situation didn't strike me as all that funny I found myself laughing too. When I got in beside him, I asked for a cigarette. He didn't seem surprised or say I was too young or anything, just brought out a pack and handed it to me.

"I'm trying to cut down on this habit," I told him, "but I still get through nearly half a pack a day. The trouble is, once the stuff gets into your bloodstream, you've had it."

He didn't answer, and again I don't blame him. When we turned out of the studio gate, he asked if I was cold.

"No," I said. "It's a mild evening."

"I don't think so, dear heart." He pressed his window closed, so I did the same. "You can keep yours open," he said, "if you really find it mild."

"No," I said. "I'm not finding it as mild as I thought."

He turned on the heater at once. It was extremely powerful, and after a minute I felt suffocated. When I told him I'd have to open my window again, he asked if I'd prefer him to turn off the heater.

"Oh, it's up to you."

He burst out laughing.

"Now what's so funny?"

"I've forgotten." He laughed again. "Now I remember. Why do you want to get drunk on Christmas Eve?"

"I honestly don't know," I said, and started laughing too. His eyes were so beautiful, they almost killed me. "I guess the main reason is to annoy Gloria and Harry." I gave him a vivid thumbnail sketch of my sister and her husband, and explained about The Dealer being kept in this home.

He frowned at this. "You going to visit her tomorrow?"

"Oh yes. And bring her a puzzle."

"It's a great Christmas for both of us, you know. I'll be visiting my sick father and you'll be visiting your crazy mother. Thank you, God!" Wade Lewis said. "We certainly thank you for all your blessings."

After that, we had a few minutes' silence. All the windows were still closed and the heater was going full blast, I couldn't bear it. I turned the heater off, half expecting him to laugh or get angry, I don't know why. But he took no notice and drove very fast.

"What's the matter with your father, anyway?" I asked.

"He's had a stroke. His second. I'm really expecting him to die. Is your mother completely off her nut?"

"Oh, she's all right if you leave her alone. In fact, according to some crazy biography of me that the studio put out, she's dead."

"Poor bitch," Wade Lewis said.

I lit another cigarette. "Gloria got herself appointed my legal guardian, you see, but the moment I come of age I'll never speak to her again. I have other plans for that day, too."

We turned into Sunset Boulevard, there was a long slow stream of traffic both ways, a huge sign TURKEYS 39¢ flashing on and off outside a market, illuminated Christmas trees in front of some of the motels. As far as I was concerned, the world never looked so awful. Wade Lewis's eyes were glistening, so I guess he thought so too.

Then "Let's brighten this whole thing up!" he said suddenly, and swerved to a stop. He told me to wait, got out of the car, and disappeared into a flower shop. I could see him talking to a woman with a white apron inside, pointing at everything, nodding and laughing. The woman picked up a huge bunch of shiny heart-shaped blooms, purple and scarlet, so bright and strange they must have come from where it's still summer, Hawaii maybe. Wade Lewis left the shop and walked up to a drugstore on the corner. Five minutes went by. I felt my legs getting cold and turned on the heater again, but nothing happened, I guess it wouldn't work unless the engine was running. The car door opened and there was the woman from the flower shop carrying a stack of roses, chrysanthemums, tropical stuff, etc., all beautifully wrapped in gold paper with candy-striped ribbon. Without a word she laid them on the back seat and went away.

I started to laugh, because when Wade came out of the drugstore he was laden with packages too, and the whole thing seemed to be turning into a routine. He threw all the packages in my lap.

"Hey!" I said.

"It's just perfume, candy, cigarettes, and I thought maybe you'd like a crazy bubble bath." Wade reached over to the back seat and added all the flowers except one bunch to the pile on my lap. "The flowers are all for you too, except the yellow roses."

"Who are they for?"

"Your crazy mother."

He started the car and drove off. I was entirely surrounded by the flowers, in fact I couldn't even see over the top. Finally I managed to push my face between two bunches and say, "Please, if you're doing all this, will you stop again? I mean, I'd like to get you something too."

Wade Lewis shook his head. "I've got enough."

I was speechless for a while. When I stuck my head through the barricades again and stammered out some thanks, it seemed to make him impatient. "I just thought this whole thing should be brightened up," he said again. His mouth looked clenched and his eyes brighter than ever.

"We're on Arcadia Drive," Wade Lewis said. "Which is yours?"

"I can't see. Is there an old Spanish apartment house on our right?" Apparently there was. "Then my little Colonial hideaway is the pride of the next block."

In a moment he was slowing down. He pulled up, leaned across and opened my door. "There you go."

"I'm not sure I can manage. I don't want to drop the liquor under my coat."

"Just hold tight to everything," Wade Lewis said.

I got out successfully, and peered at him through my loot. "I hate long good-bys, don't you? So I'll just say thanks for the ride and the presents, I've had a wonderful time, and Merry Christmas."

"And Merry Christmas," he repeated, smiling. Then he slammed the door shut and drove off with a lurch.

Meanwhile the front door of my new home had opened, and Gloria and Harry waited for me on the porch.

EXT. PORCH—MEDIUM SHOT—GLORIA AND HARRY—NIGHT

His bony arm around her shoulder. Daisy comes up, clutching flowers and packages and bottle under her coat. They've been watching the car and don't notice anything unusual about her at first.

Harry: Who was that?

Daisy: Wade Lewis.

Gloria: Why did he drive you home?

Daisy: I don't know.

Gloria (*suddenly*): You're weighed down! What's all that?

Harry: Let me take some.

Daisy: No! I mean, it's like a house of cards, Harry, if you lift one out the whole thing may come tumbling down.

Gloria: But who gave you all that?

Daisy: Just people at the studio.

Gloria: I think Wade Lewis might have helped you. (*Screams*) Are those diamonds?

Daisy: Sure.

Gloria: Who gave you diamonds?

Daisy: Melora gave me the bracelet and Mr. Swan gave me the watch.

(*Harry whistles through his teeth.*)

Gloria: Well! Baby, they certainly must be very pleased with you.

Harry: It's cold. Let's go inside.

(*They move into hall.*)

[59]

Harry: Was Wade Lewis drunk?

Daisy (*clutching bottle, which starts to slip*): Whatever makes you think that, Harry?

Harry: The way he drove off.

(*They pause under Japanese lantern hanging from ceiling, decorated with mistletoe. Harry notices it, laughs happily, puts bony arms around Gloria and Daisy and kisses both.*)

Daisy: Excuse me, I'm dying to go to the john.

And I ran up the stairs two at a time. At the top I turned around and called, "When I come down, Gloria, I'll let you wear my diamonds!" I threw everything on the bed, locked the door, flushed my toilet, and picked up a tooth glass. I removed some artificial flowers from a plastic vase and arranged the real ones in it. I dabbed some perfume behind my ears. Downstairs, the radio started playing. I sat on the bed, filled the glass with Old Heather, and held it up between my trembling jeweled wrists.

I woke up to church bells, quite a headache, and a vague feeling that I was in disgrace. The door opened and Gloria marched in, carrying a cup of coffee. She had a weird expression on her face, it looked literally split in two. I guess she was torn between being nice as it was Christmas Day and snippy on account of my behavior the night before. Also, the only make-up she'd put on was her big mouth.

"Merry Christmas, baby. Drink this. You'd better not get up."

I told her I felt fine.

"I don't believe it." She sat on the edge of the bed. "How *could* you? What got *into* you? Have you any idea how you *scared* us?"

"No," I said. "Tell me."

"You mean you don't remember?"

"I'm not sure. I want to hear."

She picked up my shell with the ocean echo—Gloria always fiddles with something when she's tense—and laid it in her lap. "You wouldn't open your door at first. We called and knocked and rattled, and all we heard was the sound of a chair falling over."

I leaned across the bed and snatched the shell from Gloria's lap. "Excuse me," I said. "I'm very fond of this thing, I wouldn't like anything to happen to it."

"You can imagine," Gloria's eyes almost bulged out of their sockets now, "you can imagine what went through our minds!"

"No," I said. "Tell me."

"We thought you'd had an accident." Her voice went high. "We thought something terrible had happened!"

"What kind of thing? Tell me."

She hesitated. "We thought, Daisy . . . you might have done something *extremely foolish*."

It's funny, I know I'm brighter than Gloria—which is not saying much—but once in a while she can take me completely by surprise. "Are you telling me," I said, "that you thought I might have tried to kill myself?"

"I'm telling you, baby, we didn't know what to think."

"Did you figure out how I might have done it? What I'd taken?"

After a moment, she admitted it. "There's a lot of pills around the Studio. A lot of people take a lot of pills there."

"Well, for Christ's sake, why should I ever try a thing like that?"

"I'm only telling you what went through our minds." Gloria frowned at the carpet. "There's still a stain where you threw up."

"I'll try some salt on it later. This is very good coffee, Gloria. You always make good coffee."

"Want some more?" she asked.

I nodded.

"Then get it yourself, you're well enough." She got up and walked out of the room, obviously feeling she'd scored a hit. Peace on Earth, Good Will to All Men, and play it cool, I thought. The day will come when you'll really tell Gloria off, so don't say too much now and take away the pleasure.

I slipped on a dressing gown and my diamond watch, and padded downstairs. There were a few presents piled under the skimpy little tree in the living room. Harry was in the breakfast nook, spreading honey on a bagel. Gloria poured me out more coffee like it was an enormous favor, then said, "I don't suppose you want to eat."

"Are you kidding? I'll fix myself some eggs."

"I'll fix them. You always make a mess."

"Why are you so good to me?" Then I smiled brightly at Harry. "No one's opened their presents yet!"

"We were waiting for you, Daisy." He sounded reproachful. "And now we're waiting for Gloria." He took a big munch of his bagel. "I never saw anyone so looped in my life. Why did you do it, kid?"

"Oh, I don't know," I said. "I guess it was just one of those things." That's a marvelous phrase, one of my favorites. It doesn't mean *anything*, but stops people asking questions.

Harry munched again, thought it over, and gave a knowing nod.

"A girl has to let off steam once in a while," I said as Gloria dumped a plate of eggs in front of me. "My, Gloria, these are good eggs," I told her. "You always fix good eggs."

As I've said before, my sister can sometimes surprise me. She did so now, for the second time this morning. She suddenly raised her hand and gave me a slap across the face. Then she turned away, breathing hard, and ran water over some dishes in the sink. I didn't think I'd needled her all that much, but obviously I had, and it was quite gratifying, even though she slapped me hard.

Harry seemed frozen in his chair. There was a long silence, until Gloria turned off the water and squeaked out from behind a cloud of steam—

"Stop riding me, do you hear!"

I started to walk out of the room and she ran after me, grabbed my shoulders, and shook them. Her face was wild, it almost scared me. After a moment, Harry came up and pulled her away.

"Gloria, I'll stop riding you if you can't take it," I said. "You have legal rights and I even have to pay you for living here, so what's the use? But just for the record you are filed in my personal black book under horse's ass, cross-filed under full of shit—"

She made another lunge, but Harry held her back.

"You told me what passed through your stupid mind last night," I went on, retreating up the stairs. "And if you really thought that, you must feel pretty bad about something. I'm glad you do. I hope you feel worse tomorrow."

She began to cry. Harry put his arm around her, mumbled something idiotic about opening presents, and led her back to the living room.

When I came downstairs again, dressed and carrying The Dealer's gift-wrapped puzzle, they watched me dumbly from the couch. They'd opened their presents, Gloria had a mink stole around her shoulders and Harry played with a shiny new golf club. I called a cab, then went to the kitchen for another cup of coffee. As I drank it, I knew they'd followed and were standing behind me in the doorway. I pretended I hadn't heard them. Finally Harry coughed and said in a nervous voice, "We were planning to eat around two o'clock."

"Okay," I said, and they looked relieved.

"I'd come with you," Gloria managed to get out, "but I have to watch the turkey." Then Harry nudged her, and she came closer. "I'm sorry, baby. I lost my temper."

I let her kiss me. It must have been one of those things as difficult to give as to receive, anyway.

"No hard feelings?"

"Merry Christmas," I said.

They sent The Dealer to the Getwell Sanatorium for Bed and Ambulatory Cases about two weeks after I made that useless phone call to Milton in San Francisco. When something awful happens and you can't stop it, you actually have to watch it happen, there's nothing to describe. I mean, there you are and there it is. Imagine a few blank pages at the end of my 4th Theme Book, write the old four-letter words across them if you like, and you're in the picture. I'll hand it to Melora, she was the only one who made any sense. I hated everything she said, but at least it was practical, and she didn't pretend like Gloria that The Dealer would be much happier in her new home and it was the right thing to do, etc. She told me that if I was going to be a singer and work in the movies and all that, I couldn't go on living with

[63]

a crazy old woman. "You see, Daisy, you're going to be very famous very soon," Melora said. "How would you like to see stories in the newspapers about your mother?" As for living with Gloria and Harry, it would only be for a few years, and I'd have the rest of my life to do as I wanted. She also mentioned she'd been brought up by an Uncle she couldn't stand, and got over it.

Anyway, although Gloria would have been quite happy to send The Dealer to some charity institution, I made them all agree that part of the money I earned would go to keep her in a decent comfortable place. (What with this and Gloria drawing expenses too, I'm not yet the richest girl in the world.) The Getwell Sanatorium is in East Hollywood, the section with a lot of weird old houses hidden away behind trees, terribly quiet. They say mainly rich old ladies and retired judges live there now. The Sanatorium itself is a converted mansion with towers and tall narrow windows, it reminds me of a movie in which Gene Tierney or someone was being driven mad at night.

It was morning now, and sunshine, and Ambulatory Cases on the porch or wandering slowly around the driveway. Some carried little presents, and I noticed a very sun-tanned old lady in slacks wearing a funny paper hat. In the hall you could smell roast turkey and hear carols coming over the radio. I met Miss Donahue, a tiny friendly nurse who always had a smile for everyone. "Merry Christmas, Daisy!" she piped out, and I wished her the same and asked how The Dealer was.

"We're very quiet." Miss Donahue didn't look so cheerful now. "I'm afraid we've been through one of our depressions. Yes, we went off our food again and refused every suggestion. We were found at sunset lying down under a tree." Then she brightened. "However, we responded quite satisfactorily to the treatment."

I felt my throat going dry. "You gave her the shocks again? The electric current?"

Miss Donahue nodded. "Yes, it perked us up."

When I first heard how they strapped The Dealer down on this table and sent electric shocks through her body, I nearly threw up. Gloria mentioned it casually the day I was going to the studio to rehearse a number called "Making Hay," and as a result I could hardly sing at all and they sent me home. Gloria couldn't understand why I felt so bad about it. She said it's a miracle of medical science. All I know is, it made me hit the roof and the doctor had to give me a tranquilizer.

"Where is she?" I asked. "May I see her now?"

"In her room," Miss Donahue said. "We're segregated for the moment. It's a shame on Christmas Day."

As we started up the stairs, the old lady in the paper hat came up with an unlit cigarette stuck in her mouth. Miss Donahue whipped out a match, but she shook her head and pointed at me.

"Ruthie wants you to light it," Miss Donahue said, so I tried to, but the old fool blew out the match on purpose every time.

"Mischievious, aren't we?" Miss Donahue took back the matches. "Enough is enough, Ruthie." This time she let Miss Donahue light the cigarette, and puttered off.

We were walking down a corridor on the second floor when I heard a quiet moan coming from somewhere.

"Don't worry," Miss Donahue said. "That's not Mrs. Clover." She unlocked a door.

The Dealer's room is dark and paneled like all the others in the place, but it has Television and they'd hung a tinsel star on the wall above her bed. The windows are barred. I could see only one solitaire, which looked as if it hadn't been touched for a while. Her head propped against pillows, The Dealer was watching some program about a zoo with a very fixed expression. "Here's a visitor!" Miss Donahue said, but she didn't look up.

I switched the television off, and The Dealer took no notice. She went on staring at the blank screen in the same fixed way.

"Hey!" I said. "Rise and shine!"

I'm afraid she didn't. Ever since she's lived in this place, it's become more difficult to get through to The Dealer, and when it happens it's only for a very short moment. I've tried explaining quite a few things to her—how I never wanted her to be sent here, and how I plan to uncommit her the day I come of age—but each time it's like talking to a stone. Miss Donahue says it's no use, she recommends just fooling around and being cheerful, etc., so that's what I concentrate on now.

[6 5]

I unwrapped the puzzle, telling her that when all the pieces fitted together she'd have a picture of the Eiffel Tower.

Nothing.

I turned up a card on the table and sang a few bars—

> *"Ten of hearts goes on the jack of spades*
> *Every card must go Somewhere.*
> *That's the rule*
> *Playing Solitaire—"*

Nothing.

"You're certainly a tough audience," I said, and she turned her face to the wall. I said good-by, and she made a little fretful movement with her arm, pointing at the television set. I turned it on again. As I went out, performing seals came on the screen and I think she connected with them for a moment. Or it may have been that the music—circus-type, a big brass band—was very loud. Anyway, I thought I saw the flicker of a smile.

When I got home, there was the smell of turkey. Frankly, this bird has depressing associations for me, and another thing I'll do when I come of age is eat something else for Christmas. Every time I smell turkey cooking I hear someone moaning behind a door and I see The Dealer lying in bed under a tinsel star, and it's not festive.

Gloria kissed me again and asked how The Dealer was.

"Just fair."

"Well, that's all we can hope for, isn't it, baby?"

I wondered how Wade Lewis was doing, he could have made my day if he called, and you can bet your life he didn't. Alex Conrad did, though, which was nice of him.

"Merry Christmas, Clover. Are you sober?"

"You should have seen me last night," I said. "I think you'd have been proud."

Later, Gloria and Harry took me to the movies. We couldn't get in to *Quo Vadis*, so it had to be *Whirlpool* with, would you believe it, Gene Tierney being driven mad again.

6

Wade Lewis hasn't called.

Wade Lewis didn't acknowledge my New Year Greeting.

I haven't seen Wade Lewis.

I haven't seen anyone who's seen Wade Lewis.

I think I've stopped growing. Maybe smoking has something to do with it. Anyway, it looks like 5 ft. 4½ in. is the nearest I'll ever get to the sky.

Screen Time magazine for February 1953 has Wade Lewis on the cover and an article called IS WADE LEWIS AS SEXY AS THEY COME? The answer is YES.

They gave The Dealer a whole slew of electric shocks last week. Miss Donahue said the results were more marked than usual, she's been asking for extra packs of cards.

Last night in Hollywood they premièred *Little Annie Rooney*. I went in Mr. Swan's party, fairly depressed because when they asked me who I'd like as my escort I said Wade Lewis— and they both looked quite stunned, and Melora said, "No, honey, I don't think so," and I was fixed up with some blond juvenile who talked about skin-diving. The rest of the party was Julie Forbes and her date, some businessman, and of course Gloria and Harry. You can imagine it didn't exactly swing.

While we were driving to the theater I couldn't really connect with the whole situation. It was like the first day I went to the Studio to see Mr. Swan. They'd rigged me out in pale lemon organdy like a bridesmaid, I had satin pumps and a ribbon in my hair. Gloria, who always picks violent shiny colors for special occasions, wore a bigger and brighter false mouth than ever. Melora as usual looked stunning, in a polar-bear coat and blue eye-shadow. Most of the time this stupid juvenile was explaining how he'd like to get me in flippers and take me down to the bottom of the sea. Just a block from the theater we turned into Hollywood Boulevard, and suddenly there were *faces peering right into our car!* I mean very rudely, and people shouting, "Who's she?" and "Is she anybody?" and "Is that Daisy?" I looked out the other window, straight into a boy's face with eyes gimleting into mine, he was on the running board. I started to pull down the blinds but Melora said you mustn't do that to fans. Everywhere the ruckus was unbelievable, crowds goggling and lurching and cops holding them back, traffic at a standstill and drivers whanging their horns. Luckily Julie Forbes's limousine drew up immediately in front of ours, and the moment she stepped out she was the center of attention, waving like a queen at the gasping, screaming hundreds. I clutched Melora's hand and scurried up the red carpet. The moment we got inside I rushed to the john, where some famous actresses were elbowing each other in front of a mirror, locked myself in a toilet, and took a pack of cigarettes I'd hidden in my organdy. The panic was hitting me now, I smoked like crazy and seriously thought of sitting out the whole thing right where I was.

Well, eventually I heard Gloria's voice calling, "Are you in there, baby? Is that where you are?" I didn't answer at once, but I guess the cigarette smoke floating over the top of the cubicle gave me away, because she rapped on the door and said, "Now come on out, they're starting in a minute!" I took the ribbon out of my hair, flushed it, and felt better. "I'm sorry," I said to Gloria when I came out, "I had the runs." "Throw that cigarette away for God's sake," she ordered, then I followed her up to the Mezzanine and slipped into a seat between Melora and Mr. Swan. The lights were just changing from red to purple.

Now the curtains with sequined suns and moons slid back, there was a jazzy fanfare of music, and the Magnagram Goddess came on the screen. I remembered The Dealer, who was scared of flying, telling me once how she felt when she had to strap herself in her seat and watch them close the cabin hatch. The audience went very quiet. I stole a look around the huge theater, all those strangers in the dark, then saw my name in tall yellow letters on the screen. The strangers gave it a round of applause. Now it's OLD NEW YORK! and a pretty street under snow, brownstone houses, a sweeper, a carriage trotting past, music like plucked icicles. We're moving nearer to one of the houses, the front door opens, and a policeman comes out. He waves, and we go up the side of the house to a bedroom window. Leaning out with elbows on the sill is someone I recognize. We speak our first words. " 'By, Pa!" We turn back into the bedroom. *Music. Her movements betray adolescent restlessness and boredom. She makes a face at herself in the mirror, then starts singing to her reflection, "Between You and Me."* My hands are shaking. Our voice sounds extremely loud! I think I *am* getting the runs! We're back to the window now, singing to ourself in the glass. It's only wind. Would you believe it, all the time I'm up there singing the song I'm also up *here* trying to slow down a fart. And the number seems to go on forever. Dot, dot, dot. *"And that's how things are, Between you and me"*—luckily the strangers applaud and I can let it out, they cover the blast.

Now that I've regained my poise, I sneak another look around. Mr. Swan's expression is definitely the cat that swallowed the canary. Gloria's sitting up very straight and giving a wriggle or two, as if she's being secretly goosed. And Melora squeezes my hand. I guess we're off to the races. Here's the first scene with my gang, we meet in an old police station condemned after a fire, and I get my laughs. Every one of them. I'm sort of tough and cute at the same time up there, and the audience certainly goes for it. Up here I'm excited and also more relaxed. Mr. Swan says what the world wants is a happy picture, and that's what the world's getting right now. So I guess Mr. Swan knows his business. Our second number comes on and it really sends them. Up here I feel like a firework that's been sputtering for a while, but when it finally gets off the ground it explodes all over the sky! I'll come right out and admit it, I think I'm pretty good. I read somewhere that the greatest moment in life is making love with someone you really love, it's more than sex and so great you can't describe it. The sensation I'm having now must be the runner-up. For some reason Twitcher's face comes back to me, and the sound of the ocean, and even the smell of seaweed and fog, it's all I can do not to stand up in front of everyone and myself and split my guts laughing.

Anyway, from that moment on, my heart beat like a hammer, and stars, as you might say, fell on Alabama. When THE END came, the applause sounded like an earthquake. I sat staring at the curtains as they slid together again; when a purple light hit the suns and moons they were spots in front of my eyes. Gloria whispered, "Oh, *baby!*" The Swans exchanged We Knew It All Along glances like mad. People I'd never met came up to shake my hand or kiss me and say, "You're beautiful!" I walked into the lobby like a zombie. A great cry went up, for a moment I didn't understand why, then fans rushed forward shrieking for my autograph. Over and over again I signed Daisy Clover, Daisy Clover, Daisy Clover, To Ted, To Marlene, To Johnny, and finally I called to Melora, "My hand's coming off!" so she pulled me into a limousine. When I was in a condition to sit up and take notice again, it was cheering to find we'd lost that juvenile in all the confusion. Mr. Swan was sitting next to me. "Well, Daisy," he said, "for a first try, that wasn't too bad." "Really?" I gave him a very wide-eyed look. "I wasn't sure they liked me." He patted my knee. "How does it feel to have the world at your feet?" "Fantabulous!" I said, "but I'll never forget I owe it all to you."

We got out at Romanoff's, where Mr. Swan was giving a supper party in a private room. I made a beeline for the john again, had a quick smoke in a locked toilet, then went upstairs. Everyone in the room looked up and smiled. I was deeply impressed. Waiters were serving champagne, there was a buffet with cold chicken and caviar, etc., all the people smiling at me seemed so elegant and on top of the world, you just couldn't believe that life was ever going to be anything except a bed of roses—the very best roses. Then I saw the juvenile. He'd turned up after all and was coming toward me with a glass of champagne. It broke the spell, somehow. It's amazing how the wrong person can do that. Here I was with the world at my feet and I could only think of Wade Lewis and how was his father? My face must have been giving something away because the juvenile stared and asked if I was all right. "No, I'm not!" I said, so loudly it alarmed him. "I'm dying of hunger!" And I walked straight over to the caviar, which I'd never tasted before. It's fairly bland. The juvenile, who followed me, said to squeeze lemon over it.

I don't know how to explain what happened next. Maybe I suddenly wanted to blow this situation sky high, maybe this ridiculous thing about Wade Lewis was getting me down, or maybe I'm not as adjusted as I think and ought to have my head examined. Anyway, I smiled at the juvenile in a provocative manner, put my mouth to his ear, and whispered, "I wish we could leave this party and go back to your place!"

Naturally I expected him to be shocked, probably drop the plate of caviar, and never speak to me again. However, the shock was mine. There came over his face the most hideous leer I've ever seen—much worse than Milton—and he gripped my arm and droned through his teeth, "You mean it?"

"Sure." My voice croaked. "Sure I mean it."

I still haven't worked out how the juvenile removed me from that room so quickly and smoothly. There must have been a side door. The next thing I knew, as they say in court, I was sitting in his sports car. He turned into a dimly lit side street, slowed down, placed his hand on my neck, rubbed the nape of it, and pressed my face quite roughly into his shoulder—all in one stupefying movement.

"Daisy, you're a fantastic kid."

Then he let me go and drove like a madman in the direction of Hollywood. The grin was still there, it transformed him. You'd never have guessed, after all that skin-diving talk, he could be so violently aroused.

"I think we should go back after all," I said nervously.

"Why?" Now he was rubbing his leg against mine, and in a small sports car there's no room to retreat. I lit a cigarette. "Everyone'll notice we've gone," I said, "and at my own première!"

He shook his head. "You felt faint and I ran you home."

"But you aren't running me home."

"I will later," the juvenile offered, and did this thing with my neck and head again.

It made me a little breathless, I have to admit, but I kept a firm hold on myself. "Turn around!" I cried. "I want to go back to Romanoff's!"

He ignored this. Soon I realized we were heading for the hills. It was distinctly cold and I had no coat over my organdy. We turned up a dirt road, no lights or houses anywhere.

"Is it much farther?"

"We're back at my place!" The juvenile stopped in front of some hillside shack with a flight of steps leading up to it. There was dark scrubland all around and crickets singing.

"I told you I'd changed my mind," I said feebly, trying to gather strength for the tussle to come. It was a long one, and ended halfway up the steps after he'd dragged me out of the car and was twisting my arm. I managed to stamp his foot hard enough to throw him off balance for a moment, then went flying down the dirt road with all the lights of Los Angeles spread out and winking at me miles below. It seemed the hills were full of dogs, they all started barking. I really didn't know where I was but kept right on running, and eventually found myself in a regular street. Then I heard a car approaching. I thought it was the juvenile coming after me, and hid behind some bushes. An old convertible nosed around the corner. The way I leaped out to thumb a ride certainly scared the driver, he braked like someone with convulsions. I stood in the glare of the headlights and tried to smile politely.

"Thank you very much. Could you help me get back to Romanoff's?"

An old fellow with glasses and a straw hat, and a big woman with a polka-dotted scarf around her head sitting next to him.

"It's all right," the woman said after a moment. "It's only a child."

I got in beside them, and we started down the hill.

"You look awful," the woman said. "What happened?"

"I can't discuss it. I'm in a state of shock."

"This is a terrible canyon," the woman said.

[72]

They were both aching with curiosity, but I kept them at bay and insisted they drop me off at Schwab's on the corner of Sunset Boulevard. I took a cab back to Romanoff's, where the doorman gave me a stare. In the john I tried to fix myself up, but my pumps were soiled and there was dirt on my stockings. I asked a waiter to go upstairs and tell Mrs. Gloria Goslett that I wasn't feeling so good and would wait in the powder room.

"Baby!" Gloria was looking very anxious and Harry peered at me round the door. "Where *were* you?"

"Suddenly it all got too much for me," I said.

Her eyes bulged, they'd caught my shoes. "But where *were* you?"

"I took a walk. I needed air."

"Let's get her out of here and take her home," Harry suggested, and I followed them to the car. I lay down on the back seat without a word and refused to answer questions. To tell the truth, I was getting what they call a delayed reaction. I'm not sure what kind of reaction, but it was depressing.

"We won't discuss this any further," Gloria said finally. "But just let me remind you, whatever you did you might have ruined your career!"

*

It's the 28th of March, *Little Annie Rooney* enters its 5th big week and I enter mine. I'm a YOUNG SINGING SENSATION, a PINT-SIZED VOCALIST and (here's a laugh) THE ORPHAN SONGBIRD. The studio's exercised my Option and I get more money, they tell me, though all I see of it is three bucks a week. Right now they're making up their minds which of two new Happy Pictures I should do next.

Gloria's attitude toward me has *definitely changed*. She'll never *like* me, of course, but because I'm famous, etc., she doesn't ask so many questions or argue so much, and goes around reminding everybody she's my sister. She's never tried to grill me about that night at Romanoff's, and when we're eating at home she even asks if there's anything special I want for dinner. Soon after the picture opened, an anonymous kidnap threat on the phone threw her into a real panic. She called the cops, and they

[73]

put a patrol on the house. She called the Studio, and they sent over a personal bodyguard. She made Harry buy a gun. She hugged and kissed me, and said, "I won't let them get you, baby, if it's the last thing I do!" One day in the street she became quite hysterical. I get pointed at occasionally, or asked for my autograph, but this time a woman rushed up and said, "I've simply got to kiss you!" Before I could answer she had me in her arms and was gasping out, "I adore you! I wish you were mine!" and Gloria nearly socked her. "I'm sure she wasn't the kidnaper," I said. Trembling all over, Gloria told me the woman was exactly the kind of decoy they use. No doubt about it, the idea of losing me really terrifies Gloria.

It was obviously some crazy joker on the phone. Nothing ever happened. They called off the police patrol and the bodyguard after a couple of weeks.

However, Gloria makes Harry sleep with that gun under the pillow.

My own problem is that, while Gloria may have changed, I'm exactly the same person. When I was with The Dealer and just wandering around those dumps on the coast by myself, it felt all right being who I was. I could even get fun out of it. I'm sure you could start with more advantages than being brought up in a trailer park in Playa del Rey, but in those days I certainly had some kicks on the side, like the old pier and of course Milton. And living in that trailer park it seemed quite natural to go out at night with no clothes on, and stuff like that, but living on Arcadia Drive with Gloria and Harry, I begin to feel all my impulses are crazy. I'd really be grateful to have fewer of them. *What's the point of it all?* I ask myself—drinking almost a quart of Scotch on Christmas Eve, or arousing that juvenile, or getting stuck on Wade Lewis after ten minutes in a car with him—and *Where's it all going to end?* You're only fifteen and a half, for Christ's sake slow down a little.

I forgot to mention that since I started working in the movies I've been going back to school, and have lessons in math, history, literature, etc. It's a bore but it's the law. Anyway, I like my literature teacher, she's an individualist and recommends good stuff to me, like *Lust for Life* by Irving Stone and *The Fountain-*

head by Ayn Rand, which is slightly far out but gutsy. Her name is Carolyn, I'd say she's pushing thirty-five and has obviously never been married. She's not bad-looking but doesn't seem to care. Sometimes she's a bit dry and impatient, and then she twinkles. Because she's the most educated person I know, I decided to have a talk with her and invited her to Will Wright's for some ice cream.

"Tell me," I said when we'd ordered the Flavor of the Month, chocolate pecan, "do you ever notice anything weird about me?"

She mentioned in a polite voice that in some respects I was old for my age.

"No, weirder than that," I said. "To give you an idea, I'll tell you the least terrible crazy thing I've done recently. I could tell you much worse things, but I won't. I'll just tell you a quite small absolutely insane thing." Carolyn looked extremely interested, she held up her scoop of chocolate pecan in the air. "The night they premièred *Little Annie Rooney*," I said, "I went and flushed my hair ribbon down the toilet in the ladies' room of the Egyptian Theater."

Carolyn swallowed the scoop of ice cream and licked her lips. "What I'd like to know," she asked, "is what you were trying to *prove?*"

"Gosh, so would I."

"I'll tell you what I think." She sounded very clipped now, she always did when she had a definite opinion to give out. "You see, Daisy, one of the artist's strongest urges is to protest against life. Artists are great disturbers of the peace. If they weren't—"

"Excuse me," I said. "How does this tie in with my action? I only disturbed myself."

"I'll begin again. Try and be patient. It's quite a long tunnel and we may not see the light at first."

"Okay," I said.

"Anyone who has something to express—as a writer, or a painter, or in your case as a singer, is a person of imagination." She leaned suddenly toward me. "Now, what is imagination?"

"The opposite of Gloria."

"That's too personal." Carolyn frowned. "If we looked up the word in Webster, we'd probably find something like—*the ability to create mental images out of things that never actually happened or that we never actually experienced.*"

"Okay," I said. "We're still in the same tunnel."

"For instance, Daisy, when you sing a song, it may be about something that never actually happened to you, but in order to *feel* it you have to *imagine* it did. Now this means that a person with imagination is also a person with some degree of madness. After all, mad people imagine things that never actually happened."

"Right!" I thought of The Dealer convincing herself that my father's body had lain up in Coldwater Canyon being eaten by the birds for three years and eight months.

"However," Carolyn went on, "the *difference* between the artist and the madman is that the artist knows he's imagining things that never happened and the madman doesn't."

I felt disappointed. "Then they're not the same at all. I certainly *knew* I was flushing that hair ribbon down the toilet."

"Of course you did." Carolyn gave a titter, very ironic. "My dear Daisy, I'm not suggesting you're mad. *All the same—*" For some reason she broke off.

"All the same what? Are you taking it back?"

"Certainly not. I just want to be sure you understand this. Sometimes the artist gets very close to the madman! This is because he lives in the world of imagination, and people living in that world see very strange and often disturbing meanings behind the mere appearance of everyday things."

"I'm afraid you'll have to explain that."

Carolyn sucked her spoon for a moment, thinking. "When I say *ocean*, what do you think of?"

"A very special shell I found," I said at once. "You hold it to your ear, and even though you're standing quite close to the real ocean, you can hear *another* ocean like three thousand miles away."

"Well, there you are." She looked pleased. "The mere mention of a very ordinary word, *ocean*, triggers off a deeply personal image in your case. You have imagination. Most kids would just say water." She paused, then suddenly threw at me "*Turkey!*"

It was strange of her to choose that word. "A woman in a nut-house," I said quietly.

"Heavens above," Carolyn said. "Well, I won't ask you to explain that one, but it certainly proves my point. What child without a remarkable imagination would ever have a response like that to the word *Turkey?*"

"I guess you're right," I said. "But I still don't feel I'm out of the tunnel. What's all that stuff you were saying before about disturbing the peace? Why do I want to do that, Carolyn?"

"Why shouldn't you?" Carolyn looked quite indignant, as if she'd like to do the same thing. "Is this the best of all possible worlds?"

"I hope not. I mean, there'd better be something better."

"I agree with you. *Now* don't you see? Most people feel what you've just said, but being ordinary they can only express their disappointment or frustration in very ordinary ways—like shall we say being unkind to animals or rude to their neighbors. But *you*, Daisy, being the kind of person you are," and her cheeks reddened and she sounded breathless, "*you* have to be original! *You* have to flush hair ribbons down the toilet at the Egyptian Theater!"

I've put all this down as well as I can remember it, because I really believe it's the most important conversation I've ever had in my life, and I'd like to be able to go back to it when my impulses worry me.

I also asked Carolyn how *she* expressed disappointment, but she looked rather secretive and said she didn't have much imagination.

Mr. Swan summoned me to the Studio after the Easter holidays to tell me about my next picture. The script wasn't quite finished, he said, but I'm to play the daughter of an old vaudevillian who wants to make a comeback. My father asks me to help him out with his act, and as a result I'm discovered and become a star, but nobody wants *him*. In the end he dies and I go on, etc. I said it sounded fine, but I felt I'd seen a picture very like that already, was this another old one they were doing over?

Mr. Swan looked cross for a moment. Then he said, "No, Daisy."

He pressed the button and that door slid open. Just as I reached it, he called after me, "By the way, how's your love life?"

It certainly stopped me dead, which was what he intended. I didn't answer at once. Something Gloria had said went through my mind, *People like that can open locked doors.* Probably the juvenile had turned mean and given me away.

"It's like my career." I laughed, and it sounded hollow as an old coconut. "I'm between engagements!"

Mr. Swan pressed the button and the door closed again.

"I thought," he said slowly, "maybe you'd have gone up to San Francisco for the holidays."

That horny old actor in *Little Annie Rooney.* He'd broken his promise not to tell, of course. I felt better. After all, it gave me the last laugh.

"Oh no," I said. "That's all over."

"*Who was he?*" Mr. Swan fairly rapped this out.

"If you don't mind," I said, "I'd rather not talk about it. It's all over."

"Will you burst into tears if you mention his name?"

"Yes."

"You're a liar, Daisy."

"Yes. I'll tell you the truth now, Mr. Swan. It's not that I don't trust you, but this boy came from an extremely snooty San Francisco family, I mean the top of Nob Hill, and his mother knows nothing about it all, and he was always terribly scared of her finding out. You know what they're like up there," I said. "That's why I'd rather not talk about it."

Mr. Swan gave me a long cool stare.

"Also," I said, "he's just got engaged to an heiress."

Mr. Swan got up and came toward me. He had an expression on his face I couldn't make out. Very cool, anyway. He stood staring down at me, then grabbed my ear and tweaked it. He

[78]

went back to his desk without saying a word and pressed the button again.

What kind of a nut is that? I wondered. He must have heard the story I gave that actor months ago, and he's been sitting on it like an old hen. Anyway, I kept my vow about not getting mad at him, just smiled and walked out of the office. I knew if I turned and looked back he'd be watching me, still with that cool expression on his face. I could feel it on my back like a draft.

Melora had invited me to lunch in the commissary, she was already waiting at a table in the important room.

"Well, you're looking chipper," she said. "Did you like the new story?"

"It's great. Mr. Swan just tweaked my ear."

Melora was definitely surprised. "A playful tweak, I'm sure, honey."

"I'm not," I said. "It didn't hurt much, anyway."

At that moment I saw Wade Lewis crossing the main room of the commissary. I waved frantically. He looked puzzled at first, then came over, said Hello to Melora and "Hi, Daisy," in a vague way to me. His skin was gray under the eyes.

"How is your father?" I asked.

He looked puzzled again. "He's fine, thank you."

"I'm glad," I said. "Last time we met, he was very ill."

"Oh, yes." From the way he spoke, you'd never have guessed he was desperate about the whole thing on Christmas Eve, you'd have thought I was playing it up. "He's fine now," Wade Lewis said.

"That's wonderful." I was furious.

He nodded and went away.

I watched him, then realized Melora was watching me.

"Honestly," I said, "he said his father was dying."

"You don't know Wade very well." Melora smiled. "That young man can't live without drama."

"He's got circles under his eyes. He should do something about that."

"Like sleep alone for a few nights." Melora's voice was suddenly hard and cutting. Then she signaled to a waitress. "We're

[79]

ready to order!" After I'd settled on Lamb Chops Barbara Stanwyck and Melora had chosen her Dieter's Special, she relaxed and lit a cigarette.

"I can't imagine," smoke poured out of her nose, "why you wanted Wade to come to your première."

I told her I wasn't serious about it, and she raised her eyebrows.

"Why are you doing that?"

"Because I don't believe you."

"Oh," I said. "Well, I'll tell you the truth. He bought me some flowers and stuff for Christmas, and I felt I'd like to do a little something for him in return."

Melora shook her head.

"Why are you doing that?"

"Same reason, honey."

"Well," I said, "I'll also admit I thought he was very interesting the first time I met him."

"And now?"

I tried a shrug.

"I hope you don't have a crush on him?" Her eyes were quizzical, she seemed amused and sorry about something at the same time.

"I certainly don't, I don't have a crush on anybody!"

I spoke more loudly than I intended. People at another table glanced up. I grabbed a cracker from the dish and started munching.

"Frankly," I said, "I'd rather not discuss my private emotions."

Melora gave no sign that she heard me. She was frowning at the Dieter's Special the waitress had just brought. She slit the hamburger patty down the middle and started filling it with cottage cheese, then mustard on top. "Maybe this is wrong of me, I don't know."

"What, Melora?"

"What I'm going to tell you about Wade Lewis."

Something in her voice made me nervous. "Is he secretly married?"

"No, dear." She hesitated. "He has a drinking problem."

[80]

"Oh, is that all?" I said.

Melora stared at me. "It's very serious. He drinks because there are things in his life he refuses to face."

I've learned something. In this kind of situation, in this kind of world—*fool them!* They're only waiting for you to give yourself away. Then they'll move in and take over.

"Thank you, Melora!" I smiled at her. "I've been wondering exactly what it was about Wade Lewis that attracted me, and now you've explained. I must call him up and compare notes. We drinkers should stick together."

She seemed surprised for a moment, then laughed and patted my hand. "I'm glad you can take it this way," she said.

"I may be laughing on the outside," I told her, "but I'm crying on the inside."

She made some remark about my unusual sophistication. What a fool Melora really is, even though she's smart. I'm simple enough not to trust her after that business with The Dealer, that's all. I'll bet that never even crosses her mind while we go on sitting here. When we finish lunch, she asks if I'd like to go shopping with her. She has no idea what I'm secretly thinking, which is that if Carolyn threw the word *love!* at me right now, the deeply personal image I might throw back is that darned automatic door in Mr. Swan's office when I couldn't find the right button.

7

A summer.

A winter.

(There's hardly a fall at all.)

A sort of spring.

And another summer.

The 21st of June, 1954. Hollywood. California. U.S.A. The World. The Universe. Hollywood.

In future, if these Theme Books are lost, kindly return to *Mrs. Daisy Clover Lewis!*

Okle-dokle. I've obviously got some explaining to do. When everything gets too marvelous or too terrible, I don't write it down at once. So for a year and two months there's been just half a blank page at the end of No. 6. Most of that blank marginal ruled paper stands for the greatest love story of all time, which of course began on Christmas Eve 1952, but didn't really get off the ground until—let's see, I think if I really make an effort I can remember—yes, around 3:11 p.m. on August 20th, 1953.

There was a heat wave outside, the high for the day was 109°. But on the air-conditioned set it was dark and cool, until they switched on the lights and Alex Conrad said, "Ready, Clover?"

The set is a stage—part of a stage, really, and the wings. Out where the audience should be is the camera and Alex and the playback machine for my number. It's the last scene of *Song and Dance!* and I'm about to become a star right after my father's died. I have to hesitate in the wings, but only for a moment, because of my grief—then I go on and give it to them.

"Ready," I said.

"Happy as only you can make it, Clover. Remember it's the end of the show and your triumph!"

The make-up man powders down my nose. The playback music starts.

"Clover!"

I hesitate. Think of my dead father, then—

Alex's voice: "Cut it!" And the music stops.

"Too long, honey." He comes toward me. "Just a very short pause is all. Can you count up to three?"

"I don't know, I've never tried."

Somebody laughs, anyway.

"Going again!" The music starts. "Clover!"

I hesitate. Think of my dead father, then—

"Alex, I'm sorry, this is ridiculous!"

Everyone stares. I had to yell, so he'd hear me above the music. It stops again and the lights are switched off.

Now it's very silent. I haven't moved from the wings. Alex climbs on the stage and asks what's the matter.

"I just don't see how I can make this happy," I tell him, "right after my father's died."

He looks surprised. "Of course it's extremely sad that your father died, and you loved him very much, but it was really for the best and you ought to know that."

Now I'm *sure* there's something wrong. *Carry me back to the beach at Venice,* I think suddenly, *and Gloria in her shiny turban and sheath dress.*

"He was a lovable old man and a great trouper in his day," Alex goes on. "But he's also washed up, and holding you back, and really he has nothing to live for."

"*You* might think so," I say, "but *he* certainly didn't. All through this movie he's been working like crazy to make a comeback. He's been living for it. Then he dies without making it. I think that's terrible."

"Clover, you old cornball, don't you understand he never *could* have made that comeback?" Alex grins at me. "He was a wreck. The whole thing was an illusion."

[83]

"Not to him. It certainly wasn't an illusion to him!"

The cameraman comes up and gives Alex a what's-going-on? look. "Take five," Alex tells him quietly. A moment later I hear this repeated to the crew, more lights go out, there's a thud of footsteps as people move to the coffee urn. Alex and I are almost in darkness. It's the kind of atmosphere, like church, that makes you whisper.

"We're making a *romantic* picture. A fairy tale! If you go realistic on me, Clover, it'll fall apart."

I find a high rickety stool and perch on it. "Well, I can't just smile and be happy no matter what happens. Do you want me to feel I'm *traveling* in happiness and every suitcase I open is just naturally full of smiles?"

"Yes, that's *exactly* how I want you to feel."

I bare my teeth, trying to look as sickening as possible. I stick my thumbs in my ears and waggle my fingers at him. I also lisp out a few bars of "Happy Talk." Then I blow a raspberry. It sounds extremely loud, and echoes across the whole dark stage. Alex has to laugh.

"It's not funny," I say. "It's just the way any normal healthy girl behaves when her father dies."

"For Christ's sake forget about your father dying." Alex begins to sound annoyed. "Do the number as if it comes somewhere else in the movie."

I shake my head. "Once I know it comes right after my father's died, I can't make it happy."

"All right." He's distinctly needled now. "Maybe you'd care to demonstrate, before we waste this whole afternoon, how you'd like to do the number. I'd appreciate that, Clover."

"I'm trying to tell you I can't do it at all. Don't you remember that day on *Little Annie Rooney* when you had to send me home? It was because I'd just heard they'd given The Dealer shock treatment, and—"

"Who?" Alex gives me a curious look. "Who's The Dealer?"

"Oh." I'd forgotten for the moment that The Dealer is what they call Not for Publication, and he'd never heard of her. "She's just an old aunt of mine. But she's really as close to me

[84]

as my mother, closer, because my mother died when I was young, as everybody knows."

"That's a funny expression. You're not exactly old now."

"I'm a good deal older than I was, Alex. Not counting strictly in years."

He sighs. "Well, here's the point. I've told you how I want you to do this number. What about it?"

I dig my feet into the rungs of the stool.

"Are you refusing?"

"I guess so."

We look at each other. Then he laughs. "You mad at me, Clover?"

"No."

"That's good. Shall we dance?"

So he's trying to kid me out of it. Okay. I nod, and he lifts me off the stool, hums "Jealousy," and starts a ridiculous old-fashioned tango. He bends me right over backward, almost drops me, then pulls me up and says casually, "Now let's get on with the show."

I don't say anything, only bare my teeth again.

He lets me go, looking suddenly like a worried dog that hasn't been given his piece of sugar after doing his parlor tricks. Then he trots away. Of course he's going to call Mr. Swan.

As Alex went off, I saw the hairdresser, the make-up man, and the script girl all standing nearby in a close excited little group. I looked nonchalant, made tracks for my stool, but couldn't get back on it because it was already occupied—by Wade Lewis, wearing a white open-necked sports shirt and white linen trousers.

"Oh," I said. "Tennis, anyone?"

He merely folded his arms and stared down at me, quite poker-faced but his eyes glittering.

"Did you hear all that?" I asked.

He nodded.

"Then please tell me something. Am I crazy?"

He nodded again.

[85]

"You think I'm wrong?"

He got off the stool. "You were absolutely right. That's why you're crazy."

More lights were switched off. The hairdresser, the make-up man, and the script girl were still watching, trying to catch every word without craning their heads. Wade looked at them, they gave nervous smiles and started to move away. In the far corner of the set, I could see Alex on the telephone.

"Dear heart, you've let in a little reality," Wade said, "and they don't know what to do."

For some reason I thought of that time I telephoned Milton about The Dealer, and imagined his face in San Francisco, very flat and blank because he wasn't interested. Then I looked at Wade, who was really tense. He took out a pack of cigarettes and offered me one.

"I'm still not supposed to in public," I said.

He took out a cigarette and stuck it in my mouth. As he lit it, Alex came back, and told me Mr. Swan was coming over.

"That should fix it," Wade said. "That should bring back the unreality."

"Would you get off my set?" Alex suddenly snapped at him. "I don't like visitors on my set!"

Wade shrugged, winked at me, and strolled calmly away.

I felt abandoned!

"He's a destructive character," Alex said.

"I'm thirsty." I made my voice sound casual. "I think I'll go and get a Coke."

I walked off the stage, opened the door to the alley outside, and saw Wade just getting into his car. It was so hot, my make-up started to run down my face immediately. As he came over, Wade looked extremely cool, which was annoying.

"Why did you come on the set, anyway?" I asked.

He put on a pair of dark glasses. "I had an appointment with a producer on the lot, and I thought I'd like to see how the orphan songbird feathered her nest."

"Oh." Now I felt my mascara beginning to run. I must have looked hideous, but if Wade thought so he showed no sign of it, which I'd say is unusual for him.

"Don't be nervous about this," he said after a moment. "Stand up to them. *Refuse to do it their way.*"

"Really?"

"*Their* way," he said, "is an insult to human dignity."

I was extremely impressed.

"I've got some vodka in the car," he went on. "Like a slug?"

"My God, do you think I should?"

"I didn't ask you that." He fetched the bottle and two Dixie Cups, poured me out a full couple of inches.

"Once you give in," he said, "you're lost. Dear heart, you're *theirs.*"

I took a sip of the warm vodka. My eyelids were smarting and I could feel huge melting beads of make-up around my throat. A group of Oriental extras walked past us, then stepped aside as a limousine came down the alley. It stopped, and Mr. Swan got out. He nodded quickly to Wade, took my arm, and said, "Daisy, let's get this thing settled."

I looked at Wade and wanted to see his eyes, but of course the dark glasses hid them.

"There's nothing worse than Seven-Up without ice!" He threw his Dixie Cup away.

"You're right!" I said, doing the same thing and for an instant feeling quite marvelous. Mr. Swan only grunted and hurried me through the door. "Throw that cigarette away," he ordered as we arrived on the stage. He sounded brisk and impatient. "And get a Kleenex or something, you look like Dracula's Daughter. That wasn't Seven-Up, either."

He snapped his fingers at the make-up man, who opened his tray and started dabbing at my face. Alex came over, giving me a fairly sheepish smile.

"Take the floor, Clover, and explain to Mr. Swan your feelings about this scene."

"My father's just died," I said, "and I'm supposed to go on and do this number grinning from ear to ear." The make-up man shook out a powder puff over me. "It's an insult to human dignity!"

"You're putting a face on it," Mr. Swan explained. "You've got an audience waiting. Are you going to let them down?"

"Yes," I said. "If my father's died."

"Would you go on the next night?" Mr. Swan asked.

I thought this over. "I guess I might."

"Then what's the difference? Have you ever heard of 'Laugh, Clown, Laugh?' "

"Sure, but in 'Laugh, Clown, Laugh' he's really crying."

Suddenly Alex gave a kind of snort. "I have a great idea! I know how to solve this whole thing!" He put his arm around my shoulder. "This number—it was a number your father used to do. Right?"

"It's the number that first made him famous," I said.

"Well, then!" Alex spoke very fast. "You do the number as a *tribute* to your father who's just died—*in his clothes!*"

"I like that," Mr. Swan said.

"You're doing it for *him!* He's living on through *you!* That way it's *important* for you to do the number." Alex paused. "And at the same time, it's very cute."

They both looked at me. Frankly, I was getting confused. That sip of vodka in the hot alley was going to my head. I wished I could ask Wade whether this was still an insult to human dignity or not.

"Okay," I said finally. "I guess that makes sense."

An hour later they had me standing under this spotlight, wearing baggy trousers and a check coat and an old hat tilted over my face. Out where the audience should have been stood the camera and a lot of well-known shadows. Behind them, the whole stage seemed to stretch away forever. I didn't really feel I was a part of it at all, because no matter where I moved I was still inside this spotlit circle, it followed me all the time and I couldn't get out of it.

When the playback music started, Alex's shadow called to me to run the number through.

I went into the shuffle and tried to think about my dead father. I couldn't get any feeling about him at all. He'd gone away. What I got instead, would you believe it? was a mental picture of The Dealer lying in that paneled room with the barred windows, staring at a blank TV screen. Maybe it was that drop of warm vodka, but it definitely made me want to cry. I knew that if I did my mascara would run, so I stopped myself. Then, as I went into the first verse of the number, I had an enormous illusion that almost threw me. I thought one of those scrim curtains you see in the theater had come down in front of the whole gloomy desert stretching away beyond the shadows, and someone began to project different slides on it, muddling them all up together, so that just for a moment all kinds of pictures would appear on it, like—

an empty beach

crazy old people in paper hats

a CHRIST DIED FOR YOU notice on an oil pump

The Dealer streaking down a fire escape in her nightgown— all of these things were in front of me and inside me, and why should they come when I'm doing a vaudeville routine?

Anyway, I went right through with it. At the end there was a long pause, and the place felt very silent again, and none of the shadows moved—then Alex ran up and hugged me, and said just for the hell of it he'd had the camera turning over, and it was absolutely sensational, and how could he ever thank me for putting him on to something so great and true and lovely? Then Mr. Swan came over and said, "I told you it was 'Laugh, Clown, Laugh.'" I was too breathless to speak, and felt a strange terrible nausea creeping through my stomach toward my throat, so I turned away and hurried to my dressing room, where I threw up on the floor. I lay down on the couch, my face icy cold and my whole body twitching under the baggy pants and check coat. When I calmed down a little, I started to laugh. Carolyn certainly hit the jackpot when she said that sometimes the artist gets very close to the madman. Maybe I've gotten close enough.

When Wade ordered two martinis, the waitress asked for my identification. Rather than be exposed as disgustingly underage, I told her I'd forgotten to bring it with me. "So let's drop the whole thing," I said. "These days, I can take it or leave it." Wade ordered a double, and whispered that he'd pour some of it into my glass of water, if I'd drink the water first, which I did.

We were sitting opposite each other in a booth in a place called The Blue Piano, on Santa Monica Boulevard, almost next door to a movie theater that usually showed dirty foreign pictures. As we parked, I noticed it was advertising *Naked Ecstasy*, Swedish I think, and I asked Wade if he'd seen it. He said no, so I thought maybe we could catch it together one evening, but he didn't want to and told me it would be a waste of time. I explained I'd never seen a dirty foreign picture. Anyway, this place with the booths was very dimly lit, just like a movie set when they aren't shooting, and the only thing you could really see was the white tuxedo worn by a colored lady quietly singing and playing at the blue piano with a bar all around it. She reminded me of a photograph in negative, pretty ghostly.

"Do you realize," I asked Wade, "this is our first meeting that isn't accidental and has a chance of lasting more than fifteen minutes? You've no idea how I appreciate that."

Wade laughed. "Tell me *exactly* how!" He hadn't changed his clothes since I saw him on the set a few hours back, only slipped a thin black sweater over his shirt. His hair was still untidy in exactly the same way.

"Well, I was dying for you to call me," I said. "And I never believed you would. I wanted so much to tell you about throwing up."

The waitress came back with his double martini and asked if I wouldn't like a Coke or something, in the kind of voice that made me feel like a child. I told her I never touched that kind of stuff.

"I wish you could explain that whole experience to me," I said to Wade. "Haven't *you* ever been in a situation like that in your career?"

"We can't start talking about my career until I've had a lot more to drink." Wade poured some of his martini into my glass.

"Why not? Everyone says you're tipped for stardom and they're always interviewing you in the fan magazines."

"Yes, I've come a long way considering I'm only thirty." Then he looked bored. "Dear heart, I'm afraid you're a fool."

He said this quite affectionately so I wasn't offended. "Tell me why."

"When I say fool," Wade picked his olive out of the martini and threw it on the floor, "I mean the kind of person nobody ever falls in love with."

This time I did feel slightly offended. But I also wanted to know what he meant. "Tell me why."

"It's just something fools have. Have you ever bought a can of perfumed insecticide?"

"Well, for heaven's sake, I don't think so."

"It makes the air smell good," Wade said. "But it has an active ingredient and it kills. Fools can be very attractive and very talented, but right down inside them there's too much despair. They know too much, or think they do. You can hump a fool, of course," he sounded thoughtful, "and you can enjoy it, but if you try falling in love, all that despair will kill it."

"Honestly, you make fools sound kind of marvelous."

"Well, I'm a fool, too." He gave me a long look, and although he was smiling I'd say it was full of despair. "You *know*, don't you?"

Dear Lord, what did he mean? Did I know about Wade being a fool, or humping other fools? Did I know about despair? About having things in his life he refused to face? I very much wanted to know the right thing. Wade was the kind of person who'd get quite disgusted and angry if I didn't. But it wasn't easy, especially after he'd had several martinis.

I decided to say nothing, just nod and look understanding. Then I gulped down the rest of my cocktail. Fortunately the waitress came back and asked for our orders.

"I'm hungry," I said. "I want two lamb chops."

Wade only ordered another double martini. Then he leaned across the table toward me, his eyes very bright, as if there might be tears coming. "I'll tell you what matters to me," he said unexpectedly. "Ever since I came out here from New York, I've been wondering what I missed most. Now I'm sure." I haven't mentioned Wade's voice before, it has deep quiet vibrations which I find extremely masculine, and also little nervous gasps and pauses like a small boy talking to grown-ups he doesn't know very well. "It's Bessie Smith," he said.

"The old singer? I thought she was dead."

"Of course she's dead. Fat and broke and drunk and ugly she's dead." Wade suddenly cupped his hands over his mouth and made a noise like a wheezy cornet. Then he sang out—

> *"It's mighty strange, without a dime*
> *Nobody knows you when you're down and out*
> *I mean, when you're down and out!"*

The Negress in the tuxedo looked up for a moment. Wade laughed unhappily. "But I wouldn't know about that, dear heart. My folks have the golden touch. Ever hear of the Slumber-Rite Mattress?"

"I don't think so," I said, "but I never ask what I'm sleeping on."

"Three to one it's a Slumber-Rite mattress. That's how popular they are."

"Do you sleep on one?"

"Sure. I get a free supply for the rest of my life. I give them to everybody for Christmas presents. And I also have all the recordings Bessie Smith ever made. Wherever I go now, I'll take them with me."

"I have a very special kind of shell," I said, "and I feel the same way about that."

"I'll play you some Bessie Smith later." Wade wasn't really listening, he watched the waitress as she came back with his martini. He poured some of it into my glass. "Unless you want to go home now."

I shook my head.

"I wouldn't blame you."

"But I like it here!"

"You ought to be bored to death," Wade said. "I bore most people to death. They say, He's got money and some talent, why's he so sorry for himself?"

"Well, why?" I asked. "Is there something terrible in your life I don't know about?"

"I'm an actor." He made the word sound as bad as murderer. "Actors are puppets who hate their strings. So why am I an actor? Because I'm a fool. And the amazing thing is," he looked at me, eyes very bright, "*you* are still a child, a monstrous child,

streaking through life like a hare with the hounds after you—
and they *are* after you, dear heart, you know—and you keep
running so bravely and you never seem sorry for yourself, yet all
the same you're a fool, too. Like me."

I started crying into my martini.

Wade looked astonished, then extremely concerned. "What is
it? You're not supposed to cry!"

"I've had a very exhausting day," I said. "And you've just told
me I'm a fool and a monstrous child and nobody will ever fall
in love with me, and the hounds are on my track and my active
ingredient is despair! Should I get up and jump for joy?"

He reached across the table, took my hand, and gave it a kiss
that was restrained but sexy. "No," he said. "I should."

The trouble with these old recordings is, you can't hear the
words clearly. Even when Wade played "Weeping Willow
Blues" for the fifth time I couldn't figure exactly what it was
about, though Bessie sounded marvelous. I'd have asked him
to repeat the lyric, but he'd told me to keep quiet.

I should explain that after I burst into tears he became extremely charming, and told me how great I was in *Little Annie
Rooney*, and did a very funny imitation of Alex Conrad, and
we laughed a good deal. Later he sat beside me in the booth,
ordered another martini, and put his arm around my waist.
We sat like this while he told me how once he'd decided that
solitude was the only answer, and he'd become a forest ranger
and lived in a tower for six months and had no company or sex
or anything. Then he burst out laughing and said, "God
dammit, not even a single fire either!"

When we got back to his apartment, which was small and
untidy, he started playing Bessie at once. Then he went to the
couch and held out his arms. I sat on his knee. He hugged me
very tight, but when I started to say something he murmured,
"Ssssh, listen to Bessie," so we stayed very still, his arms around
me and his chin resting on the top of my head.

I was afraid to kiss him.

One time, after getting up to change the record, he took off
his thin black sweater, threw it on the floor, and disappeared

[93]

into the bathroom. I snatched it up and held it against my face, for the feel of it and the smell. He came back and saw me doing this. I felt like an idiot, I said it had turned chilly and put the sweater on. (Next day I heard on the radio it was the warmest night in years.) Wade smiled, then frowned at the floor. Finally he went over to the phonograph and played Bessie again. But he didn't join me on the couch, he sprawled in a chair on the other side of the room. I noticed then that he must have taken off his socks and shoes in the bathroom. His bare feet rested on the floor, toes sticking up like a row of tenpins.

His sweater had a nice, faint, stale perfume.

After a while he stretched out his arms again—then yawned and got to his feet. "Dear heart," he said, "I must run you home."

I nodded, and took off the sweater.

"Keep it if you're cold."

"No, I don't want it."

On the way back I remember we passed a house on wheels, towed by a truck.

I have my own key now, and can let myself in. Only the porch light was burning, Gloria and Harry had gone to bed. Wade gave me a hug and I kissed him on the mouth, keeping my eyes wide open and looking straight up into his. For a moment they were extremely warm and beautiful, but then they flickered and looked away. He turned me slowly around until I faced the front door.

"There you go," he said.

I tiptoed up the stairs, though if Gloria heard me it wouldn't have mattered. She doesn't ask questions any more. It was nearly 2:30 a.m. In about five hours I'd have to be at the Studio, in the make-up department, but I didn't feel like going to sleep.

The darkness felt stale and hot, like Wade's sweater, I pulled the blankets off my bed and lay naked between the sheets. Somewhere inside me was a kind of pain that I'd never had before. It was quite strong but I didn't really mind it. I even had a crazy thought that if I *loved* the pain, it would go away. I tried, and it seemed to die down a little.

If Wade meant what he said about fools, then he'll never love me. Maybe I'll still get somewhere, though, if it's true you can hump fools and have a good time. I've also heard that a drinking problem makes you unsexy, you feel you can't be bothered, which could explain Wade's behavior tonight.

Right now, in the warm darkness, I'd rather think about something else. Wade living in that tower in the forest for six months. It's quite marvelous! Many people would call it screwy, but in my opinion it definitely makes sense. More people should go away and live in towers for a while, don't ask me why. All I know is, it's got something to do with the echo of the ocean in that shell of mine. Wherever those waves are breaking is a good place to be. Somewhere else, I mean. Way, way out. I'm serious.

8

(*Greatest Love Story of All Time, cont.*)

I might have tried more seriously to go to sleep if I'd remembered that I'd been slated to sing next evening at a big party given by Julie Forbes. Mr. Swan had conned me into this. He said that Julie had asked especially for me to entertain her distinguished guests, and it was a great compliment. I didn't feel like getting rigged out in organdy, etc., after a day's work at the Studio, but you don't turn down a star like that.

Until Mr. Swan came on the set after lunch and reminded me, I'd forgotten this shindig lay ahead, and I felt even less like going than when he first told me I must. Later in the afternoon we were waiting around while the cameraman lined up a shot, so I went to Alex's trailer and asked if he'd do me a favor.

"For you, Clover—anything!"

"I've got to sing for a big crowd at Julie Forbes's tonight," I explained, "and I'm bushed. Can you fix me up with a couple of bennies?"

He looked surprised. "What's the matter? Do some heavy drinking last night?"

"Martini after martini."

"Booze and pills, Clover, that's a dangerous route to tread."

"I know. And I'll cry tomorrow, but I've got to sing tonight."

"Just this once, then. Next time you'll have to find another pusher."

When they ask a kid to sing at this kind of party, they don't invite you to mingle with the guests beforehand. It creates a bad impression, as Mr. Swan explained, and the public might think I was being allowed to live it up in a way that would tarnish my

[96]

image. So I had to go home for dinner with Gloria and Harry, then a limousine brought me to Julie's house just a few minutes before 9:30 p.m., when I was due to go on. I swallowed the bennies as we started out, and kept squinting at myself in the driving mirror to see whether they'd dilate the pupils of my eyes. When I arrived at Julie's house my eyes were still all right, but I went to the john for a final check-up and they'd grown enormous. No turning back, of course, I had to go out there and sing and hope the distinguished guests wouldn't notice this child star was temporarily on dope.

Everyone was on the terrace this warm summer evening, or wandering around the edge of the pool, the men in tuxedos and the women checkered with jewels and little ermine stoles. I saw quite a few movie stars, but not Cary or Myrna. The Swans were there, Melora in silver with a corsage of emeralds pinned above her heart. Julie looked stunning in ivory taffeta, and a diamond choker almost as big as those contraptions you have to wear after you've broken your neck. Naturally I was trapped in one of those "simple" yellow numbers the Studio costume designer regularly turned out for me, but as I knew it was going to be a grand occasion I'd slipped on all *my* diamonds, and didn't feel a complete idiot when Julie led me by the hand to the front of the pool house, where a combo was playing "You and the Night and the Music." The music stopped and Julie announced me, and all the glittering people smiled and applauded and rushed to the bar on the terrace for refills before I got started. I looked up at the sky, which was clear as glass with a wonderful crescent moon like a slice of cantaloupe. Just as I nodded to the combo to start "Love Is Sweeping the Country" an airplane came overhead, but I wasn't going to let a thing like that stop me, and belted out the song loud enough for the passengers to hear. I'd told Mr. Swan I wouldn't do more than three numbers, but the guests encored me like crazy, and I ended up doing seven. Then Julie said, "It's way past this little girl's bedtime," and a footman brought me a dish of strawberry and chocolate ice cream on a silver tray. I ate it very quickly because I felt sure my eyes must be giving me away. Then I escaped into the limousine and gave the driver Wade Lewis's address. Wade gave me a martini but I was so tired that my eyes started to close after the first sip. He said he'd take me home, but I wanted to spend the night there. We went to bed and he held my hand and I fell asleep.

The Sunday morning after this I woke up at home and looked out the window and the sky was a dirty orange color. Gloria came in and told me there was a brush fire somewhere in the hills. Then she sat on the edge of the bed, fidgeting. Obviously she had something on her mind.

"Baby." She started very slowly, like a circus acrobat preparing for the tightrope. "We've agreed, haven't we, baby, that you have every right to a private life?"

"Yes," I said. "We've agreed that."

"And you don't have to tell me anything you don't want to. We've agreed that, haven't we?"

"Oh yes," I said.

"I intend to go on keeping that agreement, of course."

"Fine, Gloria."

"I despise idle curiosity. I just despise it."

"Do you feel anything strange about the air?" I asked. "I guess it must be that fire. The air feels very dry, it's almost like being in a desert."

"There's a Santa Ana," Gloria said. "It's terrible—twenty-eight homes destroyed already. You don't have to tell me anything you don't want to, baby, but I can't help noticing you've had dinner with us only one night this last week, and one night you didn't even come home."

"But I phoned."

"Sure. And I appreciate that. And I have no intention of asking you any questions, but have you noticed how tired you're looking?"

"That's just hard work. This darned movie'll be over in a few days, then I can rest up."

She hesitated, then gave one of her face-stretching smiles. "Just as long as you're not burning the candle at both ends." I didn't answer, and the smile vanished slowly. "Please don't tell me anything you don't want to," she said. "We'll forget this whole conversation if you like. All I ask is—don't do anything foolish! Don't drive yourself too hard! You have every right to be happy—*if* whoever-it-is is making you happy—but, baby," here came the smile again, "*please* take it easy!"

"Ram, bam, thank you ma'am," I said. "I think I will. And I'm going to start by sleeping late this morning."

I lay down again, turned away from her on my side, and closed my eyes. I heard her mutter something, then leave the room.

Frankly—and you may think I'm crazy—although I refused to discuss this whole situation with Gloria, I wanted to talk about it with someone else.

For some time now The Dealer has been perkier. She plays cards, she doesn't seem nearly so depressed, I even have a feeling she'd *like* to connect again, if she could. If we don't expect too much, as Miss Donahue said, we *may* get more than we expected.

It was a beautiful Sunday afternoon in summer, except for the Santa Ana blowing leaves off the trees like feathers from a burst pillow, and the smoky orange sky. Most of the Ambulatory Cases were out in the grounds, sitting at tables playing checkers or something, or wandering around peering into bushes, etc. Whenever there was a strong gust of wind, everybody's hair stood up on end and they looked weird, but otherwise the atmosphere was quite peaceful and relaxed.

The Dealer was sitting by herself at a small table, deep in two solitaires. She wore that old shawl and smoked a cigarette through her stained yellow holder.

"What took you so long?" was her opening line. "I've been waiting for hours."

I hoped I hadn't upset her schedule.

"I should slap you, Daisy." The Dealer reconnoitered her cards, frowned, and clicked her teeth.

"Think that one's going to come out?" I asked.

"It's in the bag."

The wind blew, and scattered some of the cards. I hadn't noticed before that there were already stray cards on the grass and the flower beds.

"Doesn't matter." The Dealer produced a new pack from her lap. She began turning them up and adding them to the cards on the table.

"Hey, you'll get two jacks of hearts or something if you do that," I said. "Isn't it confusing?"

She only shook her head and dealt a few more. The afternoon grew a little darker, because there was smoke drifting across the sun.

"Listen," I said, "I sometimes play a game with my literature teacher, which is—she gives me a word and I have to fire back with a word that her word makes me think of. Understand?"

"It's simple."

"Good. When I say the word Love—what do you think of?"

She gave me a long, fixed look. "Say that word again, Daisy honey."

"*Love!*"

Now she chuckled. "I like that game. Let's play it again."

"But you haven't played it at all yet. You haven't given me your word."

After a moment, she suddenly gave it to me. "Hose!"

I was thrown for a loop. Then I thought of the time she found my father with the little widow next door and turned the water on them. "You mean a garden hose?"

"I was giving *you* that word."

"Then you're not playing right." I grabbed the pack of cards in her hand and shuffled through them till I found the one I wanted. "*Joker!*" I said, holding it up to her.

"Hose!" The Dealer said, and chuckled again. Then she turned back to her solitaires and seemed to forget all about me.

I got up. "Well, I'm glad you're in good spirits. I'll be seeing you again next Sunday."

"Don't keep me waiting," The Dealer said.

I walked away past an old couple playing checkers. A card had landed in the middle of the board. They were both staring at it, extremely puzzled.

That night.
"Wade!" I said.

He was lying back in the driver's seat with his eyes closed. We'd gone up to look at the fire, and parked the car off the road somewhere in the hills. Nearby there were at least eight other cars, each with the lights switched off, a couple necking, and radios tuned into different stations. I heard an announcer saying on one of them that the whole thing was finally under control. The glow in the sky was fading.

"Wade," I said. "About The Dealer!"

"Poor bitch."

"Yes, and I really would like to get her out of that funny house. Do you believe that many people in this world honestly *connect*?"

He sighed. "I believe the opposite."

"Then all The Dealer's ever done is to connect a few points less than most people. And just for that they put her away and give her the shocks."

"She doesn't keep up appearances, that's her trouble." Wade's eyes were still closed. "I'd say you connect with her just as much as you do with Gloria—but you and Gloria pretend to make sense, so you're sane."

"You're right," I said. It's extraordinary how Wade is the only person I've met who understands stuff like this. Our situations are very alike, of course, he's told me how he never connected with his family, except his sister who died when she was fifteen. This surprised me at first, because he'd seemed to care so much about his father having a stroke, but Wade explained that he'd never forgive himself if his father died suspecting that his son didn't care. (He decided this during that stretch in the tower.) So whenever it looked as if his father might die, Wade felt he had to suffer. I guess that's something to try and live up to, though if Gloria ever had a stroke I'm not sure I could make the effort.

"I certainly would like to get The Dealer out," I said.

Wade laughed suddenly, and put his arm around my shoulder. I laughed too, then asked, "What's funny?"

"God dammit, there's a fire at last! All those years after I sat up in that tower, waiting for one!"

From another car I heard the sound of people laughing now.

I turned to look and saw this man holding this girl very tightly. Wade leaned forward and began fiddling with the radio. I felt like a bucket dropped into a deep dark well, let all the way down. This is something I'm growing used to with Wade, for a time it's marvelous and then it's almost depressing.

So there's his hand resting on my shoulder, and all the different radios playing, and that couple snuggled together and in the distance people putting out the fire, and the question I want to ask gone dry in my mouth. *Here it is now.* How is it possible for two people to be almost one and then extremely separate and two again? Don't try and tell me the answer's just S-E-X, because with Milton I had enough and to spare of that, and we ended up total strangers. It *may* be the drinking problem, but I can't go on blaming everything on that. Also, I'm much too scared to ask Wade about it, he might never speak to me again, especially since he told me the other night that most American women are ball cutters. I didn't understand this expression, so he explained that what the American female really wants is to deprive a fellow of his virility, they're extremely jealous of men and want to cut off their balls. I certainly don't intend to grow up that way, I'm much too impressed by virility —especially by Wade's, if only I could get at it.

In the meantime, there's his hand resting on my shoulder the way it so often does. I could kiss it, but that would mean shifting my position, and he might take it away. So I'll go on staying very still.

Sometimes, to quote the great old lyric, I'd like to give love back to the birds and the bees and the Viennese. I'd like to be pushing twenty-six and playing the field with extreme poise— on the Riviera. If anybody got serious about me, I'd tell him to grow up. "Why spoil something that's been such marvelous fun?" is what I'd say, as I went off to have dinner on yet another man's yacht.

By the end of September I'd say my condition was distinctly morbid. My movie was finished and Wade had just started one which he said could ruin his career. I was sleeping late and trying to read a book he'd given me, *The Way of All Flesh* by Samuel Butler, about this kid Pontifex who hated his father. Pretty good stuff, though not for laughs, and it certainly doesn't encourage you to get married, raise a family, settle down, etc. This book also says that there are two kinds of people in the world, the sinners and the sinned-against, and it's much better to be the first kind. I started to think about that, and where being sinned against had landed The Dealer, and I'd just decided that I agreed and maybe should do something about it—when the telephone rang. It was Belle, saying Mr. Swan would like to see me at the Studio in one hour.

Whenever I think of Mr. Swan it's that automatic door opening, and his big tanned figure in a shiny suit, and his gray hair cropped close to the skull and his quiet edgy voice saying, "Daisy Clover, come on in." This morning he didn't let me down, and as the door swung closed behind me, he pointed to the high antique chair and told me to make myself comfortable. Inside the glass case of the clock the pendulum was still swinging, and I could see Melora in her silver frame. My latest album, *Ooops-A-Daisy*, lay on the desk in front of her. Mr. Swan frowned at his nails, which looked perfect. Something else had to be wrong.

"Like some coffee, Daisy?"

I shook my head. He flipped the intercom switch and told Belle to bring one cup. Then he tapped the album. "It's not bad at all, Daisy. And we ran a rough cut of the picture last night. I think we have something there."

Well, bully for you, I said to myself, and aloud to Mr. Swan, "As we're completely alone, do you mind if I smoke?"

He nodded, and pushed a cigarette box toward me. As he snapped open his lighter, he asked, "Now what's going on with you and Wade Lewis?" And before I could answer, he said, "You don't have to tell me. I know."

I took a long draw on the cigarette and let the smoke pour out through my nose, exactly like Melora. I wanted to play it casual, and was extremely annoyed to hear my voice wobble like a schoolgirl's. "But how did you find out?"

Mr. Swan gave a thin smile. "You haven't been particularly

discreet. Would you like a list of restaurants at which you've been seen together? With a note on whether you drank liquor or not?"

"I suppose you've known about this for quite a while," I said. He nodded again. "And you've been sitting on it, just like you sat on that information about the boy in San Francisco."

I forced a laugh. "*That* was phony, you know!"

"This isn't," Mr. Swan said. "I usually wait to give people a chance. I hope they'll change their minds. We all do unwise things from time to time. We're only human, after all."

"I guess so."

Belle's voice came over the intercom. "Your coffee, Mr. Swan!"

He pressed the switch, the door slid open, and I looked longingly at it as Belle came in with an elegant little tray, cup and saucer, silver pot, pitcher, and sugar bowl.

"Sure you won't change your mind, Daisy? There's enough for two."

"No thanks," I said.

Belle went out again. The door closed. I hummed a bar or two of "They Can't Take That Away from Me."

"Stop that noise," Mr. Swan said quite sharply, opening the lid of the coffee pot and peering inside—I can't imagine what he expected to find—before starting to pour. "Has Wade Lewis by any chance asked you to marry him?"

"Not yet," I said.

"If he did, would you accept?"

"Yes!"

He stirred sugar. "You love him?"

"Yes!"

"You really think you could be happy with him?"

"Yes! I'm happy already. I'm extremely happy!"

After a moment, Mr. Swan said in a flat dead voice, "Well, it's out of the question."

I laughed, which certainly wasn't my intention, I just couldn't help it. He seemed as surprised as I was.

"You scared me for a moment," I said. "It's a way you have.

I mean, you talk like you rule the world and I almost believe it. But it's ridiculous!"

He put down his cup of coffee very slowly and came over to my chair. Then, with his thumb and forefinger, he raised my chin. His face was rigid, it might have been carved out of stone. "Daisy," he began very quietly, "we've been a success together—professionally. But personally we've been a failure. I am deeply aware that you don't trust me. I think you don't like me. This is a disappointing thing, because I'm very fond of you. You are like a daughter, a talented and unusual daughter."

Maybe it was my morbid condition, but it was all I could do to stop myself blowing smoke right in his face. I had a terrible urge to do this. Then he turned away and walked back toward his desk quite clumsily, colliding with the corner of it, almost like a blind person. I'd never seen Mr. Swan like this before. For some reason it was frightening.

When he sat down again and poured out more coffee, his hand trembled. The spoon clattered against the side of the sugar bowl. Suddenly impatient, he pushed the whole tray away. I really thought he was going to have a stroke or something. He didn't look at me, but opened a drawer in the desk and took out a bottle with a gold stopper.

"Daisy, let's have a drink."

"Okay, Mr. Swan."

He poured me an inch of Scotch, then raised his glass. "Cheers, little girl."

"Oh, down the hatch." But I only took a sip. After a year and a half in this town I'm still not a morning drinker. Frankly, I'm not a drinker at all. Martinis have a sentimental value, but Scotch reminds me of that awful Christmas Eve and I'm liable to feel nauseated.

"I'm not giving you orders now," Mr. Swan said. "I'm not trying to rule the world. I'm just asking you—as an employer, a friend, and someone with strong fatherly feelings—to put Wade Lewis right out of your life."

I took another sip. "Everyone's so *worried* about Wade. So mysterious!"

[105]

"I could tell you a great deal, Daisy, but I never listen to gossip, much less repeat it." Mr. Swan pursed his lips. "And I believe Melora's told you a little, anyway. The important thing is, you're a child."

"The important thing is, I'll be sixteen next week. That's the age of consent." Then I couldn't help laughing again. "Not that I've been asked, you know."

"Your sister would have to approve." His voice was definitely stiffening. "You can't marry anyone without your sister's consent until you're eighteen. It's the law."

"As someone with strong sisterly feelings," I said, "I'm telling you—Gloria had better stay out of this."

He gave me a long stare. "She's your legal guardian. She's involved, whether you like it or not. And if the matter should ever be taken to court—which would be extremely unwise," he sounded quite snappy now, "there is evidence that could be produced to show just how unsuitable a man you wish to marry."

"What sort of evidence?"

"We are not discussing that."

"Oh, excuse me." I got up. "Then what the hell are we discussing?"

"Your stupidity, Daisy." Very sharp and sarcastic, this. "The stupidity of a little person named Daisy Clover."

I smiled at him. "Listen, I'm young, so why not let me be foolish too?" And I started into—

> *Why is it wrong to be young and foolish?*
> *We haven't long to be.*
> *Soon enough the carefree days,*
> *The sunlit days, go by,*
> *Soon enough the bluebird has to fly—"*

"Stop kidding around!" Mr. Swan said impatiently. "Stop throwing songs at me!"

"I'm not kidding," I told him. "I believe them. Now let me out."

After a moment, he sighed and pressed the button. A strong perfume hit me as I walked to the outer office. Melora was waiting there in a lavender suit.

"Belle just told me you were here, I had no idea." She kissed me. "How would you like me to take you to lunch?"

"It sounds quite divine," I said, "but I'm meeting Wade Lewis."

She laughed. "In a few more years, I believe I'm going to be quite frightened of you. In the meantime . . ." She put her arm around my shoulder. "I just ran into Wade's agent. They have a lunch date, didn't you know?"

Belle's hearing aid gave a little crackle as she tuned herself in to this.

"You've never seen our beach house, have you, honey?" Melora said.

Melora is beautiful and ugly at the same time! I noticed this as we drove to Malibu, I kept looking at her. She has this fantastic elegance which throws you at first, marvelous poodle-cut gray hair, eyes like black opals, and a mouth that goes a little crooked in the prettiest way when she smiles. But her jaw's much too heavy and her hands are skinny and the bridge of her nose isn't straight at all, it has kinks. Maybe that's why something is always on the move, Melora knows this and takes care you never get a real long look at her, she'll turn her head away or start waving her hands around. I have to admit she fascinates me, even when I almost hate her.

I hardly listened to what she was saying, which wasn't important, only what they call light conversation.

From the highway, all you could see of the beach house was a high white wall and an electrified wire gate. Melora pressed a buzzer and it swung open. We were in a courtyard with stone angels and tubbed geraniums. The front door opened straight onto a big white airy room with more windows than walls, and the sound of the ocean hitting the rocks below. At one end there was a bar with a striped awning and a sign above it saying CHEZ SWAN. The floor around it had been made to look like a sidewalk, with small round tables and chairs instead of bar stools.

"That's pretty cute," I said. "Like you're in Paris."

"Cannes, honey."

I followed her out to the sun deck. It was like being on a pier, there was no beach, only rocks and pilings underneath. A butler appeared, very formal in white tie and tails, which I thought weird, and asked Melora if she'd care for a drink before lunch. She ordered a dry vermouth and I said I'd like to try one too.

"Make Miss Clover's long, with soda," Melora said.

I sat down on a canvas swing seat and faced the ocean. The ocean! It was really a long while since I'd seen it, and right now I felt very glad we were together again. The wind made white-caps on it, the water looked bright and glossy. I closed my eyes for a moment, just to listen more clearly to the marvelous thud of the waves. When I opened them, Melora was putting on dark glasses.

My mind began to wander. I thought how strange it was that a few miles down the coast, at this very moment, someone must be looking out at a quite different ocean, gray and sour, from a trailer in Playa del Rey. I also thought of old men playing chess on the boardwalk near Santa Monica pier, and the smell of seaweed and fish. And I remembered a whole afternoon I spent, staring out the window from behind that bead curtain in the old Spanish dump, waiting for Mr. Swan to call until the moon came up.

"Daisy, you look tired," Melora said.

"I'm fine," I said.

To shut her out, I close my eyes again—but now everything changes, the fog comes up and it feels chilly. There are palm trees creaking like old doors, sad empty lifeguards' towers along the beach, and the sex maniac stands by the shore. Melora's voice comes through, saying she's going to tell me a story. It's humiliating for her to tell this story, but she'll humiliate herself to help *me*. At first I don't listen attentively, I just think *That'll be the day!* and say nothing at all. As the butler comes back with our drinks, she breaks off and asks how I like vermouth and soda.

I try it. "It's fine, Melora. It's refreshing."

She's lying back on a chaise longue, her face just a pair of dark glasses and a crooked smile. She holds her drink in the air, and the ice rattles. She says something about having been in New York three years ago, and feeling so tired that she decided to re-lax by returning to California on the train. Somewhere before

Chicago she went to the Observation Car, which was empty except for a handsome young man she'd never seen before. He was drunk and very depressed. They started talking, and he asked her not to leave him alone, so she took him to lunch in Chicago during the stopover, and then they visited a museum with a very fine collection of French paintings. They had to leave after he made a scene with an attendant who asked him to put out his cigarette. That night they had dinner together on the train, and the young man started telling Melora about his life, how his family was rich and he didn't like them, but he loved his sister who died when she was fifteen.

By this time I was alert and knew who the young man was, but decided to play it cool and keep a poker face. I also had a definite suspicion how the story was going to end, but Melora broke off again as the butler and a maid in uniform served us lobster salad. When they left, she gave me a long stare. I speared a piece of lobster with my fork and told her it was delicious.

"This may shock you," Melora said, and took off her dark glasses. Her eyes looked very bright and expectant. "I spent the night in his compartment. It was just one of those things that happen. It didn't mean anything. It didn't even make sense."

"Oh, I don't know about that," I said. "I guess those long train rides get pretty boring."

She ignored this. "I just want you to know that from the way he made love, or tried to—"

"MELORA!" I'd jumped to my feet and was glaring at her. "All I can say is," and I honestly didn't know at first what it was going to be, I only wanted to put her down in the coolest possible manner, "Melora," I said again, *"you are one hell of a ball cutter!"*

I'm glad to report it really threw her. She put on her dark glasses again, as if she needed protection, and didn't say a word.

"And anyway," I said, "if you get picked up on a train, you're taking potluck. I mean, you may hit the jackpot and then again you may not."

I sat down and finished my vermouth.

"All I wanted," Melora said finally in a quiet voice, "was for you to know the score with Wade."

I didn't answer.

"I'm afraid I told you the wrong story." She said this in a way that suggested there was a very large Melora Swan collection of terrible stories about Wade. "I should have told you something that didn't involve *me* at all. Something about the people he's destroyed. That's what he does, you see. Like the person in New York who tried to commit suicide—"

She didn't get any further, because the ocean was suddenly sounding much too loud in my ears. My empty glass, a plate of lobster salad, the pepper mill—I knocked them all off the table. The sun deck was a glorious mess, and five minutes later Melora had pushed me into a cab. My rage was really something—red at first, like that fire in the hills, then it turned black. *They were moving in again, taking over.* As I cooled off, the Swan campaign became pretty clear to me. Old King Stag threatens, then Melora wises me up. But the game isn't over, though I suppose my next move comes under the heading of crazy impulses. When I got home, feeling extremely threatened and wised up, I was going to roar for Gloria and find out just how much of this I had to thank *her* for. ("I knew there was *someone*, Mr. Swan, and I'm not surprised it's *him!* Why? Well, I remember that Christmas Eve, she came home with all those presents he'd given her! There was even a bottle of Scotch! Yes! I've never told you this before, but—") Somehow, I couldn't face yelling at Gloria. Not right away. Also, I've heard that it's a good idea, when you're extremely upset over a problem, to try and put a distance between yourself and it, if possible consult an outside person, etc. So I went quietly upstairs and sat on my bed, to figure out who this should be.

Finally I thought of a person called Wilma Cole who runs a teen-age advice page in the *Los Angeles Post*. She seemed as outside as I could get, so I wrote this letter, which I asked her not to publish, just to give me an answer in her column as soon as possible. She does this with problems that are confidential. Then (disguising my true identity) I explained—

I am a child opera star (residing in New York but at present visiting relatives in the West) and am deeply involved with a handsome tenor (in the East) who's pushing thirty. I know he likes me a lot too—we are both non-Conformists—but when it comes to declaring his feelings, let alone making love, he mysteriously draws back (way before first base). He has a drinking problem, which naturally I haven't discussed with him, but exactly how much can I lay at that door? The impresario strongly disapproves of our dating, and is trying to break us up. He thinks it's gone much further than it really has, which I suppose is ironic when you think how much further I'd like it to go. I love this man. What shall I do?

Soprano

As I put the letter in an envelope, there was a knock at the door.

Gloria.

"I thought I heard you come in," she said.

I decided to let her have a nod and a faintly enigmatic smile—no more. Then I licked the envelope.

"My, it's warm in here!" Gloria said. "Do you mind if I open a window?"

I told her to go ahead, and waited for the next part of her small-talk routine. "Muggy enough for a storm! We should live in a house with stone walls, stone walls are cooler!" I agreed with every word. At last, keeping her voice casual but her eyes shifty, she brought out her question.

"What did Mr. Swan want to see you about?"

I smiled at her again. "Guess."

"A new picture lined up for you already?"

"Guess again, Gloria. I don't believe you're really trying."

"Of course I am. Was it nothing to do with a picture?"

"Nothing at all."

"Then I can't imagine!" She sat on the bed. "I mean, there's no reason for Mr. Swan to discuss anything," and she looked away from me, "anything *personal* with you."

"Isn't there?"

"I'm asking *you!*" Gloria said rather sharply.

I waggled a finger at her. "Scuttlebuts aren't supposed to ask questions," I said. "Scuttlebuts have all the answers."

It fazed her. "Baby, what's the matter?"

"There you go again!"

She didn't answer, only watched me with those dumb, treacherous eyes. "And stop pretending you don't know," I said. "You knew before I did."

"Will you please stop talking in riddles?" She gave a helpless shrug. "I'm completely at sea."

"I will stop talking, Period." I said. "I will never speak to you again, Gloria, unless you agree to connect a little. Just a little."

She wriggled uncomfortably on the bed. "I guess," she brought out finally, not looking at me, of course, "it had something to do with Wade Lewis."

"I knew you'd get there if you tried."

"I didn't tell him it was Wade!"

"Because you didn't know."

"I told him I knew there was *someone*," she admitted, "because you'd been out of the house such a lot."

"What else?"

"That's all."

"What else, Gloria?"

Another wriggle. "I told him I had a feeling that someone was making you unhappy."

"And you did this for my own good," I said.

To my surprise, Gloria's face crumpled up like a baby's, and she began to sniffle. "You're so *hostile!*" She stood up. "You never give me a chance! I never wanted to interfere with your life, those people *make* me!" She sat down. "I'm not clever enough. I'm a very ordinary person, not like you."

For a long time now I've thought of Gloria as a complete idiot, but I've never taken the next step, which is to figure that complete idiots can't help it and you shouldn't be surprised or annoyed at them. As Gloria sobbed quite loudly on the bed, I wondered if she was honestly miserable about this whole situation, just a helpless pawn in the Swan campaign. She almost had the benefit of the doubt, then I thought that nobody could have *made* her commit The Dealer, and the record shows that while she may be an idiot she's also something worse—top of the shit list, in fact.

[112]

A handkerchief came out, Gloria blew her nose. "Anyway, if you're serious about this man I think it's terrible!"

"I thought you didn't want to interfere."

"I don't, baby. I'm just extremely worried that you never seem to learn the difference between healthy and sick."

"What is it?"

"Sick people can't face up to life," Gloria informed me. "They can't *function*. They live off healthy people and, if healthy people let them, stop *them* functioning too."

"I don't need to ask where you get that from," I said. "But the only people who could stop *me* functioning are you and the Swans—and you're all supposed to be healthy. So how do you account for that, Gloria?"

She obviously couldn't. She looked extremely puzzled.

"And here's something else. The reason you and I have never been as close as sisters should be is that we don't agree about anything. For instance, would you say this is the best of all possible worlds?"

I could see her trying to figure out whether I thought so or not, she wanted to agree with me. "I guess not," she said finally.

"Why?"

"Well . . ." She looked trapped. "There's a lot of poverty around. Disease, too. And Communism."

"Suppose there wasn't all that kind of stuff around," I said. "Would it be the best of all possible worlds then?"

She gave me a suspicious look. "I guess so, baby."

"I knew we didn't agree," I said. "In my opinion there's a lot in life that's extremely sad, and I don't just mean people dying or not getting enough to eat."

"You don't?" Gloria stared at me. "Then what in your opinion is sad?"

"I can't put it into words, except when I sing. Then I feel it right through me, even when it comes out happy. Oh, I remember feeling sad right through on my fourteenth birthday," I told her. "Not because no one seemed to know it was my birthday, and there was a lot of fog, and The Dealer set fire to the Paradise Hotel and Apartments—it would have been just as sad, really, if I'd had hundreds of presents and the sun came out and—"

"I never knew you had such a rotten birthday!" Gloria looked as if she was going to cry again. "I blame myself!"

"For Christ's sake, I told you that wasn't the point. The important thing was, I sat down under a palm tree, sang 'You Are My Sunshine' and felt much better. Now do you get it?"

After a moment, she shook her head.

"Nobody does," I said. "Except Wade."

✳

During my account of the Swan Campaign (which *didn't* include Love in a Roomette), Wade seemed quite relaxed, just saying Um and Ah and getting up a couple of times to freshen his martini, and for the rest of the time sprawling back in his chair and giving me an intent but twinkly gaze.

"That's all they said about me?" he asked when I'd finished.

I nodded. "That's all, Wade. Just that you're unsuitable and have a drinking problem. Which is utterly ridiculous, of course."

He got up, a little unsteadily I must admit. "Dear heart, would you like to go to a party?"

"You mean now?"

"Sure."

"Are you kidding?"

"Would you like to go?" he said again.

"Who's giving the party?"

"It's a birthday party," Wade said. "We'll have to buy a present." And he disappeared into the bathroom.

I felt depressed. To shake it off, I removed Bessie from the record player, found one of Ella's albums and put that on instead. I snapped my fingers to "How High the Moon," and it helped.

When he came back from the bathroom, Wade looked much better. He must have put drops in his eyes, they were clear and bright again. He steered me out of the apartment with his arm around my shoulder, and told me that Christy Williams, the actress who was making this terrible movie with him, was giving the party for her own birthday. I saw her once, she's very realistic, the kind Hedda Hopper says is taking Glamour out of Hollywood. Wade says she's talented but won't stop improvising.

[114]

As we drove, I asked how the terrible movie was coming along. Wade laughed, he seemed suddenly in very good spirits. "Just terrible," he said, "but I'm going to be all right."

"Oh, I'm glad. Then it won't ruin your career after all."

He looked surprised. "Did I say it would?" I nodded. "Dear heart, you mustn't let me get away with saying things like that. I want you to do something for me," he said, very serious now. "Whenever you detect a note of exaggerated self-pity in anything I say, tell me to stop it. Be as rude as you like. Will you do that?"

"Okay," I said.

We stopped in front of an art gallery in Beverly Hills, and I followed Wade inside. I must admit that my reaction to the stuff on the walls was extremely unfavorable, but of course I'm not a highly educated person. The owner of the gallery was a big man with a beard and corduroy pants, which struck me as corny, and he greeted Wade like an important customer.

"This man has fantastic taste," he told me, and when Wade said he was going to buy Christy Williams a painting for her birthday, he was very complimentary about Miss Williams' taste as well. The best painting in the show, he went on, was in his opinion White on White, but Wade said he didn't care for it. Instead, he stared for a long time at Composition 3, and seemed hooked.

"It's almost as fine," the bearded man said.

Wade took the painting off the wall, put it under his arm, and told the owner to charge it. When we reached the car, he slung it carelessly in the back.

"Hey," I said, "you might chip it or something."

He only laughed.

"Don't you care about it?" I started to laugh too, though I wasn't sure who the joke was on or for. "I mean, if that's really the way you feel, I could mess it up with lipstick."

"It's just fine the way it is." Wade was still laughing. "I fooled you, didn't I?"

"I guess so. But if you think it's a piece of junk, why did you buy it?"

"I fooled that bearded idiot too," Wade said. "I have fantastic taste. The point of this whole operation," he explained, "will be revealed when I present that work of art to Christy for her birthday. Then we'll see who's the better actor."

"She won't like it either?"

He shook his head.

"Well," I said, "it's an expensive joke."

"Money is not my problem."

Christy Williams has an apartment in what Gloria calls the wrong part of Beverly Hills, I mean south of Romanoff's. I could hear a few voices coming from inside, and someone playing the guitar. When she opened the door, I could see in a way what Hedda Hopper meant, she had no make-up, snarled hair, a pair of man's black pants and a sloppy sweater. Nobody does this for laughs, I thought, she means it, and I really liked her at once.

She was smiling, but looked serious when she saw Wade.

"You didn't invite me," he said, "you didn't invite me to your birthday party, but I forgive you."

And he gave her the painting.

"Well, for heaven's sake." She looked at me, then grinned. "Wade probably told you we had a big row on the set yesterday, we're not speaking."

"No, he didn't," I said.

Wade remembered that we hadn't met, and introduced us.

"I recognized you," Christy said. "You're the Little Menace."

"To what?"

"To all of us. You've got too much talent."

"Christy, I hope you like that painting," Wade said.

"Yes. The white against the red. I like it."

"Then may we come to your party?"

"Don't make me feel terrible." She suddenly kissed both of us. "Wade, I take back every stupid thing I said."

"Oh, I do too."

"I say a lot of things I don't mean," Christy explained to me. "Especially when I'm worked up over something. I warn everyone about my threshold of tolerance."

She led us into her living room, which was like Wade's, small and untidy with a rented look. There were about a dozen people, some of them sitting on the floor, all in old casual clothes except for two men in dark suits, I guessed they were agents. A hefty-looking boy in Levis, shirt open and sleeves rolled up to his shoulders, was strumming the guitar. On a table stood a big birthday cake, about a quarter eaten, and bottles of champagne in cardboard ice buckets.

Christy went on talking loudly, above the guitar and the conversations. "That painting changes everything," she said. "Now I'm glad I didn't go on suspension." She turned to me. "You know what suspension is, Daisy?" I shook my head. "It's when you're under contract to a studio, like I am, and you refuse to do something they want you to, they take you off the payroll and stop you working for anyone else, and you sit each other out." Her voice rose even higher. "I've been on suspension five times!"

"What for?" I asked her.

"Honey, that's the question. That's what I discuss with my analyst. You have to be sure that—" She broke off, and smiled at me. "Listen, you're a fantastically talented kid, you're having a lot of success, and I hope you don't react the way I did. I mean, it started to destroy my security. That's why I always discuss going on suspension with my analyst, I have to make sure it's valid and not just the self-destructive bit. He thought I should do this picture and I guess he was right, at least it's got me this painting!" She held it above her head. "Everyone look! Look at what Wade gave me for my birthday!"

While the others admired it, Wade grabbed my arm. "Did you notice she hardly looked at it? That's her trouble as an actress, she never relates."

I nodded, then turned away and sat down on the couch. I really wanted to go home, the room seemed too small and too frantic. Christy went on talking more loudly than ever, the boy with the guitar had his arms around her and she was saying he had a great future as an actor. I heard one agent whisper to the other that he'd give it a month. The telephone rang but nobody answered it. Wade looked quite drunk again, he was eating a chunk of birthday cake and spilling pieces on the floor.

A red-haired woman, in a black dress with cigarette ash down the front, sat next to me on the couch and started to cry.

"Oh, what is it?" I said.

She lay back and clenched her fists. "You know why they asked me here? They say she's fun at a party. Sure, we have to invite *her* to the party. But then—then—" She broke off with a sob, staring through her tears at the ceiling.

"What goes wrong?" I said.

"The curtain comes down. *Down!* I've embarrassed them, you know why?" I shook my head. "I'm not successful. I have no success in this town as an actress. I'm just fun at a party, that's all."

She opened her purse and fumbled for a handkerchief.

After a moment, I said, "I believe I detect a note of exaggerated self-pity." I was really thinking out loud, and didn't mean her to hear it. Anyway—

"And who the hell are *you?*" She leaned across the couch and peered at me, her eyes streaming. "My God, it's that awful child star. Oh *well*," she said, "pardon me for sitting on the same couch. Pardon me for bothering such a famous person with my ordinary little problems."

"It's not really any bother. But frankly, you're up the creek if you think that being famous solves any problems at all."

"Oh, I know!" She sounded extremely caustic. "Success and riches just don't bring happiness, do they?"

"Don't knock them too hard, because they certainly help. They don't get rid of unhappiness, that's all."

"My God. I heard your singing voice was dubbed, but now I realize your personality must be, too. Where do you get your lines from, Daisy? Who pulls your strings?"

"Magnagram Studios," I told her. "They own me body and soul. So if my hand suddenly reaches out and cracks you on the mouth, you'll know who to sue."

She didn't answer this, but whimpered and mumbled something about being drunk. Then she apologized, so I said I was sorry too. Then I got up and excused myself. She lay back again and said, "The curtain comes down."

I decided to tell Wade that he could stay if he liked, and I'd call myself a cab, but just as I reached him Melora and Mr. Swan came into the room. They saw us immediately, exchanged glances, then Melora touched up her lips with a smile and came over. I think Mr. Swan was going to follow, but Christy blocked him and started raising Cain at the top of her voice about how terrible her movie was, and what should she do.

"Surprise," Melora said to me. "You certainly get around. Hello, Wade."

He looked at her without a flicker. There were no preliminaries. "I've just been hearing some very interesting stuff that you told Daisy about me. So maybe you'd like to listen while I tell Daisy something about you."

Melora's smile became fixed and frozen. "Go ahead."

"This gracious lady, this lady of elegance and breeding," Wade said, "don't you think she's done very well, considering where she came from?"

The whole atmosphere was beginning to nauseate me, I hated it, but I didn't know how to stop Wade and I could only say feebly, "I don't know where Melora comes from."

"About fifteen years ago," Wade said, "you could have found Miss Melora in a movie studio, just like now, except that she sat very demurely in front of a typewriter—or, which is more interesting, as I'll explain, she smiled very demurely as she took dictation from her decrepit old boss. Now this is telling tales out of school, which I agree is a bad habit, but who started it, Melora?"

His voice had grown very loud, not because he was excited, but on account of the noise Christy made as she complained to Mr. Swan. You had to listen to one or the other, whichever was loudest, and now there was a ghastly pause because everyone in the room was listening to Wade. I saw Mr. Swan coming over.

"And here's the hatchet man," Wade said. "So what brings him to this party, is there a body buried here?" He turned to me. "Your boss is certainly an expert on where bodies are buried. The first time he discovered a body—that was a long while ago too, dear heart, when you could have found *this* gracious and elegant gentleman brushing the clothes and polishing the shoes of a—"

He didn't get any further. As a matter of fact, he was lying on the floor, looking dazed, before I realized that Mr. Swan's fist had landed him there. Melora said, "Ray!" in a surprised warning tone, and put her hand tightly on his arm. One of the agents said that Wade had asked for it. Christy came up, laughing wildly, to try and save the situation. "Hey, Daisy, they fighting over you already?" She helped Wade to his feet. "If you want to go on with this, fellers, would you mind stepping outside?"

But her smile died, I guess it didn't stand a chance against all the grim embarrassed faces.

"Good night," Mr. Swan said, quite abruptly.

"You forgot her gift," Melora said.

"It's in the car, I'll get it," Mr. Swan said.

"No, I'll walk you to your car," Christy said.

As they left, I recovered my voice. "I'm going on suspension!" I called after Mr. Swan. "Right now!" Then I asked Wade if he was all right.

"I'm fine." He ran his hand through my hair, then went to pour himself some more champagne. So did everyone else except the agents, who left.

The boy with the guitar began strumming "Stormy Weather." "Daisy, you know this, don't you? Come on now, Daisy!"

I really didn't feel like singing, but Wade said, "That little trouper knows them all. Clear the air, dear heart."

"I'll need a drink first." He gave me some champagne, I settled myself on the arm of the couch, nodded to the boy with the guitar and launched into the first verse. Wobbly at first, but I managed to hit my stride fairly soon. Just as I finished, Christy came back, carrying a little gift-wrapped package. She said, "More! More!"

Somebody turned off most of the lights. The guitarist began playing "Nice Work If You Can Get It." "More! More!" I said, holding out my glass of champagne, which Wade filled. I was starting to feel good again, and somehow it was much more fun singing this way than belting out the stuff at all those people on Julie Forbes's terrace. I did "Isn't It Romantic?" and "It All Depends on You"—for Wade, of course—and also a number that I'd wanted to include in my last album but Mr. Swan said was quite unsuitable at my age. It's called "The End of a Love

Affair," and for some reason it really speaks to me, I've always seen myself doing something extremely sophisticated but sad with a glass of champagne in one hand and a cigarette in the other. People had their arms around people now, and the room was fairly dark and misty with cigarette smoke, like those New York night spots you read about. And when I got to—

> "So I drink a little too much,
> And I smoke a little too much,
> And the tunes I request
> Are not always the best,
> But the ones where the trumpets blare—"

I half expected to see dawn come up outside the window. It didn't, of course, but Christy walked over to the boy with the guitar, put her hands inside his shirt, and gave him a kiss on the mouth. Then she told Wade it must be hours past my bedtime. So we all left, except they forgot about the red-haired woman, who was asleep in a dark corner.

On the way home, I asked Wade if he knew the Swans were coming to Christy's party. Of course he did. She'd invited them because she was after a part in some movie Mr. Swan planned to produce. I was also going to ask him about Melora and the old man, and whose shoes Mr. Swan used to polish, but right now it didn't seem important. In fact, without saying a word, we agreed not to talk. It was one of those long silences that shouldn't be broken, I mean because there are times when if you say nothing you can feel very happy with someone, and if you speak you'd better be sure to say the right thing, or shut up.

He dropped me off on Arcadia Drive. "There you go," he said.

As I got out of the car, he reached through the window and touched my shoulder.

"Daisy?"

I turned around.

He had a funny expression on his face, almost hangdog. "I feel so close—" He broke off, then drove away.

9

~~~~~~~~~~~~~~~~~~~~~~~~~~~~~~~~~~~~

(*Greatest Love Story, cont.*)

It was no surprise when the phone rang next morning and Belle said to call myself a cab right away because Mr. Swan wished to see me at the Studio. "Okay, I'll be along," I told her, thinking this was the first time he hadn't sent a limousine and it must be the handwriting on the wall. An impulse made me decide to do a Christy Williams. I put on an old pair of trousers and a sweater I'd hardly worn since the Santa Monica days, and just for the hell of it tied a crumpled scarf around my head.

Gloria asked where I was going.

"King Stag's sent for me again."

"But you look terrible, baby!"

"I know. It's the self-destructive bit."

And as the door swung open I put an unlighted cigarette in my mouth.

He was sitting at the black desk, grimmer than I'd ever seen him. His eyes flickered for a moment at my outfit, but he didn't say anything. I asked for a match. He slid a lighter toward me across the desk, then pressed the intercom switch and told Belle he wouldn't accept any calls for three minutes.

"That's how long I expect this to take, Daisy. Last time we talked I told you that I usually wait to give people a chance. In your case I've waited a long time and you haven't taken it. I'm disappointed and reluctant," he sounded quite peppy and determined, I thought, "but I'm going to override my personal feelings and crack the whip."

I nodded at him through wreaths of cigarette smoke.

[122]

"I want your solemn assurance," Mr. Swan said, "that you will have nothing more to do with Wade Lewis."

"Oh," I said. "It's not available."

He didn't answer, only pursed his lips.

"So am I on suspension?" I asked.

He gripped the sides of the desk. "Daisy, what do you consider the most important human virtues?"

"You mean, why do I like people when I like them?"

"No, I don't. I'm not discussing personalities. I'm asking you in general terms what qualities in the human race you most admire?"

"Well, I admire anyone who understands what I'm talking about."

He sighed. "How does *gratitude* strike you? Do you think it's something worth feeling?"

"Oh, *now* we're getting there!" I said. "I was afraid this whole thing was going to take more than three minutes. You mean, shouldn't I be grateful to you for everything you've done?" He nodded. "Well, it's a funny time to ask me that, I mean I'm not exactly grateful to you for cracking the whip, but as for giving me my chance and stuff like that, I'm *very* grateful, Mr. Swan." I gave him a bright little smile. "So am I on suspension?"

Mr. Swan got up from his chair, walked slowly around his desk, and stood looking at me. He had the same expression on his face as the day he tweaked my ear, and I covered both my ears with my hands. With a faint smile, he reached out and tweaked my nose. Then he went back to his desk and flipped the intercom switch. "Belle, as a matter of formal record, Miss Daisy Clover is suspended by Magnagram Studios until further notice, to take effect as from September 30th, 1953."

He pressed the button and the door opened, and as I reached it he played the trick of closing it again in my face. There was something he'd forgotten to tell me, he said, which was that he was letting me off lightly. Legally my contract with the Studio could be torn up at this very moment, because I'd infringed the morals clause. I didn't know about this, and he explained that if you're a star and behave indecently in public you've had it.

"So be careful, Daisy. Frankly, I believe you're at a crossroads.

You can go Down from here—or come to your senses and continue Up."

"Okay," I said.

In the outer office Belle gazed at me with stunned reproachful eyes and said I was an extremely reckless girl.

Now for the record I'm going to write down that background information on the Swans which Wade started to hand out at Christy's birthday party. It's when you learn stuff like this that you wonder at the nerve of some people.

In the long ago Melora hit this town from strictly nowhere, but she could type and take shorthand and she landed up in the pool at some studio. This very old executive with a Thrombosis picked her out of the pool and made her his private secretary because he had the Hots for her, but Melora wasn't going to give it to him so easy. She wanted a ring on her finger and money in his will. "I hear you knockin', but you can't come in," was the song Melora sang as she crossed her knees and prepared for dictation, and after a few weeks the old cherry picker grew tired of listening, so he married her and they went to live in his Bel Air mansion, full of antiques and art, etc. Almost at once he had a relapse and they put him to bed. He was so angry about being ill and possibly dying and definitely not being able to satisfy his Hots that all he could do was weep all the time, he lay propped up on pillows with his face puckered like an old baby's. Now the newspapers made a sensation and took pictures of Melora sitting at her husband's bedside, saying, "I want him to live! I married him because I love him!" while the tears spurted out of his eyes and he clutched her hand. Then he died in the middle of one night and Melora got her million.

While all this was going on, there was a valet in the executive's mansion and his name was Raymond Swan! He and Melora had the Hots for each other, and Wade says were making it like there was no tomorrow while the old man lay weeping in his bed. I asked Wade if he thought that either of them actually helped him on his way, but he said he wouldn't go as far as that and besides it was hardly necessary. However, the other important item in this tale is that Mr. Swan, when he was a valet, had something on another rich old executive who came to the house for the Friday night poker game. It was enough to rate quite a layout in the scandal magazines, and that's how Mr. Swan got started right at the same time as Melora. It turned out to be one hell of a break for them both, since the first old executive died and made Melora rich, and the second gave Mr. Swan this job, and after what's called a decent interval they were openly off to races together.

"Well!" I said. "It's not a pretty story, is it, but what really makes me mad is to think of Mr. Swan waving the morals clause in my face this morning."

Wade didn't answer. He got up and stared out of the window, then with an impatient movement he pulled the cord of the venetian blinds and snapped them closed. The untidy room was all in shadow and when he looked at me his face was a blur.

"Daisy, dear heart . . ." Somehow the tone of his voice made me nervous. "You're the only person I know who really makes sense."

"Oh, I feel the same about you."

"And I want you to know that because I love you very much, I also respect you. We have to do the right thing."

I didn't understand. "How will we do that, Wade?"

"We mustn't let you be allowed," he was speaking so low, almost mumbling, that I had to stand very close to catch what he said, "to stop functioning on my account."

"But if I didn't go on suspension, I couldn't see you any more."

A pause so long I could hardly bear it. "The point is, dear heart, you won't see me any more for about six months, anyway."

"Wade!" My own voice sounded peculiar now. "I don't think I could have heard right."

"I finish this movie at the end of the week. Then I'm going to New York. To do a play. Don't look at me as if it's the end of the world. I'll only be in it six months, then I'll be back."

"I don't believe it," I said. "It's simply not to be believed."

"*I'm coming back.* And when I do, you'll find someone who . . . who can be responsible for you. Right now I'm not. Not responsible for anything. I'm—" He broke off, and grabbed the slats of the venetian blinds so fiercely that one of them cracked and he shouted, "Damn!"

"You're what?" I said. "What are you?"

"I've got a splinter in my hand."

He stared at his palm as if he couldn't believe it. Five minutes ago I'd have run to take the splinter out for him, but I was so miffed I could only shrug and say, "Well, it's your own fault."

Wade nodded and sat on the arm of a chair. "On the whole," he was still looking at his hand, "I mean in spite of your poor bitch of a mother being locked up, and you can't stand living with your sister Gloria, and you've gone on suspension for no reason at all because I'm going away—in spite of all this, you still think life's been pretty good to you? You still want to get up in the morning?"

"Hell, you know me. I'm just an optimist who bellyaches all the time."

"You don't know *me*." Wade frowned. "There's a lot I hope you never find out. Anyway, I usually hate to get up. And if the world was your face I might step on it."

"But you're welcome! I mean it."

He didn't answer.

"If you take a raincheck on *that* offer," I said, "I guess you've made up your mind not to be stuck with me, so you're running off."

Wade huddled himself up like a person sheltering under a tree from the rain. "No, but I *have to go away and come back*. It's necessary."

You look at someone you're angry with for putting you in a deep blue funk, and your mouth opens for a bright and bitter little crack, but it doesn't come out because you realize he's put himself in a funk even bluer than yours. It's not like understanding and forgiving, which in my opinion is a game not worth the candle, it's just not understanding at all but knowing that you're hooked all the same.

After a moment I said, "Necessary like living in a tower?"

"There you go."

"Then . . ." *It's difficult to compete with a tower, but if you*

[126]

get as far as this, Daisy, don't let anything throw you now. "Give me your hand, Wade, you ought to lose that splinter." He held it out. It felt warm and obstinate and tense. I liked it. After I'd taken out the splinter I didn't want to let it go. I tickled the palm, then looked up at his eyes. I really gasped for breath because they still sent me, even though they were shifty as Gloria's, as if he wished he was thousands of miles away.

✳

Three days later he was.

Dot dot dot.

He didn't want me to see him off at the airport, but I knew his plane left at midnight, so I took a cab down there, put on dark glasses, and joined a small crowd of people at Gate 27. I'd never been in an airport before, and it was confusing and marvelous and frustrating, almost everyone except me seemed to be going off somewhere or meeting someone, and they called out through loudspeakers the names of cities I'd never been to.

When they announced that the plane for New York was going to leave, the people at Gate 27 put out their cigarettes and went through the barrier. I didn't want to be conspicuous, so moved up to Gate 29 where another small crowd waited to go to Detroit. "Mr. Wade Lewis! Mr. Wade Lewis!" a voice called out through the loudspeaker so suddenly that I jumped. "Please report to Gate 27!" And a moment later he came hurrying down the alley all in black, polo-neck sweater and old corduroys. He looked fairly drunk but quite cheerful, which made me realize I was sober but depressed. He didn't see me, of course, but walked quickly across the field to the plane, went up the steps, and disappeared. They closed the cabin hatch immediately.

It seemed morbid to stand and watch and wait for the plane to take off, but I wanted to. The engine started to roar, drowning out the piped music, then the thing taxied away very slowly until I couldn't see it any more. It was still on the ground, though. I stared at the flight of steps left on the field and leading nowhere, then asked some official if there wasn't a place from which I could see planes go up in the air. He told me to make for the Flight Deck, but halfway there I changed my mind and decided to try and have a drink at the bar instead. With my dark glasses I hoped I could get away with being under age, but they took one look at me and asked who I thought I was kidding.

As I came out of the airport building, a plane took off. I saw its lights climbing up the sky. I couldn't be sure it was Wade's, but I waved anyway.

Next morning I'm wedged in the breakfast nook, facing Gloria and Harry across the plastic table, and it's my birthday. I've reached the age of consent, if anyone cares, but the only thing I feel right now is that the sound of a plane in the sky is extremely depressing.

Gloria and Harry, obviously acting under instructions, have been playing it cool. They're determined to be reasonable. "All we ask you, baby, is to remember that you may have to throw away a great deal for Mr. Wade Lewis, and you must be sure he's worth it." I used to think that Magnagram Studios was a front for a cannibal organization and the Swans really dealt in human flesh, but now I suspect they're onto a different racket. Zombies. This town is full of zombies, owned and operated by the Swans, and, while Gloria and Harry are two of the busiest, there's a whole slew of them, they drive limousines, wait on tables and at bars, sit behind typewriters, and answer the phone like Belle. It's really something, and it means you can't be too careful. For instance, Gloria knows that I went to the airport last night. She didn't mean to let on, but it slipped out a few minutes ago while she was scrambling eggs. She tried to cover it up and asked why didn't I start unwrapping my presents, and I just smiled and said I wanted my coffee first. Obviously zombies are being ordered now to play a waiting game. Let *her* make the first move. Okay. I take another sip of coffee and open the *Los Angeles Post*.

Here it is, Wilma Cole to the rescue, and beautifully timed too. There's a long letter from a girl who says her best friend at school is walking around pregnant and her mother wants to stop their friendship, and does Wilma agree? and then comes my birthday present—

[128]

Dear Soprano: You don't say how old you are, but obviously you've got most of your life ahead of you, so why hit the high notes all at once? That tenor will cause you to lose more than your voice, and I suggest you try harmonizing with a normal boy of your own age.

Wish I knew Wilma. She sounds like a barrel of fun.

As I put down the paper Gloria looks quickly away and starts spreading jelly on a piece of toast. She's been studying me. Harry coughs and says now I've had my coffee and my eggs, how about my gifts? So we go to the living room, which feels chilly, and they sit on the couch while I open packages. "My first beaded bag—why, thank you, Gloria! And my first *kimono*—Harry, you shouldn't have done it!" He wants me to try it on, so I go into a coy Oriental routine, giggling and wrapping myself inside it, and they think it's a riot, just for a moment you might imagine this is the snuggest, cutest little family on Arcadia Drive. The rest is a magnum of perfume disguised as champagne from Alex Conrad, *Giant* by Edna Ferber from Carolyn, and nothing at all from the Swans.

The phone rings. Gloria goes to answer it and comes back trying to smile.

"For you, baby. Long Distance."

I ran into the hall, nearly tripping over my darned kimono. Behind me, I know they're listening. As I pick up the receiver, I close my eyes to shut them out.

"Happy birthday, dear heart." His voice makes me see his eyes at once, very dark and flickering, with the painful expression they've had ever since he told me he was going away. "What are you doing?"

"I've just opened my presents, Wade, and each one of them is out of this world."

"Are you still on suspension?"

"What a crazy question. You only left last night."

"Well, it's later here. I mean I've had lunch already, so it feels like more time has passed."

"It feels that way here too. It's a real drag. Is that Bessie I hear playing?"

"Yeah, I've been playing Bessie."

"So what else is new?"

"I checked into this goddam hotel and I'm still sitting in this room. I hate hotels. I hate walking through those goddam lobbies and asking the desk if there are any messages. I hate room service and venetian blinds when it's raining outside. The only think I like, dear heart, is the card that says Do Not Disturb. I hung that outside my door right away. But now I can't go out because it's raining and there won't be a goddam cab, so I sit here trying to convince myself this god-awful play makes any sense."

"You're swearing as much as I do sometimes. And would you leave your greatest admirer on suspension and go to New York just to do a play that didn't make any sense?"

"Yeah, I probably would. That's what bothers me."

"Then it's not good for you to go on sitting there. You should turn Bessie off and go out, even if it means getting wet."

"Where shall I go?"

"Christ, I don't know. Don't you have any friends?"

"Hundreds. That's not the point. The point is—if there is any point—I'm half an hour late already for an important appointment."

"Who with?"

"The producers of this god-awful play."

"That's terrible. I mean, it's so unprofessional!"

"You're a monstrous child, you really are."

"But you need me. Look what happens when you go away, you get all screwed up and just sit in a hotel room listening to Bessie. I'm going to hang up now. I'll call tomorrow and see if you've gone out yet."

"*Daisy!*"

"What's wrong now?"

"Wait a moment. I've just looked out the window. And it's stopped raining. What do you make of that?"

"It always does, finally. You'd better get going, Wade. I hope you'll call me again soon."

"Very soon, dear heart. Any time it rains I'll call, and you'll stop it. Happy birthday again. Take care."

[130]

"Oh, be careful crossing streets yourself."

Click.

The hall's empty.

All the doors are open, though. After a moment comes the sound of running water from the kitchen. By the time I get there, Gloria's very busy throwing dishes into the sink and Harry stands by with a Detergent. They look blank and nervous at the same time. Of course they're wondering exactly what the score is, and how much longer this peculiar situation's going to last.

So am I.

Later. It's cold and the beach is empty, not even a dog around. And what is Daisy Clover, child star, doing in an empty lifeguard's tower on her sixteenth birthday?

I only know she suddenly walked out of the house, told Gloria she wouldn't be back for lunch, and took a cab all the way down to the old pier at Venice. She walked past the Big Wheel and the track machine and the pinball arcade, and nothing was changed, even the people seemed the same, until she came to Twitcher's booth. It was a hall of distorting mirrors now, and when she went inside she saw herself twelve feet tall, spindly as a totem pole, then as broad as she was long, as if she'd been run over and flattened out. She made horrible faces at herself in the mirrors, sticking out a tongue that looked big as a surfboard, then pulling at the corners of her eyes and making weird noises like a Boris Karloff monster. Finally she almost made herself sick, and went out.

Next she dawdled along the boardwalk until she reached the old Spanish dump, which hadn't changed either. She looked into the courtyard and was fairly sure the same line of washing hung over the second-floor balcony. Then she stared up at the windows of the room she and The Dealer had occupied, but they were heavily draped. Next door, the Twilight Convalarium was FOR RENT. There was a rattan chair left on the porch, falling to pieces.

Low tide at the beach, and mushy brown patches of seaweed floating in the ocean. She was alone with the long line of her footprints on the sand. There were clouds driven quite fast

[131]

across the sky because it was windy, but now the sun flickered through and made that closed-up lifeguard's tower very white and mysterious. She went up the steps, pushed open the door which was sticky with damp, then battled with the shutters until they creaked back and she could stand looking at the huge sulky ocean. It suited her mood, the way it always did. She felt marvelously cut off from everything and quite depressed too. Obviously birthdays weren't her best days. The wind had swept everything clear and the horizon seemed at least a million waves away. It occurred to her that she was trying to find out how it felt to live in a tower, as Wade had done. She decided that although she couldn't face it for six months, it was a good way to spend this particular afternoon.

She perched herself on the sill and dangled her legs over the edge. By the shore, sandpipers waddled and flapped. *The 3rd of October*, she said to herself, *1953*, Daisy in this Tower and Wade in New York and The Dealer in her paneled room probably gazing at TV. Wouldn't it make sense for these three people to get together, maybe in a nice little beach house? Yes, except that what makes sense doesn't usually happen, and what happens doesn't usually make sense. Okay. That's progress of a kind, if you can sit here quite calmly knowing that to be true, and not want to throw stones at those birds, etc. Also, if you played the old game of the sky opening and a voice that says, You can have one wish, you know now what the wish would be. That's progress, too. You've got something to live for.

It's a pity your chances are so slight, of course.

Dot dot dot. I don't know how long I stayed in the tower, but suddenly the tide was almost at my feet and the light was like being in church. There were thin pointed clouds above the ocean, as if sharks had leaped into the sky. Sometimes, when the end of the day takes you by surprise, everything looks weird. In fact, I just couldn't believe it when I seemed to hear, above the thud of the surf, some music and a voice singing. *My voice!* I gave myself a vicious little pinch in the neck, but the voice didn't stop. It was singing "So's Your Old Man," from my last picture. It was coming from somewhere along the boardwalk behind me.

Well. There was a bar, of course, and a juke box inside it. By the time I got there, my voice was deafening. They certainly liked their music loud in this place. I peeked through the open door into a dark, dingy kind of room with sawdust on the floor, a bullfighting poster on the wall, and a tough-looking woman in a matador's cap behind the counter. She grinned at me. The other people in the bar, just a few boys in sweaters and Levis, only stared and then looked away. My record stopped and another started, "Making a Song and Dance," from the same movie. A tall blond boy snapped his fingers and wiggled his hips a bit, and an older man sitting by himself at a table perked up to watch.

I went up to the counter and told the woman I could use a bottle of beer. She didn't ask my age, only my name. I told her Gloria, and she said she was Roddy. She slung me a beer and wanted to know if I lived around here. "I used to," I said. She wondered if I knew a woman called Jack, because my face was somehow familiar and she thought maybe she'd seen me with Jack. Then the phone rang and she went off to answer it, which was good. I was more interested in looking around than talking to this old butch. I remembered Milton telling me once he used to have offers on the pier, and I guessed this was where they hung out. It surprised me in a way that they should pass the time listening to my numbers, I'd often imagined my records being played in all kinds of different places, but never in a colorful little joint like this.

The blond hip-wiggling boy suddenly looked at me and smiled. He whispered to another boy and finally they both came over. "Excuse me," the blond said, very polite, "this is the craziest thing, but aren't you Daisy Clover?"

"Oh, people are always coming up and asking me that," I said. "I guess it's because I am."

"I told you," the blond said. "Isn't she divine?" He turned back to me. "I'm Carl and this is my friend Sandy. This is just the biggest thrill you can imagine. You're my very favorite singer. I've got both your albums and I saw *Little Annie Rooney* three times and I'm dying for the day *Song and Dance* comes out. No kidding!"

"How about another beer?" Sandy asked.

"Hell, why not? After all, it's my birthday."

"Isn't she divine?" Carl said as Roddy came back from the phone. Everyone else was standing around me now, except for the man at the table, who looked cross. "Roddy, you know who this is?"

She scratched her forehead, tilting back the matador's cap. "Her name's Gloria. But I've seen her someplace before."

"You can say that again. It's Daisy Clover, and it's her birthday, and she wants another beer."

"Christ." Roddy peered at me. "I'm sorry, lover, but if that's who you are, you're under age. You've got to go."

"My publicity's a lie," I said. "I'm really twenty-eight."

"Isn't she divine?" Carl said.

Roddy looked grim. "I'm crazy about you too, but it's more than my license is worth. Lover, you've got to go."

They all turned on her. "Come on, Roddy! Don't be mean! Give her a beer!"

"Well . . ." She tilted back the cap even farther, sighed, winked at me, dived down under the counter, and slung me another bottle. "Just one for the road. I'm not being unfriendly, I want you to know."

They were really sweet boys. They raised their bottles and sang, "Happy birthday, dear Daisy," and Carl asked if I had plans for later, because he'd like to throw a party for me and I could have all the liquor I wanted. For a moment I was seriously tempted. Only the thought of the morals clause stopped me. Frankly, there's nothing like real fans to make you feel good about your work, and when Carl said he'd read about my suspension in the newspapers and I just had to get off it because the world couldn't live without Daisy Clover, I agreed with him. I could see he really cared. "You're a big hit with the boys, you know," Roddy said. She was mellowing, and offered me one more for the road. Then Carl played another of my numbers on the jukebox and started to dance with Sandy, and she bawled them out. They told her not to be mean. "Lover, I'm not mean," Roddy said, "but you've really got to go. They're getting too excited." "Can't I dance with Carl?" I asked. "Wouldn't that be all right?" We started to do it before Roddy could say no, then someone shouted that a police car was stopping outside, and everybody went still.

After a moment, Roddy seized my arm without a word, pushed me through a door at the back of the bar, and slammed it hard. I was locked in the men's room! If the cops break in and find the Orphan Songbird here, I thought, her career couldn't end with more style. I also read the stuff on the walls, which topped anything I've ever seen, let alone written.

The door opened. It was Roddy. "Okay, lover, you can come out now. And please go home."

Almost the end of October now, and I'm still sitting it out. No word from the Swans, but home in zombiland my instincts tell me that the master has a plan, and nothing happening is part of it. Gloria's unbelievably calm, so someone must be controlling her. I'd say the general idea is to teach me a lesson, wait for the crack in my armor, etc. It's quite smart, except there's not going to be any crack. Frankly this is a bad time of year to have nothing to do except count your fingers and read *Giant* by Edna Ferber, but I refuse to go under.

Wade's play is in rehearsal now and he's moved out of the hotel and taken an apartment, and when we talk on the phone he says he's okay. He doesn't like the way my suspension lingers on, but when I explain that if I go down on my knees and ask them to take me back it's an insult to human dignity, he has to agree. Sometimes his phonograph is playing, and I can hear Bessie wailing faintly at the end of Long Distance, exactly like the ocean echo in my shell.

November's in. I've taken some driving lessons, and yesterday I passed the test. Gloria agreed to let me have a hundred dollars out of the Trust Fund to buy a jalopy, so I chose this nice beat-up convertible with a BUY GIRL SCOUT COOKIES sticker on the rear fender. I drove it away from the used-car lot and five minutes later the brakes gave out. Gloria started to yell because we were going downhill. "The emergency, baby!" she gasped as we nipped through a red light, "for God's sake, where's the emergency?" She panicked me so much that I was almost ready to close my eyes and meet the Casting Director in the Sky, but finally I got the old rattletrap to stop right on the railroad tracks that run along the middle of Santa Monica Boulevard. Gloria was shaking, a real study in yellow, and I had an impulse. "Get out quick!" I told her. "There's a train coming!" Well, when the chips are down, you know where you are with Gloria. She was out of that car and across the street, without a thought for me, before she realized it was a joke. She didn't speak to me for half an hour, but when we got home a newspaper reporter called, and she recovered herself completely and gave out quite an interview. In fact she became very chipper for the rest of the day and said it was good publicity.

Next morning the paper had a snappy little headline, DAISY CLOVER ENDS ON WRONG SIDE OF TRACKS, etc., and a picture of the child star's jalopy and a description of her sister, Mrs. Gloria Goslett of Hollywood, admiring my courage. She bought six copies.

November's on the way out. My brakes are fixed. Gloria told me this morning that she's been "informed" there's to be a sneak preview of *Song and Dance* tonight. Zombies have been instructed to attend, but I said I didn't want to see it.

"You don't want to see your own movie, baby?"

"I threw up making it, remember."

"That was because Wade Lewis fed you warm vodka!"

"Am I invited?"

"Of course you are. I know you're on suspension, but they'd never turn a star away from her own picture."

"How do you know, Gloria? Did the Swans ask you to bring me?"

"They said they're keeping three seats."

"Honestly, you're too easy to trap."

"Now what is that supposed to mean?"

"I knew you were in secret communication with the enemy, anyway, but you let it out as naturally as a dog drops—"

"Baby, you're not to finish that sentence! You know how I feel about vulgarity!"

"Okay. Have a good time, though. Why don't you get Harry to take you out to dinner for once? I'll fix myself a sandwich and watch television and be perfectly happy."

Harry came home beaming because he'd sold a house that afternoon, so Gloria put on her biggest mouth and a shiny dress and they went off to eat Chinese food. I placed a call to Wade, but there was no answer. Fairly soon it was time for Plan B to go into operation, and just before the movie was due to start I parked my jalopy in an alley behind the theater and snuck up carefully to the ticket office. There was quite a crowd. In the lobby I could see the Swans, and thought he looked a little heavier and Melora a little paler. Alex Conrad went by in a blue suit with thick white stripes, laughing with some blonde, and Belle gazed anxiously around as if she wasn't quite tuned in. It felt marvelous not to be with them, obviously we didn't belong together at all. They were like a school you take a vow never to go back to after you've left, except to blow it up. So maybe this was my last movie? I got very tense and saw myself as a teen-age Garbo—but it didn't last, it was a bore, and next I got angry because in fact I hadn't sung for months. It was definitely a temptation to rush into the lobby in my sweater and jeans and give the whole crowd "Isn't It Romantic?"

They were moving up to the mezzanine now. I put on dark glasses in case there were unidentified zombies lurking around, paid my dollar, and tore into General Admission downstairs, just as the lights were dimming. As I found a seat my name came up on the screen, there were gasps of surprise and then a big round of applause, and I felt extremely gratified. It was going to be a different experience from the last time, when I'd been upstairs in yellow organdy with the gang, and didn't know who or what I was. Sitting alone now and feeling quite private even though my Public was all around me in the dark, I could separate myself from my image up there, and look it up and down as coolly as if I was pricing a cabbage or something in the market. I guess I'm becoming a pro. In a couple of numbers I really excited myself. In some of the others I'd say I took the easy way out, just letting the world know how cute the little trouper is, which is a lie, because she's not. I used to think I was, and Mr. Swan agreed, but it's obvious now we all kidded ourselves. I'm crazy for serious, that's all I know. If I weren't, I'd never have worked so hard to make that awful last scene in the movie pay off. When I finish the number in memory of my dad, there's this big close-up of my face with the hat tilted down my forehead, wet swollen eyes under the brim and a gashed smiling mouth under the eyes. I really tear the strips off this routine, and the same thing happened now as when I did it in the studio. The audience went numb, and didn't start to applaud until the curtains were halfway closed across the screen.

To give the others time to leave, I stayed in the theater and watched a newsreel about American G.I.s going home from Korea. Then I went out the side door, drove to a drugstore, and bought a large jar of bubble-bath mixture. Gloria and Harry were back already, and when they asked where I'd been I showed them the jar and explained that I'd just nipped out for some bubbles because I felt like a good soak before turning in.

"How was the movie, Gloria?"

She said it was fantastic, and they both cried, and she'd never heard such an ovation. The only criticism she had, which wasn't really important, was that they shouldn't have ended the picture with such an unflattering shot.

Surprise telephone call next morning, with Melora on the line as if nothing had ever happened, and how would I like to come out to the beach house for lunch? When I told Gloria, she was very excited, and said obviously the Swans were so impressed after last night that from now on I could write my own ticket.

"Just one thing, baby. Don't go out there looking like a tramp. How about a nice crisp blouse and skirt?"

She needn't have worried. It's no use trying the beat-up act with Melora, she looks right through you as if it's a terrible bore and you aren't feeling well.

Second surprise, though, when Melora opened the door looking definitely beat-up herself, in an old dressing gown. I'd never seen her like this before and I wouldn't have believed it possible, she always gives the impression that she even wakes up in the morning like a star in the movies, not a hair out of place, lipstick and stuff absolutely top-notch, her whole face fresh as a salad straight out of the icebox. Her hand pressed my shoulder, she said, "It's good to see you, honey," and as I followed her to the living room I realized she wasn't particularly sober. She sat down at a café sidewalk table, picked up a half-full drink and raised her glass. Her eyes were slightly red-rimmed, too.

"Here's to talent." She drained her glass. "But I wish you hadn't disappointed me last night, honey."

I felt myself bristling. "You didn't *like* it?"

"I adored it. But you didn't show up. Believe me, you'd have swallowed your pride if you'd known what a personal triumph the whole thing was going to be. I just wish I could do what you can do."

"Hot damn! You mean put over a number?"

"I mean make anything phony seem genuine. I'm not sure it should be allowed."

I wriggled modestly. "Coming from you, Melora, that's really—"

"I didn't say you could get away with it in real life!"

A crowd of gulls mewed past the window, the sound really shrieked across the bare open room. Melora was on her way behind the bar to mix herself another drink. She turned her head to watch the birds as they dived low over the ocean, she blinked and muttered something, and I thought how she looked like some kind of bird herself this morning. An owl in daylight, maybe. *What the hell has happened to her?* I wondered. She mixed the drink very slowly, not coordinating too well, then sat on a stool under the striped awning, resting her elbows on the counter and staring at me with her chin just above the rim of her glass. After a moment she raised the glass again. "Well, honey, up yours."

"Oh, and with turpentine, Melora." I was beginning to feel nervous, not because she was drunk, but she's been fixed in my mind as someone to whom poise is as natural as rock to Gibraltar.

"But what does one have to do to get *through* to you?" She

leaned across the bar, pressed my shoulder again. "Tell you everything, I guess, and then hope . . . Did Wade Lewis finish that story he began at Christy's party?"

I nodded. "Is it true, Melora?"

"It's completely true. And completely unimportant. I mean, so *banal*, honey!" I suppose I looked blank. "That's bee-a-en-a-el, it means trivial, corny, boring. So let's forget it."

"Okay," I said.

"Let's talk about the important subject."

"Do you mind if I make myself a vermouth on the rocks first?"

"Go ahead." She got off the stool, wandered into the middle of the room and flung out her arms wide, more like a bird than ever. "Can you imagine a desperation, honey, that has no *banal* reason—I mean, like losing a leg or a lover?"

"That's very interesting, I once tried to explain the same thing to Gloria and got nowhere."

She looked pleased. "I knew you'd understand. It takes an artist."

"And it takes one to know one!" I said.

"You can cut that out."

I rattled the ice around in my glass and had a flash. "Melora, is that how you felt when you first came out here and hit that pool?"

"Oh, I felt it before that." She sighed. "And after that, too. And a lot of the time in between. Honey, I'm not talking about conscience or anything, because I don't have any. All that's not important. But have you ever been in Arizona?"

It was definitely turning into a dance I didn't know the steps for, but Melora was leading so I followed.

"You know I've never been outside the Orange State."

"Well, I was born in a town called Stumpville." She leaned her back against the window now, tilting up her head to stare at the ceiling. "You wouldn't believe that town, honey. It only happened because someone found gold there, but then the gold gave out and they turned it into the Dude Ranch Capital of the World. It was really a ghost town that wouldn't admit it, of course, surrounded by other ghost towns that *had* admitted it, and other mines that had given out, and those awful beautiful mesas—red sandstone mountains, honey, with sheer sides and flat tops, all the color of dried blood. They were so proud the town hadn't changed, they kept all the old hitching posts in the main street, and the men rode around in cowboy hats, making healthy outdoor sounds of boot against saddle. Puritans, of course. That's why I hate Westerns." She moved back to the bar to freshen her drink. "And there was a little river that passed through Stumpville, a river with an Indian name and a tiresome Indian legend. They said that if you ever drank its water you'd never be able to tell the truth again in your life."

"Oh, Melora," I said. "Did you drink any?"

She shrugged. "The river was dry, honey, that's life in a ghost town. Anyway, my father ran a café that was open twenty-four hours around the clock, and my mother died, and there was no one to give Melora all the loving care she needed. So they packed me off to live with my uncle in Dicken."

"Was that any better?"

"That was a *real* ghost town. I mean, a showplace of the nation." She gave me a pitying look. "My uncle was one of its caretakers, and when I was fifteen he gave me my first job. I sold tickets at a museum which showed what a beer saloon was like in the old rootin-tootin days, with player-pianos and colored glass lanterns and a picture of Lola Montez. Well, I walked out of that and I came here and worked in a drugstore and learned shorthand and typing at night, and finally . . . It's really a great place to live, you know, most of the time, but some mornings I wake up with this terrible feeling. I feel this place is slowly turning into a ghost town too, maybe the biggest one in the world."

"And is that why you're a bit crocked right now?" I said. "Just on account of this ghost-town thing?"

"Yes, that's the real reason. I could give you a banal one too, but it's completely unimportant."

"Well, give it to me anyway," I said.

She was back at the window again, looking at me with blurred eyes. "I hate anticlimaxes, but it just so happens that someone I really love very much called this morning to say he's decided not to see me any more."

[141]

I was genuinely stunned. "Melora . . . you can't mean Mr. Swan?"

"Oh, that'll be the day. Anyway, it's not important. So let's forget it."

"Okay," I said.

"Let's talk about the important subject. I've been trying to explain that if this town's not to become a ghost town, it needs *you*. You're the gold, really you are!"

"Well," I said, "if that's true, who closed the mine?"

Melora didn't seem to hear this. "You're the greatest single thing in Ray's career, if he'd done nothing else but discover you, it'd be enough. And I don't have to tell you that being Ray's wife is the greatest single thing in *my* career—my life, that is. The rest is . . . it's one of those things that just happen." She went back to her perch behind the bar. "I'll get over this one. This one's really too *banal*. Honey, it's not what people *do* that counts. It's what they feel!"

"Then what I feel about Wade Lewis certainly counts."

"You can say that again. That's so true we don't even have to talk about it." She nodded several times, then gave me a smile. "As far as Ray and I are concerned, the problem of Wade Lewis no longer exists. Besides, he'll be in the East for quite a while." She got up suddenly. "Excuse me, will you?"

As she went out of the room her dressing gown slipped open, and I saw she was wearing nothing else.

There was so much going on in my mind, I didn't know what to start thinking about. I couldn't have imagined a more round-about pitch to try and get me back to work. Was it Melora's own idea, or had she discussed it with Mr. Swan? Maybe he'd asked her to soften me up first, but then this fellow had ditched her and she started boozing. Or maybe she started boozing and for some reason called me up? I suppose Melora carrying on with someone else shouldn't have surprised me—after all, I knew she once picked up Wade on a train—but it felt extremely spooky, and I wondered if Mr. Swan knew, and how often it happened, and whether she always went off the rails when a stud left her.

Ten minutes passed and Melora didn't come back. The sky

had clouded over and the room felt cold. I called out her name but there was no answer. There didn't seem to be any servants in the house today, either. I went upstairs and heard some sighing and muttering behind a door. She was lying across this big rattan four-poster bed with her eyes closed.

"Honey, I'm afraid there isn't going to be any lunch."

"Don't worry."

"There was a Chinese philosopher, honey, who believed that *any* action corrupts! In other words, the moment you do anything, you've had it."

"That's pretty deep stuff."

"I know. And sometimes we can't help doing things, usually things we shouldn't do. The only way to remain a decent human being is to *feel* good after we've done them."

"Then go out and do them again?"

"I knew you'd understand." She waved an arm. "I'll get over this one, though."

As I walked past the angels and geraniums in the courtyard, I heard a car drawing up outside. The gate buzzed open and Mr. Swan hurried in, his face quite gray and tense. He looked extremely annoyed when he saw me, then managed a stiff smile.

"Is Melora here?" I nodded. "Is she all right?"

"She's getting over it."

The smile vanished, and he stared at an angel with a chubby stone face and wings stretched out for the take-off. "I hope I can ask you not to mention this."

I nodded again and he walked past me, up to the front door. His shoulders were slightly hunched.

"I'll call you later," Mr. Swan said as he stepped inside. Then, before he disappeared: "The picture's pretty good, Daisy!"

10

(*Greatest Love Story Winds Up*)

When zombies get the green light from Mr. Swan, they're like bats out of hell. Late that afternoon Belle phoned to arrange for a limousine to pick me up next morning, and before you can say Back to the Salt Mines I'm sitting in that cozy office, we've had a friendly let-bygones-be-bygones interview, Uncle Ray presses a jigger, Alex Conrad steps in with a grin, a kiss, and a script under his arm, Belle crackles like a damp squib and brings us coffee, then we're off to lunch in the important room, Melora joins us and has obviously gotten over it, she couldn't put on more dog, and even the old girl from Wardrobe comes across with an album of costume sketches. A month flies by like gulls on the wind, and—

2nd of January, 1954. Here I am in a new portable dressing room on Stage 11, back in the old orange make-up, if I stretch out an arm I'll knock over ten dollars' worth of flowers from Alex or the Swans, there's a knock on the door, and the assistant calls, "We're ready for you, Daisy!" so out I come, picking my way across cables to the center where it's very bright and the crew is huddled around waiting.

Something's new, though. A person on the sidelines who wasn't there before! It's Wade Lewis—and I give him a wink as the cameraman almost sticks a tape measure up my nose. Unexpected? You can say that again, and here's the inside story.

When Mr. Swan explained that maybe he'd made too much

of this whole situation with Wade and he realized now you have to let these things work themselves out, and there was certainly plenty of time for that because Wade would be in New York for several months yet, he didn't fool me. I played it extremely cool and said no hard feelings, etc., but I could see his mind ticking over as clearly as the pendulum inside that glass clock on his desk. *By the time Wade's finished his run of the play,* old King Stag was thinking, *one of them's bound to have met someone else and cooled off, so don't worry, we can put her through another movie anyway before he gets back.*

This was the Master Plan, and I didn't need psychic powers to perceive it. I *could* have used them, though, to be ready for the next move on the board of life, which came three days later. I'd read the script and said it was great, we had a starting date and everything, and just as I got home from singing practice the phone rang. It was Wade on the line from New York, his play was a terrible flop, thumbs down from every newspaper in town, and he was hopping a plane back to California at the end of the week.

I saw him in the crowd of passengers crossing the field, he wore the same old black sweater and corduroys, and it was as if no time had passed at all. Then he saw *me,* and I caught my breath all over again at the beauty of his eyes and his thin relaxed figure and the springy way that he walked. He was also completely sober.

We didn't speak at first, he put his hand on my head and I felt his fingers in my hair, then I pressed my face against his sweater and didn't care who was watching.

"You're paler!" I said, looking only at his hand.

"No sun, dear heart."

The quiver in his voice too, that was like a touch all the way down my spine. I could have stayed against his sweater forever, but he moved away, and the next five minutes were rather long and nervous, tagging along while he got his luggage and a cab. He wasn't in a talkative mood either, in fact he didn't say anything at all. As we drove off he shifted in his seat, smiled at me, sighed, and gazed out of the window. I told him all the Swan news and then the story of my new movie, which took quite a while because it's complicated. I play two parts, a ghost and another girl. I haunt the house where the other girl lives, she's the only one who can see me, and she has problems exactly like I did, only I died. We sing to each other (trick stuff), I stop her making the same mistake as I did, and then she can't see me any more. It's a change of pace, anyway. By the time I'd finished, we were back at his apartment.

He dumped his suitcases in the middle of the room, opened a venetian blind (the slat was still broken), then lay back in a chair.

"Well!" I said.

He nodded.

"How are you, Wade? You look marvelous."

"I'm on the wagon."

"Really? Shall I make some coffee?"

"Christ, no."

"Okay, then tell me about the play."

He shrugged. "I've told you all that matters. It was a bomb. God, it's depressing to be back."

I watched his body hunch up slowly. He folded his hands, rested his chin on them, and frowned at the floor. I felt extremely discouraged and couldn't think of anything to say. Nor could Wade, apparently. Finally I got up and put a record on the phonograph.

"I'm going to have a drink," he said, and went into the kitchen.

I heard the clink of a bottle, the slam of the icebox door, and was so miserable that I almost decided to walk out of the room and not be there when he came back. He'd never see me again, I wouldn't answer the phone or anything. However, I just lit a cigarette, or tried to. I had a book of dud matches, not one of them would strike, and I was swearing at them when Wade returned with a glass in his hand. He took some matches from his pocket and gave them to me.

"Thank you very much," I said. "And please tell me what's the matter. Have I changed? Am I not the girl you abandoned two months ago?"

He laughed, and touched my hair again. I immediately kissed his hand.

"Dear heart, I'm sorry. It was being on the wagon in a plane. It threw me."

"It threw you right off, I guess. How long have you been on it, anyway?"

"Almost three days. I got so drunk when the play folded, I despised myself." He sprawled in the chair again. "My great gesture folded, too. Just like when I lived in that tower. Nothing happened. Shit."

"You mean, all that stuff about going away and coming back responsible?"

"There wasn't time," Wade said. "You see before you exactly the same ridiculous irresponsible person. One more fiasco under my belt, that's all."

"Nothing's happened to me either." I went over and knelt beside him. "And I couldn't care less. As far as I'm concerned—"

Suddenly he pushed me away. "Who cares what you care?" His voice was sour and biting. "I'm not talking about *your* concern!"

"Wade—"

Then he caught me and hugged me so hard that the tears came to my eyes.

"Dear heart, dear heart, dear heart."

"Yes?"

"I'm still the last person in the world for anybody to expect anything from."

I was recovering from my confusion. "Just don't ever do that again!" I said.

"What?"

"Refuse a drink on a plane!"

Then we were both laughing.

"And furthermore, don't ever *get* on a plane again. Without me, that is."

I sat on his knee and for a while we just listened to the phonograph playing—not Bessie but classical, because it happened to be on the top of the pile. Concerto for Orchestra by Bartok. It's

[147]

quite romantic when you get the hang of it, and made me think about the day I'm hoping for when Wade says What a fool I've been, I love you, why was that always so difficult to say? etc. Then we'll get The Dealer out and find a beach house.

∗

Alex Conrad certainly has a low opinion of Stanislavski. The Stanislavski business started because I said to Wade that sometimes I found it very difficult to stop myself being cute, especially when everyone liked it. So he brought up Stanislavski, and I had to admit I'd never heard of him. Now I've got all his books, tough going, I don't think I'll read them right through unless someone invites me to join the Old Vic, but in the meantime with Wade's help I can pick up a pointer or two. For instance, the reason I get too cute is *vanity*. Stanislavski says that any serious actor has to study at least half the year to purge himself of vanity, otherwise he'll end up just another obvious whore selling his charms. This kind of study isn't like school, where you make the grades and get out, it lasts till you die. Even Sarah Bernhardt after she lost her leg did an hour's fencing every day.

When he came to watch me work, Wade said it was amazing because you couldn't tell where instinct left off and technique began. I couldn't either, and Alex said it didn't matter. Wade thinks Alex has a very commonplace mind, which is the result of confining himself to the movies and never getting a whiff of the keen stimulating air of the theater. When you work in the theater, even in a flop, you realize all over again that an actor can be the prisoner of his mechanical responses. Anyway, my instinct makes me do a lot of things that Stanislavski teaches, and they're right. Frankly this doesn't surprise me, because I've studied in my own way, and I really knuckled down when I made all those recordings on the pier, thinking about the songs and the feelings they gave me, etc. However, Wade points out that even if you start with a rare natural gift, the world will corrupt it. You have to be a very special kind of person to stand up to the world and say no. Even though I said no to the last scene of *Song and Dance* and I don't intend to sing unless

[148]

I believe in it, according to Wade the whole experience is insidious and the world tricks you into believing your own lies. That's what happens when I go cute.

There's certainly something in this whole business, and I may get fascinated. Wade also finds that I've neglected my speaking voice for my singing one, and it shows through in dialogue. I need a greater command of inflections, and once or twice I teeter on the brink of monotony. The kind of lines I'm given to speak don't strike me as worth doing exercises for, but Wade tells me I'm arguing from the wrong end and surely I want to develop? He's right again, of course, which is why I'm going to see this person he calls The Breathing Woman. The secret of voice control lies in the lungs, and once you master it you'll be astonished how your range increases. The Breathing Woman has taught Wade for three years, and he swears by her.

Her real name is Mrs. Rauch, and she has an apartment in Hollywood just behind Schwab's drugstore. She's tall and slim, white hair with a blue rinse, wears leotards and you'd never guess she's pushing seventy-five. We go into this elegant room with books along two walls from floor to ceiling, a *pink* grand piano and a Siamese cat with a tinkling bell-chain. Mrs. Rauch sits on a black leather ottoman and tells me in a slight foreign accent that she's a fan. Then she explains that she's going to say a few words which I have to repeat without taking a breath.

"I'll not put the Dibble in earth to set one slip of them," she gives me, "no more than were I painted I would wish this youth should say, 'twere well, and only therefore desire to breed by me. Here's flowers for you."

It sounds like a very fancy tongue twister, but Mrs. Rauch says it's Shakespeare. I tell her I'll have to memorize it first, and while I'm doing that I'll hold my breath for practice. Then I mutter it through to myself, and it's really quite easy. "Okay, Mrs. Rauch, here it comes," and I'm perfect on the first take. She's distinctly impressed and says I have control, which is natural in a singer, but the instrument can be developed and she'd like to help me. There are two basic exercises, and if I work hard at them I'll start getting results in a month. "Number

[149]

one!" she says, going to the piano, striking a note, chanting, "The bawdy hand of the dial is now upon the Prick of noon," keeping her voice all on the one note like they do sometimes in church. "Number two!" She stands with her arms outstretched and holds her breath. After a while she bends her arms, clenches her fists over her knockers, and lets out her breath very sharply, asking, "Who? Why? When? Where?" It sounds crazy, but she explains that if you blow hard on the aspirates, you tone up your glottis. Maybe this is how Wade got his sexy vibrations.

"Okay, Mrs. Rauch, I'll give it a run. But when I hit that note on the piano, do I have to say Shakespeare?"

"You don't like Shakespeare?"

"I don't think so, but is that last line you spoke as dirty as my mind tells me it is?"

"The bawdy hand of the dial . . . ?" She looks pleased. "By all means."

"And do you give it to all your pupils?"

"I only offer it as a guide. Most of them find it makes the exercises more enjoyable."

"Can you give me another one?"

She looks thoughtful, then strikes middle C on the piano and goes into her routine. "Virginity being blown down, man will quicklier be blown up."

"Jesus. Maybe I should try reading Shakespeare again."

I like Mrs. Rauch, she's certainly more down to earth than Stanislavski.

When Wade isn't on the set, I go to my portable dressing room between takes and read Shakespeare. I started with *As You Like It* and *Twelfth Night*, both of which are pretty clean and have no parts I'd like to play. Only the clowns get numbers. But now I'm halfway through *The Tempest*, and I think I see myself as Ariel, especially if the lyrics have good music. I mention this to Wade, and to my surprise he's very enthusiastic and wants to play Prospero opposite me.

"Now that's crazy! You're so beautiful, why go and play an old hermit?"

But Wade says it's a great part, and no more crazy than a girl wanting to play a boy. He thinks maybe we could do it at the Pasadena Playhouse, but I'll have to get permission from the Studio.

25th of February. When Alex told me they've cut together about forty minutes of *The Willing Spirit* and Mr. Swan thinks it's going to be my best yet, it felt like a good day to ask about playing Ariel at the Pasadena Playhouse. I've avoided the subject so far, because since Wade came back and started visiting the set two or three times a week, Mr. Swan has been distinctly mumpish. If he runs into Wade he's polite enough, but in a double-edged way. "I can't believe an actor as talented as you is still out of work" is the kind of needle he likes to stick in, and I know I'll get a jab too if I expose a tender spot.

Anyway, while they lined up a shot this afternoon I went to a corner of the stage and did breathing exercises. I let out "Who? Which? Where?" a few times and wondered frankly when some results were going to show. Then I saw that Mr. Swan had come in and was staring at me.

"What's this?" He sounded extremely suspicious.

I knew that if I told him Wade had sent me to Mrs. Rauch, he'd disapprove. "I read some article in the paper," I said, "about toning up your vocal cords, and I thought I'd give it a whirl."

He didn't answer, but still looked suspicious.

"I hear the picture's coming along okay," I said brightly.

"Any reason why it shouldn't, Daisy?"

"Why, no! It's a great script. And Alex Conrad is a great director. And listen, when we've finished shooting, would you have any objection if I played Ariel in *The Tempest* at the Pasadena Playhouse?"

Mr. Swan shuddered. "I don't think I have to ask who put that idea in your head."

"It's my own idea. Girl Scout Honor. I've been reading the plays of Shakespeare and I like the part of Ariel. Wade Lewis wants to play Prospero and thought of the Pasadena Playhouse, but I started the whole thing."

[151]

"It's out of the question," Mr. Swan said in his most final voice.

"I honestly think I'm ready for it."

"It'll take your mind off the picture."

"But I wouldn't think about it till I've finished the picture."

"Then you'll have another picture to think about. I have no objection," Mr. Swan went on dryly, "to Wade Lewis playing Prospero. He can go on the road with it for all I care. But Daisy Clover as Ariel is definitely out."

"I'd get to sing."

"OUT, Daisy."

He started to turn away, and I felt pretty sick having been polite for no reason. So I cleared my throat, went Mi-mi-mi to find a note, and gave a powerful singsong. "Virginity being blown down, man will quicklier be blown up!" It echoed right across the stage and stopped him dead.

"What was that?"

"Just toning up the cords, Mr. Swan."

"And you read it in the newspaper?"

"No. In Shakespeare."

He was standing over me, I recognized a tweaking mood and ducked. Then the assistant called, "Ready for you, Daisy!"

"It's about time," I said. "The sooner we get this piece of crap in the can, the better." I was in a tweaking mood myself, and felt like saying no to the world, considering it had just said no to me. As I walked back to the set, I thought about the scene I had to play. This week I was the ghost, advising the girl not to run away from home. We tried it through, and at the end I gave a long sigh.

"I don't know, Alex," I said. "I just don't know."

"What is it, Clover?"

"It seems to me this stuff is pretty corrupt." And I collapsed on the Early American couch and buried my face in my hands. When I looked up, both Alex and Mr. Swan were staring quite coldly at me.

"She darned well *ought* to run away," I said. "I certainly would if I lived in that household of old farts."

"Daisy, you know that's not true!" Mr. Swan sounded quite

shocked, as if he'd never told a lie in his life. "If she runs away, that friend will lead her straight into a life of crime."

It was annoying, I couldn't think of an immediate answer.

"And remember this. You've told me on numerous occasions how much you like this script. So just get in there and do as you're told, or I'll read you the riot act."

"People have no respect for actors in this town," I said.

"How can you say that when this town made you a star? You weren't even *thinking* about that scene, Daisy. You were mouthing obscenities in a corner of the stage, I saw and heard you."

"Clover, you been at the bottle again?" Alex asked.

"You're a one-joke man," I told him, "and it's beginning to show in your work."

There was a moment's silence, then Mr. Swan grabbed my arm and pulled me off the set so fast I almost fell over trying to keep up with him. He really dug his fingers into my wrist, and it hurt, and he wouldn't let me go till we were inside my dressing room. He slammed the door and pushed me on the couch, my head bumped against the wall.

I was definitely scared, like the time Gloria made a lunge at me, but in spite of this I felt a mood of open defiance rising up inside. "If it's to be brute force, I'm helpless!" I cried. "But you'll never crush my spirit!"

"I know where this nasty destructive mood comes from, and that's what I intend to crush."

"Stop blaming Wade, I've got a nasty destructive crush-proof mood of my own."

Mr. Swan didn't answer this, but reached out, threw me across his knee and began hitting my ass with a script bound in a heavy folder. I was so shocked that I couldn't even react at first. The pain was minor but the humiliation wasn't, so I let out a series of ear-splitting yells that must have been heard all over the Studio. It alarmed Mr. Swan, and he let me go. I ran out of the trailer, there was quite a crowd outside, everyone looked horrified at my appearance, and I clutched the old girl from Wardrobe, who'd just wandered up with a box of hair ribbons. "He beat me up!" I said. "Mr. Swan of Magnagram Studios beat up his own star!"

The fiend came out of my trailer now, tight-lipped but calm. "I spanked her," he announced, "with her own script. She deserved every blow." Then he had the nerve to put his arm around my shoulder. "I'm really disappointed in you, Daisy. We've had our spats, but at least I admit it when I'm in the wrong. How about *you* admitting it for once?"

They were all against me, I could feel it. They were smiling at a child who just had a tantrum. They weren't absolutely wrong.

"Well!" I said, ignoring Mr. Swan with dignity. "I'll certainly admit I'm all mussed up. I'd better get my hair fixed before we shoot that scene."

I went back to my trailer and sat down in front of the mirror. After a while I stuck out my tongue at myself. "Pumpkin-head. You lost that round." Then, in the mirror, I saw the door open behind me. Mr. Swan came in, his face surprisingly anxious and sad. He looked like a whipped dog, which was ironic under the circumstances.

"Daisy."

"My make-up needs a little repair work too," I said.

"I'm still disappointed in you."

"Well, that's your problem."

"I don't think so. I believe it's yours. If you could see your heart now, it'd look harder than it used to." He gave a long sigh. "There are moments when I almost don't recognize the little girl who came to my office in a white dress."

Jesus, I thought, first he beats me up and then he gets sentimental about little girls in white dresses. "That's because the dress fooled you," I said. "You've got a definite thing about me as a little girl in a white dress. Or a yellow one."

Another sigh. "Daisy, I'll admit it again. *There are times when I've been wrong.* Doesn't that mean anything to you?"

"We all make mistakes," I said cheerfully. "I was wrong about that scene. It's not exactly Shakespeare, but it'll play."

He picked up my script, which was still on the floor, laid it on the table, and went heavily out.

Wade advised me to examine my contract, and see whether Mr. Swan could really stop us doing *The Tempest* at the Pasadena Playhouse. I didn't have a copy of it, but I was sure

Gloria kept one under her bed. She denied it, but said she remembered all the details.

"First of all, baby, they've got you for seven years!"

"My God, how are they allowed to do that?"

"By picking up the options. They can pick up those options for five more years."

"If they do, I won't be free till I'm twenty-one. I'll have given Magnagram Studios the best years of my life."

"Baby, you've got more best years than that!"

"You're an optimist, Gloria. Is it true I can't work for anyone else?"

"Not unless they give you permission. You're exclusive."

"And what else does an exclusive person need permission to do?"

"Let's see." She gave a big smile. "You can't leave California!"

"WHAT?"

"You can't go out of state unless you notify them. Of course they won't *usually* object, unless they want you here for some reason."

"They *own* me. That's all there is to it."

She seemed surprised. "I thought you realized that. You're their most important property."

"Gloria, I think you made a rotten deal."

"Baby!"

"You sold your kid sister into slavery for seven years. It was heartless and cruel."

"You're making good money. Very few girls your age have such a healthy Trust Fund. Every time they pick up an option, they have to pay more for it."

"Is there any way they can drop an option? That's what I want to know."

"If there was, I wouldn't tell you."

"Wouldn't they drop it if my pictures stopped making money? Or if my talent ran dry? Suppose I lost my voice, wouldn't they drop it then?"

"People don't lose their voices, baby. Or if they do, a doctor can fix it."

"I could bust a gut at my breathing exercises."

"Put that out of your mind. And if you tried to *pretend* you'd lost your voice, they'd find out afterwards and sue you."

"Then I've been sold down the river. No matter what happens, I have to go on singing for them for another five years. How many days is that?"

"I don't know, baby."

"Well, guess."

"Two thousand, maybe. But you don't have to sing every day."

"How do you know? I have to do anything they want."

Gloria looked as if she was going to cry. "I'll never understand you. You put yourself on suspension and nearly go out of your mind because you're not singing. Now you're back at work you complain about *having* to sing."

"Yes, I'm a mass of contradictions. But what the hell, Gloria? All that matters is, our little life is rounded with a sleep."

"That's the most morbid thing you ever said!"

"Oh, Gloria. You're just an insubstantial pageant, that's all you are."

✳

We were sitting in The Blue Piano.

"Wade," I said as the waitress brought us another round of martinis, "do you realize I'm completely trapped? Gloria made this lousy deal with Mr. Swan, he's got me all to himself for another five years."

He nodded. "You can still fool him, though. You can be *in* the world, dear heart, but you don't have to be *of* it."

"That's pretty deep. How do I pull it off?"

"Mr. Swan *thinks* he owns you because he's got a hundred clauses to prove it. But what is *you*? Is it just someone called Daisy Clover who sings and clowns around and makes a lot of money? Is that all *you* are?"

"No, it's only stuff that dreams are made on. And I told Mr. Swan yesterday he could never crush my Spirit."

Wade smiled. "So what is *you*?"

"Now isn't this fun?" I said. "What is me? First of all, it's a

[156]

person who thinks *you* are too wonderful to be true." His eyes flickered. "I mean it. Whatever *you* is, I'm crazy about it." He didn't answer. "So what is you?"

"I started to tell you that," he looked away, "before I went to New York."

"I know, but you didn't finish."

"Because I couldn't. I still can't. It's like—" He broke off as the waitress came back to ask if we'd like anything to eat. "No, only to drink," he told her. "Two more martinis." She went away, and he said, "She annoys me, she's so stupid. Hasn't she the stupidest face you ever saw? God dammit, that face of the stupid everyday world when it raises an eyebrow or looks snide because somebody's drinking too much or crying in public, that face ought to be wiped off the face of the earth." He picked up a French roll. "The least I can do is throw something at her."

"You might miss. Wouldn't that be humiliating?"

"Dear heart." He laughed. "Why do I worry about you? You handle the world much better than I ever will." He stared sadly at the roll, then put it back on the plate. "About your question, it's like asking a man with one arm why he never took up the violin."

"I've never heard the answer to that one."

"A man with one arm," Wade said in a strange, dry, matter-of-fact voice, "is mutilated. He's a cripple." I must have looked blank, because he made an impatient gesture and sighed, the way I do with Gloria. "Do I have to spell it out?"

"Yes, Wade, I'm afraid so."

"All right." The colored pianist was playing a very quiet slow blues, and Wade listened for a moment, his face had such a helpless expression that I almost panicked and told him to change the subject. The waitress came back with our martinis, he didn't even notice her. I took a quick gulp, and whether because it was my third, or I was nervous, everything reeled for about five seconds. "I'm a cripple!" Wade was saying. "Don't look so startled, I'm not talking literally, I mean that I'm totally incomplete. I make sounds and send up signals, but nobody hears or understands or answers."

"I hear them," I said. "And I answer them, even if I don't always understand them."

"Oh, you're the cripple's nurse."

"And you've just won the solid gold chamber pot."

"It wasn't an insult, dear heart. Some people have that faculty, they attract cripples."

"I didn't hear you."

Wade opened his mouth to answer, but he laughed instead. It was loud enough to make people turn around. "They ought to be wiped off the face of the earth!" I said indignantly, but he didn't seem to mind now. "If that's how you feel," he said, "if that's your last word, if it really is . . ." He picked up his martini and chinked the glass against mine.

"What are we celebrating?"

Sweat broke out on his forehead. "Would you like to get married, Daisy? Would you like to marry me?"

"I think so. Jesus!"

And for the second time in my life I fainted. Call it monotonous, but I went through *exactly* the same sensation as when that test was starting. It's so dark inside The Blue Piano that after I regained consciousness I thought I was back on that set, I could hear the other piano player and blinked at shadows. Then it was marvelously refreshing and I wanted to float.

"I thought that kind of thing went out with Lillian Gish," Wade said.

"No, it's still good."

When we got to the car, I started shaking.

"For Christ's sake, what's the matter with you?"

I put my arms around his neck and kissed him several times. "Merrily, merrily shall I live now!" I said. "Under the blossom that hangs on the bough."

He dropped me off at Arcadia Drive and told me to go to sleep immediately. I just sat on my bed in the darkness, staring out the window at that old devil moon. It beamed on my shell. I listened for the ocean echo, the waves sounded louder than I'd ever heard them. Like a roar.

I called Wade from the studio next morning and asked if the deal was still on. He said yes, but not to break it to the Swans yet because there'd probably be a story in the papers on how I fainted in The Blue Piano. Two reporters had called him already and there were various rumors going around town that I was pregnant, had a weak heart, etc. He thought it would be a good idea if I acted very bright and cooperative, so I wore a big smile for everybody (which wasn't difficult, as I was in a marvelous mood) and even exchanged a couple of blue jokes with the assistant director. When I came back from lunch, there was a copy of the midday paper on the couch in my dressing room. DAISY POOPS OUT. Obviously a present from King Stag. I read something about how I slumped across a booth, then they were ready for me, so I went on the set with my smile brighter than ever and no one made any reference to it. Toward the end of the day, when I was writing this Theme Book between takes, Mr. Swan came in without knocking. "Hello there!" I said. "What's new?"

He sat down on the couch and stared at me, bunching his lips together.

"It's going just beautifully today," I said. "Everything plays like a dream."

"All right, Daisy, now tell me what happened."

"Last night, you mean? I only know what I read in the papers."

"Are you sick?"

"I'm perfectly fine. It's sweet of you to worry, but I'm honestly colossal and definitely super-duper, and I'm staying that way right through this picture." Greatly daring, I gave him a pat on the cheek.

"You sure you're not sick?"

"I swear to you," I said, "I'm the Top. I'm the Nile, I'm the Tower of Pisa, I'm the smile of the Mona Lisa! I'm an O'Neill drama, I'm Whistler's Mama—"

"You've convinced me," Mr. Swan said. He looked extremely relieved.

My only big disappointment right now is being unable to make The Dealer understand that Wade and I are going to be married. Or maybe she *does* understand, you can't tell, because in recent months The Dealer has refused to speak any more. At the Getwell Sanatorium they say she's decided to withdraw. She's still very involved with her cards, she'll chuckle and nod and frown, but they can't get a word out of her. The doctor says that for some reason she's rejected language as a means of communication. He's trying to find out why, but since she refuses to communicate he's not making any progress. Not even Sodium Pentothal loosens her up, she lay on the couch completely deadpan for a couple of hours.

She was on the sun deck, very wrapped up, with the shawl around her shoulders, when I took Wade to see her. She's grown much older, not that her hair's turned white or anything, but her eyes look so heavy and tired. Miss Donahue says she's really quite happy, but that sounds like Gloria-talk to me. I have a sneaking suspicion that The Dealer knows what she's doing. She's so extremely fed up with where she is, she's cut herself off from it. She won't even admit to it that she's there. I've tried to persuade her to let me in on her game, but she never reacts. That's when I feel bad, because she seems to include me in everything that's useless and boring, maybe she thinks I'm to blame.

"Listen," I said. "I've brought your future son-in-law to see you."

She shook her head and turned up a card.

"His name is Wade Lewis," I said, "and we're going to be married, and I'm extremely happy. Also, we'll be taking a house and you can live there too. We can all go back to the ocean!"

The Dealer glanced up at the sun, which was shining brightly, and drew the shawl closer around her shoulders. Then the old nut with the cigarette-lighting routine wandered up.

"Jesus, it's Ruthie," I told Wade. "She wants you to light it."

Wade struck a match and she blew it out at once. The Dealer watched, and gave a deep satisfied chuckle. Ruthie almost doubled up with laughter, the two of them nodded at each other, The Dealer reached out and gave Ruthie an affectionate nudge. I felt turned to stone.

"Hell, I can't take any more of this," I said to Wade.

I didn't look back as we left, but I was sure they were laughing and pointing at us.

*

This afternoon, 18th of March, in the small-town street on the back lot, I told Melora. We stood outside the church, waiting for sun.

"Well, honey, I can't say it's unexpected."

Not exactly enthusiastic, but at least she wasn't going to raise the roof.

"We'll do the whole thing, of course. I'll speak to Ray."

At first I didn't understand what she meant, I only knew she sounded as if some great sacrifice was expected of her, and she'd make it. "Melora, what will you do?"

She turns up her high collar because it's chilly, then takes my arm and walks me to the church entrance. Right inside the door are a couple of lamps with MAGNAGRAM on them, and for some reason an old-fashioned sofa with red velvet upholstery. Melora sits on the sofa and explains that she and Mr. Swan will Give the wedding! Wade and I will tie the knot right at her own poolside, just as soon as the weather gets a little warmer and she has some fancy new tiling put in. It's important to have her pool ready for the ceremony. Also she'll provide the minister and the champagne and most of the guests. I tell her that Wade and I would be very happy to go off somewhere and get married quietly, maybe in Las Vegas, but Melora won't hear of it. "That's no good," she says, "it'll look as if you don't want people to know." Apparently it's important to have this town on my side about marrying Wade, which can be arranged so long as I leave everything to Melora. Frankly I can't get with this attitude at all, but Melora warns that this town can hurt you, take her word for it. There's always nasty gossip and rumors flying around, and when you're a public figure they can descend on you like a swarm of bees, so you'd better be protected. Considering that Melora once told me herself she picked Wade up

[161]

on a train, and wasn't very gracious about it either, I wonder what she means by protection.

"Well," I say, "I guess you know more about all this than I do. Don't think I'm ungrateful, but I'd certainly appreciate it if you also wished us happiness or something."

"Honey, of course I do." She brushes dust off her skirt. "That's why I'm going to all this trouble."

When I told Wade, he only laughed. "Give them their unreality," he said. "I mean, let them pay for it."

I asked him to explain about this town, etc., but he said it wasn't important. Everybody talks, he said, and when two people decide to get married they like to find reasons why it'll never work.

"What kind of reasons, Wade?"

He shrugged. "Only one, really. He's cheating on her or she's cheating on him." Then he gave me an odd suspicious look and went to the kitchen to get another drink. He stayed out there quite a long time, so I went after him.

"I think you'd better tell me, dear heart." He stood by the window, arms folded, and spoke so quietly I had to move nearer. "Just tell me what you've heard."

I was taken completely by surprise. "Nothing, I've heard nothing."

He obviously didn't believe me.

"People hardly ever tell me things," I said. "They always imagine I've still got ribbons in my hair. Sometimes I find things out, but that's because I just happen to be around and they can't stop me. Like when Melora was drunk and gave me a few installments of her childhood and boy friends and stuff." My voice sounded strange, too quick and more high-pitched than usual, but I couldn't stop. "Otherwise all I get is dark hints! Then people think they've gone too far and clam up. Isn't that ridiculous?"

"Then give me a dark hint." Wade had the same untrusting look on his face. "Go on, give it to me," he said, louder now.

"All right, Melora once told me about you and her on that train and I couldn't care less."

"That bitch." It really shook him. "That ancient bitch." He

[162]

slammed the ice tray on the draining board, all the cubes spilled out. "What else did she tell you?"

"That's all."

Wade mixed the drink rather clumsily and walked back to the living room. He sprawled in a chair and sank into a silence so deep and frowning I couldn't try to break it. Finally he reached out and touched my hand.

"Listen. I find it very hard to give love. I can accept it, all I can get I'll accept. One thing they'll never say about me is that I ever turned it down." He was smiling now. "And I want to give it to you. I really do."

Then he drove me home.

And in the still of the night I'm going to write down my most secret thought, outburst, and confession. People can imagine as many ribbons in my hair as they want, the truth of this situation is that I'll flush them all down the toilet the moment I'm alone. Of course all kinds of dark hints are roller-coasting through my mind now, including one that Melora threw me (which I'm keeping to myself) about somebody who attempted suicide on account of Wade. Well, I wouldn't attempt that. I'd *do* it. So if in the end Daisy Clover throws away her life for a pair of dark bright eyes, and the way someone touched her hand and stroked her hair and generally made sense, and even when he didn't, had wonderful vibrations in his voice, if that's all there finally is, just a hope and a promise but no beach house, she'll still go out smiling. Maybe even with a song on her lips.

✳

Swan headquarters are a rambling white Spanish house off Coldwater Canyon which I've always called Stage 28. It was originally a convent, but for some reason the nuns cleared out and left town, and the place was remodeled. Melora's bedroom was once the Mother Superior's private wing, the bar is where the chapel used to be, you can tell by the shape of the roof and the rafters, and every closet is as big as a cell. On the afternoon of my wedding the garden looked like a back lot. Some of the grass lawn was a bit thin, men were putting in artificial green squares on the bare patches. They'd set up rows of chairs, the new tiles with a camellia pattern glistened in the pool, and on a nearby platform stood a harp. The terrace had been turned into a dance floor with a bar, a marquee, tables and chairs, an orchestra was going to swing from a second-floor balcony.

Melora was on the phone somewhere when I arrived, but Mr. Swan met me in the hall. He looked fairly depressed, and wore a suit black enough for a funeral.

"Well, Daisy." His voice somehow suggested it was too late to draw back now. "How do you feel?"

"The script's just great," I told him, "and I'm crazy about my leading man."

He nodded reluctantly. "I guess this one was made in Heaven."

"As God is my director."

We both gave terrible phony laughs, they echoed through the empty hall. Then Mr. Swan shifted his feet, stared at his polished black shoes, and became very serious. He was stepping into the father role, I could tell. "Personal happiness is very important, Daisy, I believe we all deserve it, but it's not everything. This may surprise you, especially as you're about to become a bride, but people like us have to look beyond happiness. It's our work that fulfills us and makes life real."

"You mean," I asked, "that your work is more real to you than Melora?"

"I don't mean that at all." Mr. Swan's eyes flickered. "I mean that Melora is a part of everything, and I'm proud to admit that I need her, like air to breathe." He looked vaguely ashamed. "I could never have done what I've done without her."

Then he turned away suddenly and left me. I watched his bulky black figure hurry out to the terrace, and tried to figure out exactly what he was trying to tell me. Maybe he wanted me to know that he didn't mind Melora cheating because she was still his wife and helpmate, etc., or maybe he was warning me that if Wade cheated I'd have to look beyond it—but anyway I didn't want to stand in this empty hall trying to figure out stuff like this when I was due to be married in an hour. So I went upstairs to Melora's room to get dressed.

I'd absolutely refused to get married in white, it's ridiculous, and frankly I'd have enjoyed most of all saying "I Do" in a pair of old jeans somewhere down by the ocean, however Melora insisted on getting this man who did all her clothes to create a number for me. It hung now from the canopy rail of her bed, and it was yellow, which is supposed to be my color. I ran my fingers down the skirt and at the same moment came the sound of that harp being played. I moved to the window and saw a tall lady harpist, she wore a bright blue flowing gown and was tuning up by the pool while Mr. Swan watched.

"I really do appreciate all this," I said as Melora came into the room. "It's certainly a slick production."

Melora took down my dress very carefully. "In you get!" she said, as if it was a cold bath or something.

And soon enough I'm hooked up and my veil's at the ready and Melora's handing me the bouquet of (yellow) lilies. This town is waiting in the garden below, and the harpist plays a dignified arrangement of one of my hit numbers. Standing in front of Melora's mirror I see a reflection which is simply not to be believed. "Hey!" I want to say, "what the hell are *you* doing here?" and then I remember Wade telling me that though I may be *in* this world, I'm not *of* it. So I tell myself that although Daisy Clover *seems* to be a vision in yellow and is being put through this wedding which the Swans wish to God would never happen but are still paying thousands of dollars for, she doesn't believe a word of it. The Swans could spend a million dollars and still not make it click.

"It's adorable, honey!" Melora touches my arm, I look up at her face, and in a strange way it's sincere, almost maternal. It throws me. But I guess if you're spending that kind of money you take things seriously.

"I wish The Dealer could be here to see it all," I say. I'd wanted to put her on an upstairs balcony, I was sure she'd be all right with a table and a pack of cards, but the Swans wouldn't risk it. After all, she's still officially dead.

Melora looks busy and practical again, casts an eye at herself in the mirror, nods, and says it's time. We go downstairs, where Mr. Swan is waiting in the hall. He leads me out to the garden, we stand on the edge of a strip of carpet that runs all the way to Wade and the Minister. The harpist switches to the Wedding March. Wade has his back to me, but this town gets to its feet, turns around, and smiles. Julie Forbes is all in white. Thank God I can't see Gloria and Harry. There's Carolyn and old Mrs. Rauch, I asked them specially, someone gave them rotten places. It feels like a première, I get the old urge for a cigarette in the john, but I've reached the end of the carpet and I'm standing right in front of the Minister, who's surprisingly cute and reminds me slightly of Cary. Wade sends out a quick signal with his eyes, which I understand immediately. It means he's on to the whole racket and it's mildly hilarious. Also, it gives me a marvelous sensation. For the first time in my life I'm not by myself in public, but *alone with someone else*. Usually when they dress me up and start taking over it's a serious ordeal, in fact as Carolyn explained it makes me protest, but now I'm relaxed and friendly. I can't get over it!

The rest is like an album of photographs when someone turns the pages too quickly and you can't get a proper look. The ring goes on my finger—the Minister shoots a cool line about how the blood in this finger is supposed to connect by direct vein with the heart—we make our exit—Wade needs a drink at once—we're back on the terrace—music! champagne!—I get a silly twinge when Melora dances off with Wade—Gloria's swacked, turban and big mouth all crooked—Mr. Swan wanders off gloomily to the pool—Mrs. Rauch in purple satin gives a breathing demonstration to Christy Williams—who's brought her guitar player—who asks me to cha-cha—no one talks to Carolyn, she scares them off fast—Julie Forbes loses an $80,000 diamond sunburst—Harry finds it!—Alex Conrad's swacked, but makes time with some bouncy starlet—it's dusk, butlers in tails light Hawaiian torches—Wade touches my sleeve, wants to cut out—I take a last gulp of champagne—it's over.

I must have fallen asleep soon. I know I was moderately pooped myself, and when Wade wanted to drive all night I didn't give him any argument, even though it struck me as a wild idea. He said we had to reach open country. I said a honeymoon in Playa del Rey would be okay by me, it didn't matter, I had this good feeling about us being the only two people in the world. A couple of times I woke up and it felt chilly. We were in the middle of some desert, very flat and clear and spooky, thin twisted trees pointing their arms in the moonlight. Around dawn I woke up completely, reminding myself that I was a bride and after sixteen years and nine months on my first trip outside Califorina. Wade looked the same, only he was beginning to need a shave, but everything else was certainly different. It was still a kind of desert, dry and rocky, more scraggly trees and cactus, and no one around as far as you could see. In the distance was a wall of red mountains that you somehow felt had never been climbed.

It was wild country! The country was definitely wild. It really looked as dead as the moon. I couldn't believe the size of it either, it made Wade and me seem less than tiny, I mean too small to live.

"Jesus, where is everybody?" I asked. "Where are the Indians?"

He laughed and told me we hadn't reached Indian country yet.

"Why are we going there, anyway? Maybe I won't like it!"

Wade pointed his thumb over his shoulder. "It'll wipe out everything back there, dear heart, all the contracts and close-ups and pools and premières. It's beautiful and appalling, and there'll be absolutely no one we know."

"Oh," I said.

"Doesn't that appeal to you?"

"I'm not sure."

"You really like it back there. It's your town, as they say."

"I'm used to it, anyway. I've never been anywhere else." I pointed at the red mountains ahead. "What's on the other side of all that?"

"More desert." He sounded pleased. "Then more mountains."

"Don't you think there's just too much *land* around here? And what are the Indians really like, anyway?"

"What would *you* be like if the first thing you opened your eyes to was *this*?" The desert and the mountains seemed to grow bigger and emptier as he spoke. "How would the world seem to you then, Daisy?"

I thought it over. "Like it hadn't really got started, I guess. I'd imagine I was some kind of prehistoric baby. Maybe later I'd start wondering where everybody had gone."

Wade switched on the radio. We heard Spanish voices and then, as he switched stations, a singing commercial for smoked bacon.

"Where the hell can a person get breakfast in this country?" I said.

Two hours later I felt hungrier than I'd ever been in my life. We had nothing but vodka in the car, the first sip nauseated me, but after the second I began to feel better. The mountains didn't bug me so much. We whizzed through some little place, from the distance it looked like a ghost town, when we got nearer people actually lived there, I saw an old shack with the sign BREAKFAST. Wade said it was bound to be depressing. As we climbed higher, there was a sheer drop from my side of the car and I had to close my eyes. Near the top I peeked back at the desert we'd crossed. When I looked ahead again, there was another one below. You'd think that was how the world went on forever and ever, in a very sharp clear light with no shadows, and I understood what Wade meant about waking up to such a scary view, I was grateful to have seen the light of day at Hermosa Beach.

Finally we reached a little oasis of oak trees and billboards. There was a town coming up, it seemed to mean business. WELCOME TO STUMPVILLE! I didn't react to the name at first, then it hit me. "Wade," I cried, "we are entering the birthplace of Melora Swan!"

"God dammit."

A handful of motels, a signpost to a Dude Ranch, and then we were in the main street. I felt we'd driven hundreds of miles and somehow landed up on the back lot at Magnagram. It was definitely unimpressive, just more motels, a few stores and restaurants. Some of the stores had false fronts, like in Western movies. Two men rode slowly by on horses and stared at our car. The red mountains loomed over everything. I noticed a dingy café with a notice saying it was open around the clock. I asked Wade if we could have breakfast there, not only because I was hungry, but the man who served us scrambled eggs might be Melora's father. "If he's still alive," I said. "And if he hasn't moved on somewhere else. Melora never told me."

The café couldn't have been fixed up since Melora left town. If there hadn't been a ceiling, you'd imagine the whole place had been lying around in the open for about thirty years. There was a wooden counter with paint flaking off, pies under smeary glass cases, a coffee urn with streaks of rust, a poster advertising a Rodeo on the stained white wall. At a table by the window sat four men in cowboy hats, pouring syrup on piles of pancakes. No one spoke, you could hear the silence.

The man who took our order had skin like old leather, hands covered with freckles, and a mouth that turned down at one corner with a sour, tired expression. I'd say he was pushing seventy, and he had Melora's eyes, or vice versa. They were almost black. When he asked, "What'll you folks have?" he smiled, and the sourness went away. He was really quite friendly, just fed up with this around-the-clock deal, I suppose. As soon as he went off to cook our eggs, I told Wade I'd like to ask if his name was Swan. Wade said that would be pretty stupid, since Swan was Mr. Swan's name. The vodka had confused me, and of course I didn't know Melora's family name. So I'd either have to ask if he had a daughter called Melora, or shut up. When he came back and put the food in front of us, it looked awful. The eggs were desert-dry, the coffee tasted scalding hot and bitter. Somehow, in front of this complete silence and the middle-aged cowboys eating pancakes, I couldn't go up to this tired old joker —who was mopping the glass of the pie cases now and trying to get a shine on it—and ask that question about his daughter. It wouldn't have seemed right. So I nibbled the toast, which was okay, and tried to make sense out of being in this rundown joint in the middle of nowhere, with Wade who I'd just married and had gone to the john, and a cowboy coming out of the drugstore across the street.

By late that afternoon we were in Indian country. You couldn't see anybody. First I was drunk on clear blue sky, red mountains, endless sagebrush and cactus, then I had a hangover.

Wade seemed to enjoy the monotony, it relaxed him, but I was beginning to hate it. I could understand why men went crazy in the desert. It's an overdose of nothing. "Stop the car!" I said. "I want to get out." He pulled to the side of the road. I was definitely in the grip of an impulse, I ran very fast into the scrub, then stopped and looked around. Just me and hundreds of miles of Indian country. Not a sound anywhere. The sun was on its way down behind the red mountains. I stretched out my arms to them and broke into a Jeanette MacDonald soprano.

> "When I'm calling You-oo-oo
> Will you answer too-oo-oo?"

It must have echoed all the way to the Rio Grande, and back again. That's what happens when the movies get in your blood.

I don't remember where we stayed the night. Maybe it had no name. It was very late and very dark, we'd been traveling for hours. Frankly I thought we were lost, but Wade disagreed. Sometimes, out of the clear blackness, we'd see a cluster of lights ahead, but they were always off the highway and there seemed no way of reaching them. I drowsed, then woke up and felt cross with Wade. This driving kick had definitely gone too far, and something was wrong. The last time I woke up, he was just stopping the car. A motel at last, it looked closed except for one light dimly burning. Wade knocked on the door, a dog barked, and this cheerful stout little woman came out. She might have been waiting for us, she showed no surprise at all, only asked for ten dollars in advance and unlocked the door of a room, while a big mangy hound sniffed at our ankles. I was so tired that I told Wade I couldn't even fetch my overnight bag from the car. He said he'd do it. As he went out, I noticed that his eyes looked like the dead of night, even darker than the country we'd been traveling through. For some reason I called his name quite loudly—"WADE!"—but before I knew whether or not he'd heard and was coming back, I'd fallen on the bed and dropped like a shot bird to sleep.

11

~~~~~~

Melora said that Mr. Zidell was the man to handle it, and Mr. Zidell said that to discuss personal tragedy in an office, however elegant, was not conducive. So I went to his house in the Hollywood hills. It reminded me of the Getwell Sanatorium, it had narrow pointed windows, a turret, and a huge paneled front door that swung open very slowly. Inside, there was a priceless collection of antiques, heavy carved chests, statues, tables with dragons' heads sticking out, etc. Paintings covered every inch of wall, classical stuff, landscapes with ruined temples, and nude ladies eating grapes. At first I couldn't see Mr. Zidell anywhere. When I finally spotted him, he seemed to have crawled out of the woodwork. He was quite small, wore a shiny olive suit, and had a face like a baby alligator, drooping eyelids and a snappish greedy jaw.

He took my hand and gave it a squeeze. "Daisy. Poor child. You can trust me."

"Oh, fine," I said. "Really?"

He pointed to a long couch covered with tapestry, and I sat down. More dragons' heads came out of the arms. A tape-recorder stood on a marble-topped table, next to a pair of silver candlesticks. Mr. Zidell started the reels going, then almost disappeared into a chair with high velvet wings.

"Relax and tell me everything, Daisy, in strictest confidence. I promise not to use it."

"Then why should I bother to tell it?"

"I have to know the real facts of a case in order not to be able to present them."

"I'm not sure I know the real facts. I only know what happened."

"Let's go back four days," Mr. Zidell said. "To your marriage ceremony. Ray and Melora handle everything with style, don't they? I'm only sorry there were so many people that we never got to say how-do."

"I didn't see you there," I said, wondering if it was really style to invite a famous divorce lawyer to my wedding.

"Around nine o'clock that evening you started on your honeymoon, but I understand you never reached your destination."

"You can say that again, Mr. Zidell. Frankly I'd no idea where we were going. I guess Wade told me, but it didn't register."

"I believe that's the first time I ever heard of a wife starting on her honeymoon without knowing where her husband planned to take her."

"Well, I had this feeling, you see, it started at the wedding, I felt it didn't matter *where* I was with Wade, there'd always be just the two of us. Does that make sense?"

Mr. Zidell nodded. "You loved him and you trusted him. You closed your eyes and let him lead you—to the Sunset Crater Motel on the Navaho Reservation in northeast Arizona."

"Yes, Mr. Zidell, I *do* know I was there."

"Then tell me exactly what happened after you checked in at this motel."

If I looked at the tape-recorder and listened to myself speaking, those reels turning slowly made everything I said sound ridiculous. If I looked at Mr. Zidell I couldn't see him properly. Unless he leaned forward, he was like an imp in shadow. "I immediately fell asleep," I said to a bowl of artificial wax fruit that was held in the hand of some little nude cupid. "Well, it was extremely late, like one o'clock in the morning, and we'd been driving almost non-stop for more than twenty-four hours, and I knew Wade was disturbed, but I was too tired and maybe too confused to start anything then. I just fell asleep on the bed. Wade went to the car to get our bags, and—well, Mr. Zidell, you know I haven't seen him since."

"Poor child. Did he bring your bags?"

"Yes, when I woke up next morning they were in the room, also a half-full bottle of vodka. I don't know whether Wade left, right away, or slept a bit and then vamoosed before I woke up. I'd guess he slept a bit and drank half the vodka. Anyway, I wasn't worried at first. I thought he'd just gone to the drugstore or something. Then I noticed *his* luggage wasn't there. Then I looked out the window and saw there was no drugstore. There was no car, either. There was nothing at all, except that darned Indian country and this motel with a gas pump set down in the middle of it."

"You couldn't have a clearer case of desertion than that."

"Are you kidding? But I didn't care to face the fact right away. I just sat gazing stupidly at this Reservation stretching away forever, and the road that ran straight through it forever, and I felt sure I'd see the car coming back."

"I know you were brave," Mr. Zidell said.

"No, I was just stumped. When I realized I was definitely on my own, I looked in my purse to see how much money I had. Three dollars and fifty cents, Mr. Zidell. I took a shot of vodka, then went to the office to explain to this woman who ran the motel that I was in a spot of trouble. I wanted to borrow enough money from her to get back to California somehow without the world knowing, but she wouldn't part with a cent. She didn't know who I was and my situation smelled fishy to her. I said I was Daisy Clover, but she'd never heard of me. I explained I was a movie star and had jewels and credit, but she laughed, and I cried. Finally she agreed to let me call Melora collect. She stood by the phone, and to spare myself any further humiliation, which I couldn't have borne, I had to let Melora know that I was up shit creek, if you'll excuse the expression, without making it clear to this woman just how I'd been left without a paddle. But you know how smart Melora is, she got my message right away and called Mr. Swan. They had a quick discussion on how to get me off the Reservation. It wasn't easy, you're really cut off in that part of the world, a Studio car would take at least a day and a half, the nearest airport was miles away, and Mr. Swan said the only answer was a helicopter. He

[173]

told me to wait in my room, and a helicopter would come down from somewhere and pick me up later that afternoon. I finished the vodka and finally this thing landed back of the Sunset Crater Motel. When I got up in the air I looked down at the desert and stuff. It seemed more like the end of everything than ever, the meanest place in the world for anyone to dump anyone. I felt honestly miffed, and couldn't restrain my language."

"And who can blame you?" Mr. Zidell said. "I understand no one's found a trace of Mr. Lewis yet."

"Not yet. Mr. Swan's put a watch on his apartment, and they've contacted his family, who don't know anything, never did, his father was too ill to come to the wedding. I'm pretty sure Wade's hiding out in some tower."

Mr. Zidell leaned forward sharply. "How do you work that one out, Daisy?"

"When he has a real problem, a bad one, Wade goes to a tower. Or he did once, anyway. He joined the forest rangers for six months."

"A young man of peculiarly violent decisions!"

This sounded sarcastic, I didn't care for it. "The only one I don't go along with," I said, "is the last one."

"Have you any idea, any suspicion, *why* he left you?"

"Oh yes. He wished he'd never married me."

"Did he say so?"

"It wasn't necessary. Just the way he wouldn't stop driving, I knew he was regretting the whole thing."

"That's not really evidence, Daisy. I'm going to be very direct with you now. Exactly how far did your relations with Mr. Lewis ever at any time go?"

"Melora asked me that already," I said. "Not ever at any time terribly far."

"Did he ever suggest going further? Did you refuse?"

"I kind of suggested it. He refused."

He sighed. "One handles all kinds of cases. One hears and sees a great many things. And the lesson one learns, over and over again, is that human beings are not basically logical. All the same, I don't understand how you could know Mr. Lewis so long and actually marry him without having any suspicion that he was sexually abnormal?"

"Although he didn't make love to me," I said, "I knew he loved me. We talked about it. He explained he was mutilated."

Mr. Zidell raised an eyebrow. "Where?"

"Inside."

The eyebrow went down. "A figure of speech. I see."

"When something's over," I said, "when it's all finished and dead, *then* people start telling you things. They explain how they *tried* to warn you, but they didn't want to say *too much*, it wouldn't be *fair*, especially when you're making a movie and you have to be *protected*, or your work might go to pieces. Once the picture's in the can you're allowed to go away and suffer, and as Mr. Swan told me yesterday, maybe you'll come back a bigger person and can use it as an artist. JESUS!" I was getting carried away. "Mr. Zidell, I'm just part of the great human stock market, that's all. It's my averages that count and a slump at the wrong time can rock the corporation. If I don't recover, I'll be written off!"

It startled him. He said, "Poor child," again, then asked if I'd like a drink. I told him I could use a vermouth on the rocks. He explained that we had to prepare for every eventuality, which was why he felt obliged to probe me. "Suppose Mr. Lewis were to reappear quite suddenly, and for some reason contest a divorce? He sounds impetuous enough. He's also a wealthy young man, remember, and he may contest the settlement we have in mind."

"There's no settlement in mind," I said. "Just a divorce."

"Daisy, you must try not to be bitter."

"I'm not bitter. That's why all I want is a divorce."

"It's a negative attitude. Why should this man betray you and go free? His father has the biggest mattress business in the country."

I stood up. "I don't care to listen any more. I don't even care for a vermouth on the rocks. I just want to go home."

"Don't worry." He came over and squeezed my hand again. "We've made a good start. You've given me enough on Mr. Lewis to feel confident. All we have to do now is find him. And

[175]

if he doesn't contest a plea of simple desertion, you can go to court, describe what happened at the Sunset Crater Motel, and get a divorce in ten minutes."

"Okay."

"And remember this. When we've had a several emotional shock, life threatens to overwhelm us with its futility. It's a natural reaction but we must fight it." His jaw gave a snap. "Fight, Daisy!"

"Okay. I'm a born fighter, I think, everyone says so. Which reminds me of something." I sat down again. "Mr. Zidell, you may not know that I have a Mother. She's officially dead but actually they keep her in the Getwell Sanatorium, my sister arranged it with Melora. I want her out, one of the things Wade and I talked about was how when we were married we'd all live together. Now I want to make a home for just the two of us, but I have to be legally of age to get her out of that place, because my sister definitely wants her to stay there. Aren't I legally of age now? If I've made movies and been married and deserted and will soon be divorced, how can I still be a minor?"

"Let me discuss it with the parties involved." Mr. Zidell gave me a doubtful look. "But are you sure you feel equal—after your recent experience—to removing your poor mother from an asylum and living with her?"

"She may cause a little unsteadiness on the market at first," I said. "But we'll rally."

"You have to stop talking that way, Daisy, and start trusting your friends, who are deeply concerned about you." His eyes were quite reproachful under their alligator lids. "They are all so anxious for you to be happy."

*

I'm not living on Arcadia Drive any more. I've moved to Stage 28 until I find a place of my own, or Melora finds it for me. Anything's better than Gloria and Harry, I won't speak to them, in fact I've refused to accept Gloria's calls. Swan headquarters are roomy and I don't have to see anyone unless I feel like it. They've put me in a guest cell not too far from the Mother Superior's wing, but smaller. Probably some little nun lived here and whipped herself at night. I know about the whips because a girl at school had a sister who took the veil and joined some way-out order where they weren't allowed to speak, just meditated and then brought out their black snakes at night for exercises. I recommended it to Gloria, but she only got annoyed.

Anyway I'm mortified enough these days, I don't need exercises. I concentrate on my objectives every morning—getting The Dealer out, finding a nice place at the beach, and going back to work—and I keep up my breathing routines. I thought I'd have to give them up because they'd remind me too much of Wade, but they're paying off. My notes are rounder. Before all this happened, I also had a thought about suicide which I wrote down here. It came back to me while I was waiting for that helicopter to take me off the Reservation, and I might have done something about it if I could have found the right way. I didn't feel like going out on the road and throwing myself under the first truck that passed, I can't explain why. I considered waiting until the woman who owned the Sunset Crater Motel was asleep, creeping into her kitchen, and sticking my head in her oven, but I was afraid that dog would kill me. In the end I took a long walk and found a beautiful piece of rock, white and smooth with reddish purple crystals. It turns out to be porphyry, extremely rare but not worth anything, but I'm keeping it anyway.

Every week is Be Kind to Daisy week now, the Swans invite me to go everywhere with them, I've sat at quite a few fancy dinner tables and heard a lot of talk about the business. Naturally no one mentions my tragedy—except Christy Williams, who called up and asked me to lunch and wouldn't talk about anything else. She looked terrible, she'd just been to the dentist and her cheek was swollen, she couldn't eat much but carried on quite cheerfully about the difficulty of finding happiness with a man. She gave up the guitar player two days ago, he wasn't strong enough. Christy says we're very alike, both strong women, and we have this same problem of needing an equal partner but never getting one. She also came right out about homosexuality in our time. She's studied it. Since she's been out here she's fallen deeply in love twice with very attractive queers, though she didn't marry either of them. At least with the guitar player she broke the pattern, but he didn't want what she calls a full relationship, in fact he wasn't capable of it, too narcissistic, etc. I remembered Wade once telling me that it's strong American women who drive men queer, because they're ball cutters, but Christy said that's ridiculous. "You'd better face it, Daisy, he's a real lousy pretentious person and actor." I said that wasn't fair, he had problems and certainly put himself through hell making up his mind to marry me. "Didn't he put *you* through hell too?" Christy asked. I had to admit it.

She's not giving up, though. She definitely believes that somewhere a full relationship is waiting for her, and she also wants kids.

✳

The Dealer was sitting in the hall of the Getwell Sanatorium, next to two beat-up suitcases. They'd dressed her in the best she had, a black dress with a darn in one sleeve, and she insisted on keeping that ratty old shawl around her shoulders, she fretted when they tried to pack it. Miss Donahue came up, followed by Ruthie, who glared at me with a face like thunder. Miss Donahue explained that Ruthie didn't like The Dealer going away. The Dealer didn't seem to care one way or the other.

"Hey," I said, "we're going back to the beach!"

She looked at me as if I was trying to put over a fast one.

"It's true, I've rented a little shack on the ocean. You'll have your own room with TV, and you can step right out on the sand."

No reaction. Miss Donahue said they'd all be very interested to know if at any time The Dealer decided to speak again. Just for the record, if she broke her silence in the future would I call and inform them?

"Okay," I said.

I took The Dealer's arm, she followed me quite obediently to the car. She noticed the BUY GIRL SCOUT COOKIES sticker on the fender, wagged her finger at me and gave a chuckle. Then

[178]

she got in. There was a commotion when Ruthie tried to get in too, and Miss Donahue pulled her away, and she cried.

"Want to take a last look?" I asked as we drove away.

The Dealer shook her head and glanced back.

"You know I'd have gotten you out before," I said, "if I possibly could. I'd never have let you stay in that dump for two years if there was anything I could have done to stop it. They're only letting me take you away now because they're afraid *I'll* flip my lid if they refuse." She didn't seem to be listening, she was gazing out of the car now. There wasn't much to see except traffic, but I guess she found it interesting after all this time. I still had the feeling that she understood more than she let on, and whether she did or not, it was quite restful talking to her as we drove toward the ocean. "Another problem," I said, "is that I've been pretty busy. While you've been holed up watching TV, *I've* made three movies, been on suspension, fallen in love, and gotten married. Now I'm getting divorced. I brought the guy to meet you, but I don't expect you remember that." The Dealer nodded. "Does that mean you do or you don't?" She nodded again. "Well, forget it. The point is, my marriage didn't turn out so well, it only lasted a day. I was crazy about him but he had problems which I couldn't help him to solve. Everyone says he should never have married me, it was a terrible thing to do to a girl just after her sixteenth birthday, but I can't hate him for it. Even if he'd told me everything beforehand, I believe I'd still have gone through with it. You know me, don't you?" The Dealer shook her head. "Oh, come on, yes you do. I'm Daisy." She shook her head again. "Well, forget it. The point is, he's disappeared now and they can't find him. A private eye's been on the case three weeks, not a trace. They want to find him to serve the papers, you see, otherwise I have to wait seven years to prove desertion. That's too long, don't you think?" The Dealer shrugged. "But suppose one of us falls in love again and wants to get married? I agree it's not likely in Wade's case, because you know what he needs? He needs to settle down with some extremely nice boy and stop feeling guilty, and I hope he does. And I hope that I meet someone as attractive as Wade who likes girls, and who also likes *you*. Then we've all got it

[179]

made." The Dealer whipped out a pair of dark glasses, stuck them on the end of her nose, and peered at me. "Well, there's no harm in dreaming," I said. "And have you ever thought of this? What do we have in common that makes men run out on us? I'm referring to Mr. Clover and that business of going to Seattle five years ago. It won't be long before you can prove he deserted you, if you're interested." She gave a chuckle. "You think that's funny?" She shook her head.

Just for the hell of it I decided to take a long way round and drive The Dealer through Venice. I wanted to see if the old landmarks gave her a thrill. I even had a wild idea that the sight of the pier, or the smell of beans, or something like that, might encourage her to open her mouth and start talking again. So I parked the car in St. Mark's Square and asked if she'd like to take a walk. She shook her head and got out immediately, setting off at a smart pace. I had to run after her and hold on to her arm. "Remember this piazza? The bingo parlor's still closed up over there." We turned the corner into the boardwalk. "And how about that?" I pointed in the direction of the old pier. She tugged impatiently at my arm and seemed to want to go straight to the beach. Being July and Saturday afternoon, it was fairly crowded. The Dealer's shawl billowed in the breeze as she hurried across the sand in her old black dress. We were heading straight for the ocean. Near the shore she broke away from me, walked into wet sand that squelched all over her canvas shoes, then entered the water. A medium-sized breaker was bearing down. "Hey!" I ran after her and pulled her out just in time. A few people stared and laughed, but The Dealer merely took that old yellow holder and a pack of cigarettes from the pocket of her blouse, and lit up. Her dress was splashed and water poured out of her feet, but she stood there puffing and looking extremely gratified.

"Shall we head on home now?" Luckily she didn't object. She let me take her arm and steer her back to the car, smoking grandly all the way.

"Well," I said as we drove off again, "you really were glad to see the ocean, weren't you?" She shook her head. "I could tell how cooped up you must have felt all this time, and how pleased you were to be free. There's nothing freer than the ocean, is there? I feel the same way too, that's another thing we have in common."

Melora didn't approve of the house I'd rented, she thought it was practically a slum, but then she sighed and said she guessed it went with my car. It can't compare with her beach palace, it's just a shingle house snuggled away at the end of Topanga Beach Road, and the furniture is what you might call basic, but there's a nice room for The Dealer, with a card table, TV, and french windows opening straight to the beach, and a room right above it for me, which faces the ocean too and has a veranda with one broken deck chair. Also, Melora's sent over a lot of rattan she doesn't need.

When I showed The Dealer her quarters and asked if she liked them, she went straight over to the bed, climbed in, and lay down without taking off any of her clothes.

"You don't have to do that," I said. "From now on you only have to do what you like. Are you sure you want to go to bed?" She shook her head but didn't move. I took off her wet shoes, then unpacked her things. They weren't much, I felt terrible about the shabbiness of them all, blouses so tacky with cheap laundering, skirts that hadn't been pressed for months, a weird old girdle. "Tomorrow," I said, "we'll take a little trip to Saks Fifth Avenue." The Dealer frowned and lit another cigarette. "For Christ's sake be careful about smoking in bed," I said. "Remember what happened once before?" She chuckled. "And just how long are you going to keep up this silent routine?" She nodded. "You mean you *are* going to keep it up?" I was putting out all the cards in stacks. She watched very closely and her eyes grew bright. The decks really mesmerized her. "You've worked out some pretty cunning business for this no-talk act," I said, "but don't forget I'm an actress and catch on quick. When you nod it means no. When you shake your head it's yes. When you chuckle it's not funny. When you frown it is. Now, would you like me to turn on the TV?"

After a moment, The Dealer sighed.

"You old devil, you've pulled a new one on me."

She chuckled.

"It's not funny?" She shook her head. "It *is?* Then why did you laugh?"

She peered at me over the top of the bedspread, then blew a slow deliberate ring of smoke.

Later. The sun's going down over the ocean and I'm sitting on my veranda. There's a lot of noise from The Dealer's room, she's turned on the TV, and from the sound of all that gunfire must be watching a Western. I wonder if she'd like a dog. If she's not going to talk, it's really the best companion for her.

Melora called a few minutes ago to ask if we'd got settled. She's been fairly busy, tied up some baby-sitter under exclusive contract to come in and stay with The Dealer when I'm not here, had a talk with her private eye, he's pretty sure Wade's left the country, and is going to cast a wider net. Also, a famous lady columnist from New York is out for a look-see, and as she's an old friend they showed her a rough cut of *The Willing Spirit.* She raved. In fact, she's standing next to Melora, still raving, and would like to speak to me.

"Daisy Clover?"

"Hi."

She went right on raving, and explained that although we'd never met she had to tell me about my knack of expressing universal emotions.

"Okay," I said.

"At times it's almost too poignant."

"You mean I ham it up?"

"My dear, you know perfectly well that's the last thing in the world I mean. It's too poignant because it's so simple! That's what makes the world identify with you."

"Are you sure? I don't identify with the world, you know."

She laughed. "I simply refuse to believe that's true."

"Well, bully for you. But if you'll pardon the punch line, it's a case of mistaken identification."

Melora said the columnist was quite surprised, she hadn't expected me to be so articulate.

12

~~~~~~~~~~~~~~~~~~~~~~~~~~~~~~

Last day of August. They've found Wade!

Melora's private eye says the whole set-up is not to be believed. Everyone wants to spare my feelings, Melora says if I insist on details it'll be painful. I insist, and promise it won't disturb my work. (I start a new movie next month, thank God.) What Melora finds hard to forgive, and expects I will too, is that Wade seems extremely happy. He's taken a house in Acapulco and has been living there for over a month with a fellow called Malcolm.

"Who the hell is Malcolm?"

Melora looked enigmatic, so I knew she knew. "Remember the day I told you about someone in New York who tried to commit suicide on account of Wade?" I nodded. "Well, it was Malcolm."

"So who is he?"

"A young painter. I've never seen his work but I hear it's not bad."

"I bet it's not abstract, anyway."

She stared at me.

"Wade never liked abstract stuff," I explained, remembering the time he bought a painting for Christy Williams.

"It goes back a long way," Melora said. "Part of the time they were together and part of the time Wade would go off with some woman, which never worked, honey. When he came out to California he wouldn't bring Malcolm with him, and Malcolm tried to kill himself. When Wade went back to New York to do that play, the *real* reason was to see Malcolm again."

"So this other fellow's been my rival all along and I never knew it. Did *you*, Melora?"

She was lighting a cigarette and answered me through it. "Of course not. I suspected it, though."

"You always knew more about Wade than I did. In fact, you're the expert."

Melora said she wouldn't go as far as that, but it was true she was aware of Malcolm's existence, and it had occurred to her that a tug of war might be going on behind the scenes.

"My God, how could you splurge on that wedding?"

She looked surprised. "You forced our hands. We were just giving in gracefully."

I felt weak, and had to sit down. "Melora, is my ass in a sling."

"Poor baby."

"Took all the wooden nickels in circulation."

"*Don't.*"

"Push-over and pumpkin-head of all time."

"Honey!"

"It's *ironic.*"

"What?"

"It had *better* be ironic. Otherwise it can only be something much worse." I remembered the first time Wade called me from New York and didn't want to leave his hotel. I guess I sent him on his way to Malcolm.

You can take it, baby. Sure you can. Don't let them feel they've got to get out the crying towel for you. Not yet seventeen and a star already! Get back in there and sock out those numbers. Belt out the heartbreak, kiddo, get going with the beat of sorrow. They'll pick up your options anyway.

*

The Dealer still hasn't broken her silence, but I know she's made an important discovery. She realizes that after all this time she's free again, can come and go as she likes, nobody's imposing a routine. The first morning she got up early and sat out on the back porch, looking very confused because there was no sun, it doesn't hit that side of the house until later. "I suppose they herded all you jokers at the Sanatorium out into the sun at this hour," I said. "Well, that kind of thing is all over. From now on the world is your oyster." She didn't seem to believe me at first, but now she's got the message, sleeps extremely late, takes a stroll along the beach when she feels like it, puts enough bubbles in her bath to reach the ceiling, and even does a little silent shopping at the market, bringing home the beans, etc.

Since she wouldn't speak, I thought maybe a blackboard and a piece of chalk might come in handy, so if occasionally she had an idea she felt like passing on, she could write to me. When I explained this, she nodded, took the board, drew some squares on it, marked one with an O, then handed it back for me to play ticktacktoe with her.

"You know," I said, giving her an X, "I believe you make more and more sense every day. You've decided, haven't you, that we connect better if you *don't* talk. And you're right. When I look back on the days we made a kind of conversation together, it certainly never got anywhere. In fact I usually didn't have the faintest idea what you were talking about. This way we haven't had a single misunderstanding." She shook her head. "Considering your situation," I told her as she drew the winning O, "you really are the most fantastically intelligent woman that ever lived."

It was a day in September of gusty winds below canyons, of the story breaking in the newspapers (CALLED STAR TERRIBLE NAMES ON HONEYMOON, TEEN-AGE SINGER'S ORDEAL, DAISY'S DESERT BLUES, etc.) and I'd just come out of Mr. Swan's office at the Studio after a conference on the script. As I made my way to the parking lot and my old jalopy, someone called my name. I turned and saw this young guy in tight black pants and a check sports shirt with the sleeves rolled up to his shoulders. It was the guitar player who'd broken up with Christy Williams; I was slightly embarrassed because I couldn't remember his full name, I just knew he was Artie. However, he called himself Ridge Banner for the movies now, so it didn't matter.

"So what are you doing, Daisy?"

"Getting ready to face the cameras again."

He wondered if I ever found time to eat dinner.

"Oh yes," I said.

"Well, so do I. But I guess you're pretty booked up."

"Oh no."

"A big little star like you?" And Ridge Banner offered me a cigarette, then a match. Because of the gusty winds I had to cup my hands over the match, and Ridge Banner had to cup his hands over mine.

"I don't have a lot of friends in this town," I said. "Honestly. I've never crashed the movie set, I'm the wrong age. And the Studio doesn't like me going to big parties and driving home stoned in my old jalopy at two o'clock in the morning."

"That's a shame." Ridge Banner was looking very directly into my eyes. I threw back my head and blew out smoke. Next evening I called in the baby-sitter and drove down the highway to Santa Monica Canyon. A drink at Ridge's place before we went out to dinner. He lives on the top floor of an old building with a laundromat and barber shop directly underneath it, and he's made it Japanese, which means hardly any furniture at all but a lot of pillows, also his guitar on the wall and some bullfight posters.

"Oh, I like it," I said. "It's adorable."

"I like the beach," Ridge Banner said.

"I couldn't live anywhere else," I said.

"What's your poison, Daisy?"

"Vermouth on the rocks, Ridge."

"Hell, I don't have any."

"Then anything on the rocks. Except vodka."

We had dinner at a little Mexican dump. He didn't ask me where I'd like to eat, and the moment I stepped inside and got a whiff of refried beans I was taken aback, but then I realized it's the cheapest food and Ridge didn't have much money. I decided to make the best of it, and toyed with an enchilada.

"So what are *you* doing, Ridge?"

He looked rueful. "Not much. Rode in a couple of Westerns last month."

"That's a shame."

"A lot of guys like me don't stand a chance."

"How's that?"

"You know this town."

"Not really. I'm *in* it, you see, but not *of* it."

"I can see that. It's what I like about you."

"Oh. Ridge, could I have a double vermouth on the rocks?"

"Hell, they only serve beer or wine."

"A bottle of wine, then. Now tell me about this town."

He glanced around, then spoke in a low voice. "It's been taken over by the Faggots."

"I never heard that before."

"A lot of guys don't stand a chance if they don't play along. And you should see State Beach on a week end." He glanced around the restaurant again. "That booth right at the end! See it?"

"It's kind of dark in here. Oh, you mean with the two boys?"

"Faggots."

"Ridge, I'm not crazy for that kind of talk." I peered at the booth again. "And I know those boys, anyway. I met them at a bar down in Venice. Hey!" I called. "Carl! Sandy!"

They heard me, and looked up.

"Who's that?" Carl said.

"I can't see without my glasses." Sandy put them on. "Why, it's Daisy Clover!"

They jumped up and came over, absolutely thrilled.

"Ridge," I said, "I'd like you to meet two friends of mine, Carl and Sandy."

He only grunted, very sullen.

"Hi, Ridge," they both said, very friendly.

Carl smiled at me. "It's divine of you to recognize us."

"I never forget a true fan," I said.

"We're charter members of the Club," Sandy told Ridge. "We really are."

Ridge didn't answer.

"Well," I said. "Lovely to have seen you again."

"Can't wait for *The Willing Spirit*," Carl said. And to Ridge, "Nice to have met you."

"Good-by," Ridge said.

"That was mean," I told Ridge when they'd gone away. "They're very sweet boys."

"I'm sorry." He looked slightly ashamed, and I realized he was basically a very sweet boy himself, just not too bright.

"Anyway," I said, "Christy Williams is no Faggot and didn't she help you?"

"Christy made a lot of promises. You know her trouble? She talks your ear off about people relating to people, but she can't relate to anyone except herself."

"Yes, I guess she's narcissistic."

"In spades."

"And that's the way it goes." I gave a long sigh, God knows what for, except the wine was setting up a pleasant buzz. But Ridge looked at me with very brown sympathetic eyes.

"Poor kid. You've really been taking it on the chin, haven't you?"

As we left, he asked if I'd care to come back for a nightcap. Also, if I felt in the mood, he'd take down his guitar.

Now don't ask me why I liked the sight of a hefty sun-tanned arm with a thin silver bracelet around its wrist, and strong fingers plucking at a guitar, and the sound of Ridge's voice singing "I Gave My Love a Cherry," etc. (In fact, don't ask me anything for the rest of the summer.) I only know it was a crazy sight and a cool sound, and I also liked relaxing on pillows and the way this music drifted out through open windows across the highway and got lost somewhere on the warm empty beach.

If I stop to pause and reflect, which I won't, and didn't, I'll get truly worried about being in a way back where I started, and how S-E-X in the end seems to have nothing to do with whether you really like a person or not. Ridge doesn't give me the Absolute Strangers sensation I had with Milton, but I can't pretend I'm on cloud seven either. Maybe that's my fault, because I believe he loves me, he even refused at first to let me take him out to dinner at non-Mexican joints. Still, the only person I loved never made love to me, and while I don't love Ridge, he makes love to me a lot of the time. Which is a problem, but then everything is till you solve it. In the meantime we both know what we're doing, as you might say, and we certainly do it. The moment we get back to his place I get terribly worked up, and so does Ridge, I can't think about anything else, and afterward I just sleep it off.

It's made me late to the Studio a couple of times.

∗

The word for my new movie is Americana. It's called *Love to Spring Valley*, and it's about a girl from a family in the Middle West. She's the youngest, makes trouble, is very adolescent, etc., and goes off to join a touring musical show. The leading man tries to make her, she won't allow it, he has her fired, you take it from there. The numbers are pretty good, anyway.

We're shooting at night on the back lot. The scene's supposed to be winter in Wisconsin, but of course it's late summer in California and extremely warm. They've planted leafless trees in the small-town street and sprayed the ground to show it rained recently. I'm all muffled up and perspiring inside a thick coat, a sweater, scarves, and gumboots, and when Alex Conrad says action I've got to shiver. All part of the business and naturally I'm not complaining, but I have to meet a more serious challenge than just pretending to be cold when I'm hot.

I *am* cold! Something's freezing me up inside. Christy Williams once told me it's important to find images when a scene doesn't come alive for you, and usually I don't have to search for them, they just come. All this week my only images are no help at all. Most of them have to do with Ridge and they're quite unsuitable. If they ever invent a camera to X-ray your subconscious, heaven help me. You'd think I was making a dirty foreign picture, not family fare. Anyway, they were taking a long time to line up this shot, so I peeled off most of my clothes and wandered off across the lot to where they had real trees and stuff. I found myself outside the church where I'd told Melora that

[189]

Wade and I were going to get married, take it or leave it. Inside, I sat on the old-fashioned sofa and it sent up a cloud of dust. On the floor lay a torn poster that had drifted out of a Western, it offered $200 reward for information leading to capture of any of the Younger Brothers. Through a big crack in the roof I could see the moon, very full and pale, and a few stars twinkling, and through the open door the small-town square, then winter and the lights that glared down from scaffolding. I sat in this place for a long time and got steadily more depressed than I'd ever been in my life. I tried a breathing exercise, gave out What? Where? Why? to the moldering church, but it didn't help. Ridiculous tears splashed down my cheeks. Finally I heard distant voices calling, "Where's Daisy?" "I saw her going *that* way," etc., and I sat very tense and still, *couldn't move.* Cold as a frog and staring at that moon.

The door gave a creak and Alex Conrad said, "What is it, Clover?"

"Oh, are you ready for me?" I still didn't move.

He sat beside me on the sofa. "You might feel better if you talked about it."

"No, I'd feel worse. Come on, don't you want to get this shot?" I made myself get up, but he caught my hand. "They're waiting," I said. "I heard them calling my name!"

"Something's troubling you." He looked very solemn. "For one thing, you're too darned agreeable. We haven't had a spat since the picture started, it's not right. And what were you doing just now with tears in your eyes?"

"I don't know. Maybe it's the full moon. I'm a Libra, you see, and I think the full moon has upset my scales. But as long as it doesn't show through in the dailies, don't worry."

"That's exactly why I *do* worry, Clover."

I stared at him. "What? You mean I'm not good in the dailies? Something's wrong? You're not satisfied?" He only shrugged. "Don't beat around the bush, I want the truth!"

"You're okay." I didn't like the way he said this at all. "There's nothing we can't use."

"Alex, will you stop that?"

"I guess no one can be great all the time." He gave me a long expressionless look, then let go my hand. "But there's a wonderful thing about movies, you can edit a performance, snip snip snip, Clover, and concentrate on the high spots."

I felt suddenly dry-eyed and much warmer. "So you've been letting me get away with less than my best. How long has this been going on?"

Another shrug. (I could have killed him.) "Since we started shooting. But I'm not really worried."

"A moment ago you said you were."

"About the *cause*, Clover, not the result. As I told you, there's nothing we can't juggle around with in the cutting room. All I care about now is *you*, and what's holding you back."

"I'm thrown for a loop. Why didn't you tell me before? Has Mr. Swan noticed?"

"He felt I should say the first word."

"All these weeks I've been slipping and didn't know it. We'll have to reshoot everything!"

"I told you, it's not that bad. We haven't got to the stuff that really counts, anyway. But before we do," his eyes looked beady behind their spectacles, "I want to find out how to get through to you."

"Frankly, I'm having difficulty getting through to myself. The line seems to be out of order."

"Why?" He took my hand again. "The cause, Clover, the cause."

"Maybe I'm anemic. Or need vitamins. I'm a growing girl, remember, and sometimes—"

"You're not leveling with me. You're searching for ridiculous excuses. *Running away from yourself*."

"I am?" I was desperate enough to believe anything he said. But not ready for what actually happened.

Breathing very hard, the little fellow took me in his arms and gave me a long painful kiss on the mouth! Then he let me go. "I know your trouble, I know what's been going wrong with you. You've got all the signs, Clover, of a girl who needs to get laid."

After a moment I burst out laughing. There was nothing else I could do. I fell back on the sofa and practically kicked my legs in the air.

"I'm not saying I'm the person to lay you." Alex sounded hurt but dignified. "I'm just telling you to get wise to yourself."

"That's not why I'm laughing," I managed to get out between convulsions. "It's just—just nervous evasion."

Alex stared down at me, slightly alarmed now. "Listen, I certainly had my hand on the trigger, but I'd no idea—"

"Stop it!" I gasped. "If you don't stop it, I'll die laughing!"

He must have decided to finish what he started, he slapped my face not very hard a couple of times, then kissed me and held me. The misunderstanding was so great that it worked completely, and in a minute or so I was calm.

"Well!" I said. "What do you know?"

He looked a bit sheepish, but definitely pleased with himself.

"Let's get this show on the road, Alex, or people will talk." I got up and did a little shuffle down the aisle of the church, singing, "Always have an ace in the hole." "And am I glad you took off the kid gloves. Any time I don't come up to snuff, just give me hell, baby. It's what I need."

Four o'clock that morning I drove home slowly along the coast highway. Radio was turned up very loud, playing old show tunes. Moon looked much smaller. I thought again about S-E-X having nothing to do with L-O-V-E, and this time it made me laugh. I honestly believed in nothing, and couldn't have been happier. *You certainly can take it.* Didn't you play that little scene right through to the end? Called up baby-sitter after shooting, told her you'd be very late, followed Alex back to his apartment, took off your clothes, and let him go to work. Wasn't he proud as a peacock afterward? Sat there in his birthday suit, sipping brandy out of a huge snifter, number one Don Juan of the world. Explained to little Daisy that it was just one of those things that happen in a relationship. Won't happen again, no, that would be wrong for both of us. You remembered him saying once that the basis of our relationship was kidding, but you kept your mouth shut and let him feel *good*. You got dressed, told him it had been a lot of fun, thanks for everything Alex, and went out into the night. Baby, you certainly can take it.

So don't ask me anything for the rest of the summer. Just—

Try the old trick of counting up to ten. *Slowly*.
Okle-dokle.

When I got back to the beach house, there was only the porch light burning. Baby-sitter was asleep on the living-room couch. I looked into The Dealer's room, she was asleep too. It felt very warm. I went upstairs and opened all my windows. In the distance I heard faint thunder.

Later the storm came overhead and woke me up. I heard windows banging somewhere and rather liked listening to the rain. It didn't last long. I woke up again around 7:30, and although I'd only slept three hours I didn't feel tired at all. On the contrary, very alert and nervous. I wanted to get up and make myself some coffee. As I went downstairs, I heard sounds of TV from The Dealer's room. It struck me as odd, she doesn't wake early, then I thought maybe she'd left it on again all night and it had just started up by itself. For some reason I wanted to check, and opened her door a few inches.

To my surprise she was sitting up in bed and watching the early-morning program, somebody lecturing on Faith. The room was extremely untidy, the wind had blown every window open during the night and scattered all her cards, they lay across the floor and the bed. There was even a jack of diamonds stuck in her hair. She didn't look at me, and a moment later I realized she wasn't looking at the TV either. I didn't even have to touch her cold hand to know she'd played her final solitaire.

This only happened yesterday. I guess it would make more sense to miss someone very sane and practical, but the way I am, I miss a crazy useless person, someone not to talk to. In a strange way, The Dealer was always the most solid thing in my life. I've kept her old shawl, and this morning I put it around my shoulders and sat on the veranda staring at the ocean. I don't think I moved for a couple of hours, except maybe to light a cigarette.

When the phone rings I'm sure it's Ridge, and I won't answer.

Some time ago I read an article in a magazine called "Your Nerves and You." It was by a doctor who said that the commonest sign of a breakdown was when you picked up a book or a newspaper and couldn't concentrate on it, the words meant nothing at all, the effort to follow a single sentence was just too much to bear. But as long as you could read the newspaper and it *made sense*, you were okay. It struck me as pretty morbid to sit with The Dealer's shawl around my shoulders and not answer the phone, so I picked up yesterday's newspaper and read some stuff about politics, sex crimes, etc. I felt thoroughly informed and knew I was still on the ball. Then I got out a Theme Book and started writing, and on the whole I'd say I'm fairly shaken but not to pieces.

13

~~~~~~

Yesterday, 2nd of November at the Studio she hardly knew what she was doing. Only this pill saw her through, feeling like somebody else and having no connections didn't scare her so much when she'd swallowed it. Everyone anxious and patient, etc., saying to be sure and have a good long rest this week end, Melora inviting her to spend it at headquarters, Mr. Swan asking if he can't help, Alex suggesting we drive down to Tijuana, and Daisy crying: No! she wants to stay out at the beach. She woke up in the middle of the night, Ridge's body very close, arm and the silver bracelet against her thigh. She couldn't bear it, jumped out of bed, and he found her smoking on the stairs. She took a pill for sleeping and let him put her back beside him again. But in the morning she sent him away. He was relieved, of course, he really can't take much more of this and she doesn't want his disgusting helpless pity. When he'd gone she ripped the telephone cord from the wall, then made a lot of ice-cold martini and put it in a silver flask. She went on the beach in her slacks and Ridge's Mexican shirt he'd given her.

Near the shore was a black decaying pile of seaweed, very spooky. She gave it a wide berth, sat down on wet sand, and drank martini from the flask. No one around, at last she was perfectly alone, and started to like it until things changed. They really changed. Behind her, the cliffs grew very TALL. The ocean became unusually DEEP in front of her eyes. And the clouds in the sky were much TOO LOW. I have to admit she sat there shaking and nipping and trying not to scream. If she screamed, what about the publicity? DAISY FOUND SCREAMING ON BEACH! And the crowd gathered around, whispering of course, "Why, she's crazy! *That Girl Is Out of Her Mind!* Did you see that old Mexican shirt she had on, and the flask of liquor in her hand, she can't get away with it!"

Well, she certainly wasn't going to let that kind of thing happen. Even though the cliffs were getting TALLER and the ocean DEEPER every minute, and she felt completely trapped between land and water, she'd sit it out. She gave those clouds a dirty look, and it worked, they backed up at once. She decided not to drink any more, and threw the flask into the ocean. Alcohol is basically a depressant and so are *you*, the combination on this particular day might be fatal.

Then I believe she went to sleep, and woke up feeling extremely damp but much better. Also, someone had taken that pile of seaweed away. She walked back to the house and flicked through a newspaper. It made pretty good sense, but all the same she had a definite conviction it was time to cut out, make a run for it. She just didn't feel like expressing universal emotions any more.

14

~~~~~~

21st of May 1962. Hotel Imperial, Atlantic City, N.J. Room 304, Parlor Suite, quite comfortable, radio and TV, kitchenette, private tiled bath, resident Dietitian, etc. Also, view of the ocean.

I'm in a good mood, God knows why. After checking in much too early at this dump, I took a stroll along the boardwalk in the rain, then realized I had hours to kill before I even rehearsed. So I dropped in at some weird Believe It or Not exhibition, CAPTURED SOVIET CARS! and stared at this red and gray jalopy called a Zis, roped off with a "Do Not Touch" sign. It was what my old friend Melora Swan would have called *banal*, honey, just like some American family model of fifteen years ago. Couldn't see it was worth capturing, let alone exhibiting. I walked past a pinball place, empty except for a couple of kids trying to tilt a machine, and found another room with more fancy stuff on show. In glass cases around the walls were shrunken human heads, a flute of death made from human bone, and a Mysterious Ivory Ball (from ancient India). This town's idea of entertainment strikes me as offbeat, to say the least. Maybe that's why it signed *me* up.

A middle-aged lady sat under the Ivory Ball and a loudspeaker piped some choir singing, "Happy am I in my Redeemer." Business looked poor. The lady told me this whole deal was in aid of the Veterans, so I tossed her a quarter, she gave me a small red badge on a pin, and I cut out. In a drugstore I bought a 9 by 6 Theme Book (35 cents plus tax, which shows how much the cost of living's gone up), and walked back to my Parlor Suite. I opened the book and stared at the first empty page. Back in my New York apartment, stashed away in a closet, I've got a whole pile of these books, all about my life from fourteen to seventeen, when as the saying goes I passed out of the picture. After that happened, I laid down my pen, and that part of my life went in the closet along with the books.

Now I'm beginning again, picking up the pieces, trying to refresh the inner girl. The question of the day is, will Daisy Clover pull herself out of it or slump back with the others? You know who the others are, they live in an old mansion high in the Hollywood hills, or a chic and lonely East 60s penthouse, or a castle in Spain, or Cuernavaca or quiet old Rome, scared of age and refusing to do television. Of course I'm slightly younger than this crowd, only twenty-four, but I've noticed a tendency in the Papers to make me part of it when they interview me. Maybe one reason is that by the time I was nineteen my hair had turned prematurely gray, and I was tagged the Gray-haired Teen-ager. But people always try and make you part of something, it's a move in the Taking Over act. Since I dropped out of sight I've heard and read some pretty good stuff about myself, and none of it really hit the point. People have said the point is Wade, or The Dealer handing in her chips, or the Studio pushing me too hard, or just plain sleeping around from an early age—but honestly, honey, isn't all that too *banal?* All I'm prepared to admit is that after some pretty sharp encounters with life and death, etc., I didn't feel I was getting anywhere special. In other words, if there *was* a point, I couldn't find it. (And still haven't.) But I absolutely refuse to blame anyone, including myself. If I've learned a single lesson, it's that when you make a decision— always carry it out but never explain it. It gets to be a terrible drag doing the right thing for the wrong reasons.

I certainly remember trying to bite the ambulance man. I was sitting in the driveway of Swan headquarters, confused but still not ready to give in. After starting out in my jalopy with the intention of maybe reaching Carmel that night, I somehow landed up outside Stage 28 reading this newspaper. When Melora found me, I told her not to worry, I could still concentrate. She called the ambulance, and then I got really angry with the man who tried to pick me up and put me inside it. "I'm definitely not having a breakdown," I said. "Can't you see I'm reading Walter Winchell?" Then I sank my teeth into his wrist. He answered as you might say in kind, by sticking a needle into my arm.

Quite a while later I used to lie in bed at the beach house, staring at the windows which had thick drapes drawn across them. I got fairly disturbed if the smallest chink of light showed through, made the nurse pin the drapes down so it couldn't possibly happen. The result was like a dark blank screen in a movie theater, and I felt fine so long as it stayed blank, but one day they started showing a movie, a very dull annoying one in which a girl sat in this swivel chair and clenched her fists. I used to turn over and count up to fifty, telling myself she'd be gone when I looked back. Sometimes it worked, sometimes not, then came the time that I dropped off to sleep, woke up and saw *she had come into the room.* JESUS! I thought, if I'm not careful it'll turn into a case of Come One, Come All, and I'd better fix her. I gave her a long fishy stare. She only swiveled and turned her back. I started to gasp, because I felt Mr. Swan's thumb pressing on my neck.

Well. A few weeks and sedations later, I was sitting up in bed and had the drapes drawn back. I rather enjoyed listening to outside sounds, the ocean of course, some bulldozer clearing a hillside, a dog barking or a kid shrieking on the beach. I felt basically okay again, except I had no intention of getting up. I told this to all visitors when they remarked how much better I seemed. "Yes, I'm better," I said, "but I am definitely *not getting up.*" It worried Mr. Swan so much that he hardly ever came to see me. At first he tried to lure me out of bed by saying all the wrong things, like I was a ham at heart, but I only shook my head. "I like it here, Mr. Swan, in bed, just the way it is." Then he'd ask if I thought I might get up next week. "I can't say," I told him, "maybe next week, maybe next year." He had quite a serious problem, of course, because *Love to Spring Valley* was only about three-quarters finished. "I'd like to help you," I said. "Honestly, I'd really like to get off my ass and see that picture through, just for old times' sake, but it's not possible."

"Daisy, I would like to understand you. What is your objection to getting up?"

"I have no objection. I'm just not moving, that's all."

Melora as usual made crazy sense. Because of that day at her beach house, she felt we had a secret understanding. "I know what it's like, honey. Believe me, you'll get over it." She suggested that I get up immediately, finish the movie, then take a long trip. Around the world, maybe. If I liked, she'd come with me. "Isn't that a pretty good offer? Think it over, honey."

"Okay."

"You think you might be able to reach a decision?"

"I'll certainly try."

"When do you think you might know?"

"I can't stand pressure, Melora."

In the end they shot around me and released the picture anyway. There was also a number from an earlier movie that was never used, a piece of me stored away in some old can. They got it out and stuck it in the last reel. Not surprisingly, because everyone knew what had happened, the critics said I showed great signs of strain, which in the final number became almost unbearable. I believe *Love to Spring Valley* didn't do at all well.

Gloria couldn't be kept away, though I always made it clear the moment she arrived that I was extremely sleepy, and would only keep awake for another five minutes. Her first visit, she was very bright and anxious and tried to make jokes. "Looks like I'm the only stable member of this family, baby!" It was a clinker even for Gloria, and I closed my eyes at once. As time went on and I didn't move and always felt sleepy, she made fewer jokes. Her eyes grew more and more shifty, she threw me quick dense furtive glances and fidgeted a great deal. Obviously she had something on what I suppose is her mind.

"So what is it, Gloria?"

"I've been trying to figure out what you think would happen if you got up."

"Nothing," I said. "That's the trouble. I could get up right this moment, and rattle around the house for a while, maybe

look at television and scramble some eggs too. But where would
it get me?"

"It would get you *up*, baby."

"It would get me to Magnagram Studios. Don't you understand, the moment I start walking around they'll come and put
me to work."

"That's ridiculous, you can't stay in bed the rest of your life."

"I may have to, and it's entirely your fault. You made that
lousy contract, remember."

Gloria brightened. "But they'll let you out! Melora said so.
If you'll just get on your feet and put in two weeks' work—"

"Will you never learn? Will you always fall for their cunning
promises? Anyway, I couldn't do it. The fog would come in and
I'd go to pieces again."

"What fog is that, baby? You never complained about any
fog before."

"I could always sing 'You Are My Sunshine' to it, that's why.
But it doesn't work any more. That's what's changed, Gloria."

She didn't answer, but I knew what she was thinking. She'd
decided I was seriously crazy, that's all.

Carolyn brought me two books, *You Can't Go Home Again*
by Thomas Wolfe and *Our Inner Conflicts* by Dr. Karen
Horney.

"Thanks a million," I said.

She perched on the end of the bed. Although Carolyn never
wore spectacles, she always gave the impression, when she looked
at you, of peering over the top of them. "Still lost your sense of
purpose, child? Still wondering what there is to get up for?"

You could always rely on her to be at least one move ahead
in the game.

"Are you afraid?"

"Maybe that's it," I said.

"What of? Not being able to function?"

"Maybe that's it."

"A groundless fear. Talent doesn't simply vanish in a puff of
smoke. Unless, of course—" She broke off.

"Don't stop now. Help me out of the tunnel."

Carolyn hesitated. "There are certain flames, you know, that burn very bright but not very long."

"So that's what you think!" I sat up. "Let me tell you, Carolyn, I haven't even hit my stride."

"Good girl! I see I touched a raw creative nerve." She smiled at me. "So why not get out of bed and hit it?"

I lay down again, sighed, and closed my eyes.

"You're scared the world won't *let* you hit your stride? You see nothing ahead except a Treadmill of false emotions?"

I gave a weak nod. "Ahead and behind, Carolyn. That's it."

"You've transmuted lead into gold before, haven't you?" I didn't answer. "I can believe you might be bored if you got up now and finished that picture, but I can't believe you'd be scared. It's so *unlike* you."

I opened my eyes very wide. "But what is *like* me? You think what you see on the screen is really *myself*?"

"Of course not. And it's extremely fortunate. The real you would scare most people out of the theater."

"That's a terrible thing to say."

She took a maddeningly long time to light a cigarette. "I brought you the book by Thomas Wolfe not only for its passages on the hollowness of success, which I think may interest you, Daisy, but because it's an important example of the neurotic drive behind an artist's work."

"You certainly switch around. What was Thomas Wolfe's problem and why should I care?"

"Be patient. His problem was universal." She blew out an impressive amount of smoke. "The search for the Mother."

"You mean his mother disappeared or something?"

"She died when Tom was very young. When he grew up, he tried to recapture her image in the women he met. It stopped him *really* growing up. Now suppose, child, *your* drive is really the search for the Father?"

"And I should go to Seattle after all this time and start making inquiries?"

"I don't think you meant that seriously. When I throw the word *Father* at you, what do you think of?"

"A garden hose."

She looked extremely interested. "Is the water turned on or off?"

"It's going at full blast."

"My God, how sexual. Now do you see my point? When an audience watches Daisy Clover on the screen, all it sees is a charming, talented and mischievous child. It has no idea this is a child who secretly doesn't want to grow up and has a fantastically erotic Father image."

"I'll need time to think that over."

"You blame the world for holding you back, but part of you *wants* to be held back." Carolyn was beginning to sound breathless, so I knew we were getting close to the payoff. "It's the child that's taking refuge in those pillows now. The real reason you refuse to get up is that when you finally decide to leave that bed and go back into the world, you'll have to become a Woman!"

"Jesus, what a mind," I said. "The way your mind turns over and over and then comes out with it is truly something. I couldn't be more impressed. But I wonder if it could turn over just once more and tell me this. If I get up and become a Woman, what'll I do? Where'll I go?"

"It's not a question of doing or going." She sounded impatient. "It's being! You can be yourself anywhere, Paris, London, Cairo—"

"I don't want to go to places like that. Not on my own. I'd be scared."

"Then where would you like to go?"

"I've been thinking about Playa del Rey. It's pretty restful back there."

Carolyn shook her head. "You can't go home again."

I had a definite feeling she was letting me down this time. "Then I'll stay where I am. All you've done is scare the shit out of me, I'll *never* get up now, not after all this talk about Thomas Wolfe and turning into a Woman. You make it sound like that fellow who had an operation."

And I closed my eyes and pretended to sleep. The moment she'd left, I got out of bed and walked to the window. I felt wobbly, but otherwise exactly the same. "They're all wrong about me!" I said to the ocean. "Of course I could make myself

[203]

strong enough to go back and finish that movie, if I wanted to. I could travel around the world with Melora and even think about my dirty Father image. I'd still be a bit scared and confused and resentful, but what the hell's so special about that?"

The surf broke very high and grand. As I watched it, I thought how strange it was that everyone had been so anxious about my mind, they never spared a thought for my body, and what might be inside it.

A Joker.

Once I knew I had this Joker on the way, I couldn't get up until I'd decided whether to let it come right out or have it disconnected. For reasons that were probably wrong and certainly had nothing to do with the Everything That Lives Is Holy deal, which is another game not worth the candle, I made up my mind to see the situation through. Maybe I couldn't think of a strong enough reason *not* to see it through. If The Dealer could bring up a couple of kids, I felt I ought to be able to manage one. I never liked kids personally, but I thought I might react differently to one of my own. It would be what they call Something to Love, and for a few years at least the relationship couldn't be too complicated. And since I was fairly grown up at twelve, and earning big money at fourteen, I figured that the way times move faster now, any kid of mine would be leaving home around eight to fend for itself.

So I called up Ridge and asked him to come over. He didn't want to, he thought it better to agree that the past was the past. "Normally I wouldn't argue about that," I said. "But sometimes it has a way of catching up with us." From his attitude, I had a feeling that Ridge was extremely occupied with the present (which Melora had told me answered to the name of Julie Forbes), and seemed reluctant to take even fifteen minutes off from it.

He walked carefully into the room, wary as a lion that's smelled a human being on its track. He wore a fancy Italian sweater and tennis slacks.

"You look great, Daisy. I'd no idea you'd be looking so well."

"You're sexier than ever, Ridge."

Normally he adored flattery, but now he was embarrassed. All the same, he glanced at himself in the mirror, and the silver bracelet on his wrist glittered for a moment as he raised a hand to smooth down his hair.

"So what are you doing?" I asked.

He moved away to the window. "Not much. You know how it is."

"Ridden in any more Westerns?"

"No, I'm trying to get away from all that." He hesitated. "Got a small part coming up in something."

"That's good. What kind of something?"

"It's a picture with Julie Forbes."

"Well, that certainly is something."

He smiled at me, but his eyes clouded over. I wanted to tell him not to be such a big beautiful pumpkin-head, and make a short speech about taking what we can while it's there, no regrets, etc., but it wouldn't have been a very suitable preamble under the circumstances.

"Would you like a drink, Ridge?"

"Too early in the day."

"Today you might like one early in the day."

"Why?"

"If I tell you why, you'll have the shock before you have the drink."

He stiffened slightly. "You have a shock for me?"

"I hope not but I think so."

"Well, I can always get drunk afterwards, can't I?" Another glance in the mirror, and a nervous laugh. "You really do look great," he said. "When are you going back to work?"

"That's part of the shock. I'm not."

"I heard you'd been talking about giving it up, but I never believed it. What'll you do?"

"Bringing up a child is a full-time occupation."

He stared at me, then laughed again. "I guess so, but how about getting pregnant first?"

"It's been attended to."

"What?"

"Yes. It's been taken care of."

He came toward me now, slowly. His face had a look of simple unbelief. "Are you kidding?"

I couldn't help giggling, which bewildered him all the more. "You made a pun," I explained.

"You told me Wade Lewis never—"

"He didn't."

"Hell, I don't know what you're trying to say."

"Just that you're not to worry. I will never create a situation. But I've thought it over and I'm going through with it, that's all. If it's a boy I'll call him Cary, if it's a girl, Myrna."

After a pause, Ridge asked where I kept the liquor.

"In the closet, there's a portable bar with ice and everything."

He opened the door. I heard him open a bottle, then he muttered, "I just don't want anything to do with this."

"You don't have to. You've done your part already."

Ice clattered.

"I'm sure you feel that marriage would be an extremely embarrassing situation for both of us," I said.

Ridge came back with a glass of Scotch in his hand. "You're not divorced yet, anyway."

"Well, I believe that could be arranged. If Wade agreed, I could get a quick one down in Mexico. But you don't want that, do you?"

"Hell. What do *you* want?"

"Oh, Ridge, you're forcing me to say that terrible line about only wanting what's best for the three of us."

He sat with his head in his hands, and the cold glass against his forehead. "I'm up a tree. This has never happened to me in my life before."

"Well," I said, thinking that I saw exactly what Christy Williams meant about narcissism, "nor to me either. So it's a first for both of us."

"Listen!" He got up suddenly. "Get rid of it. Why don't you get rid of it?"

"I honestly don't know. Maybe it's too much of a responsibility."

"It's a bigger responsibility to have it. You know it is."

I shook my head.

[206]

"Why isn't it?"

"Ridge, I've been trying to put myself in *its* position. You could try that, too. Suppose that you and I had never been born because it was the first time it ever happened to our parents, and they weren't married."

"That's ridiculous. That's special pleading, Daisy."

"There but for the Grace of God, all the same."

"You really believe what you're saying?"

"It makes more sense to me than getting some shady doctor to nip this thing in the bud. You've got to remember, Ridge, it's a confusing situation. In fact, when you look at it from all sides, it's about the biggest darned muddle anyone could get into."

"If you get rid of it, there's no muddle. Honestly, I can't see any muddle at all if you get rid of it." He sounded hopeful.

"Yes, it would solve everything, you could go on the way you are, and I could go back to the way I was, and there'd be no muddle at all. There'd be nothing. I don't like that, though." He stared at me. "I know what you're thinking, I understand that honest look in your eyes. Night after night you held me in your arms, etc., and never realized what a nut you were cracking. Okay. But I'm still going to take the simpler way out. I'm not getting rid of it."

Ridge's face was sullen and helpless, it had that mean touching expression of being up against something he didn't like or understand, faggots, muddles, women who broke promises. "I don't want it," he said. "I hate the idea of it. You make me feel terrible."

"But if you don't want it and hate the idea of it, why feel terrible? Just put it out of your mind."

"It doesn't seem right, Daisy."

"What seems right to you? Getting rid of it? You wouldn't feel terrible then?"

He went to pour himself another drink. "I just don't want to have you on my conscience."

"I promise you I won't be there, Ridge. I've got other places to go."

"Well," he said, scowling obstinately at the glass of Scotch, "I hope you know what you're doing."

[207]

"That's just about all I know." He still looked angry and somehow offended, and I wasn't feeling too chipper myself by now. "I wish I could think of something that would make us both happy," I told him. "If I have this kid, you'll hate me a little. If I don't, I'll hate *you* a little."

Ridge thought this over. "If that's true," he said finally, "you're really having it because you don't want to hate me." He brightened, I could tell he felt definitely reassured, though still puzzled. "I guess I ought to appreciate that, Daisy. In a way that's a wonderful compliment."

Now that I could see a kind of future ahead, I decided to get up and prepare for it. When I took the muddle to Mr. Zidell, his eyelids drooped even farther.

"Poor child. You wish first to get divorced from a man you never slept with, then go off secretly and have an illegitimate child. But you realize, of course, that by the time you appear in court you'll be visibly pregnant. This requires thought."

He met with Wade's lawyers behind closed doors, as they say, and after a week—quite a tough one, he said—managed to make a deal. Their client agreed to give his name, etc., to Mr. Zidell's client's child on condition that I waived a property settlement and accepted a small monthly check to support the little joker. "Originally I'd hoped for a much better deal," Mr. Zidell said. "But under the circumstances we're lucky to get out with our feet not too wet."

I explained to the judge how Wade insulted me in the desert and after our first night told me that our marriage was a mistake and left me stranded. Fifteen minutes later I waddled out of court with an interlocutory decree.

The nuns were fairly tight-lipped but decent. They obviously couldn't imagine why I'd checked into their little hospital at Long Beach, why no anxious father paced the corridor, and nobody at all came to see me. I heard that Melora Swan telephoned to ask if mother and child were doing okay, but that was all.

Myrna Clover was born on the 5th of June, 1955, quite a big

girl, 7 lbs., with dark orphan eyes exactly like mine and a couple of tufts on her head that suggested she might grow up one hell of a blonde. No guns were fired to celebrate her entrance into the world, but she didn't complain, in fact she started giggling immediately. I cheered myself up by remembering the old proverb about it's a wise child that knows its own father.

15

I headed for New York because I didn't like the stuff in the papers. It made me understand what Melora once said about having this town on your side. I certainly didn't. You hardly needed to read between the lines to know that I'd always been strange, now I'd become impossible, and no studio would ever touch me. *Screen Time* asked WHY DID DAISY HAVE HER BABY IN LONG BEACH? and showed a blurry photograph of Wade Lewis and Friend splashing around in the ocean at Acapulco. A scandal magazine carried a rough piece on Ridge Banner, called WHAT IS HIS STAIRWAY TO THE STARS? It printed faked-up pictures of poor Ridge climbing this staircase with Julie Forbes, Christy Williams, and me standing at intervals on it. Even baby-sitter sold me down the river by writing something called THE SNAKE PIT BY THE SEA for *Strange Confessions*, a very unkind account of The Dealer and her ways and the nights I didn't come home. And some darned photographer got a picture of me leaving the hospital with Myrna, it turned up in *Time* with a caption about an Aging Cine-Moppet. All things considered, it seemed unfair of this town to be anti-Clover but completely pro-Swan, but I suppose it was just another case of what everyone calls the way the wind blows, like some letters I received from outraged mothers and disgusted teen-agers.

However, I'd be cynical if I didn't remember that a few decent kind people came to my rescue. I had an extremely friendly letter from a man who owned a toy shop in Columbus, Ohio. He was my devoted fan, still believed in me, wouldn't listen to the muck that was going around, and asked me to marry him. He was sixty-four, but looked and felt younger.

To avoid reporters, I left town on a very late flight and got airborne without anyone noticing. When I took off my dark glasses and looked down from the sky at a crazy winking network of lights, I thought, *Good-by, you few million of the millions I made laugh and cry and identify with me. I'm going out of your lives and it won't make the slightest difference to you! You'll wake up in the morning as if I'd never happened.* Then I drank two glasses of champagne and read *Kitty Foyle* by Christopher Morley until the bed was ready for Myrna and me.

We got to New York around nine o'clock in the morning. It felt like the tropics, fantastically hot and sticky, and I remembered Wade telling me never to go there in midsummer. I checked in limply at Hampshire House, with a soaking Myrna. An elevator launched us to the 27th floor, and we were dumped in this air-conditioned suite overlooking Central Park. I fed Myrna and we both went to sleep.

When I woke up I felt hungry myself, and thought I'd like to walk across to the zoo in Central Park and have some lunch there, also buy a buggy for Myrna. I couldn't go on carrying her, she needed wheels. However, they wouldn't let me leave Myrna at the desk while I went out to get one, so I shot up to the 27th floor again, feeling definitely trapped, called room service and ordered a couple of lamb chops and a bottle of vermouth. After a drink or two I realized I was behaving like an absolute idiot, I'd forgotten I was an ex-movie star and shouldn't have to do things for myself. I called a department store and told them to send round a buggy right away. "This is Daisy Clover speaking," I added firmly. By the time it arrived, the day was cooling off. Only mildly looped, I wheeled Myrna right across the street and into the Park. The zoo cheered me up, it was feeding time and very noisy, a touch of carnival in the air, which always makes my heart beat faster. Myrna was too young (only nine weeks) to appreciate it, but she lay very still with enormous eyes apparently staring at the sky. I sat down and watched the crowds, looked at the skyscrapers, etc., and felt I was starting to get my bearings. Then carousel music drifted faintly in my direction, and of course reminded me of the old pier at Santa Monica. I caught myself sniffing for a whiff of salt on the breeze, even straining my ears to catch a thud of surf. A pretty ridiculous thing to do while you're at the zoo in Central Park. I decided I'd like to see Times Square and the Great White Way. It was a longer haul than I expected, I wheeled Myrna fifteen blocks and the lights hadn't come on when I got there, it was too early. I landed up outside a theater where *Love to Spring Valley* was playing, my own face smiled down at me from a brightly colored poster. They'd found a favorable quote from somewhere, "Daisy Makes the World Feel Young Again!" No one went in. Myrna was growing restless. I started back against the tide of the crowd.

A few days later I found this apartment, a third-floor walk-up on East 9th Street at Second Avenue. It was an old building, not a classy district, but the atmosphere reminded me of the Paradise Hotel and Apartments. People sat on front door steps in the heat, tough-looking boys played baseball on the sidewalk, cats sat on the fire escapes, somebody was playing the piano, an ice-truck cruised slowly, and I liked it.

As I parked the buggy in the hall and started to carry Myrna upstairs, a breathless English voice called after me.

"Excuse me, are you the new person?"

I turned and saw a tall, pale, red-headed girl with a bunch of yellow tulips.

"I'm coming to live in Number Four, if that's what you mean."

She smiled at me. "I say, don't I know your face? Good Lord, aren't you from Hollywood? I mean, you're Daisy Clover!"

I admitted it.

"Good Lord. Perry Pierce will go out of his mind."

"Why?" I continued up the stairs.

"Because he thinks you're so wonderful." The English girl followed. "My name's Triss. Triss Whitelaw. I have the apartment next to yours, I hope you don't mind. And if there's anything you need, you know, like sugar, anything one constantly runs out of, please call on me. Oh, let me open your door for you."

"Thanks, Triss. And do come in."

"Are you sure?"

"I'll put Myrna down, call up the liquor store and we'll have a house-warming."

"Really? May I give you these tulips?" Triss said. "A sort of a welcoming thing, you know."

"Well, thank you. Yellow's my favorite color."

"How marvelous." She smiled again. She was so tall and breathless and achingly friendly, I couldn't resist her. "Perry Pierce will go out of his mind," she remarked again.

"Now exactly who is this joker?"

"He's a really lovely boy from the West Indies, the most elegant creature I've ever seen. He dances in some primitive troupe at a little theater in the Village, and thinks you're the greatest thing that ever happened in the American musical."

"Does he live in this building too?"

"He has the apartment below. He's made it so elegant," Triss said. "I absolutely adore Perry Pierce."

"Well." I sank into a rather tacky leather armchair. "You never know what you're getting into."

"Isn't that the fascinating thing about New York?"

"I guess so. Where's the nearest liquor store?"

"Shall I ring them up and order it for you?"

"I'd certainly appreciate it, Triss. Dry vermouth is my peculiar poison, but we'd better get in some Scotch and vodka as well."

While she gave the order on the phone, I took the tulips to the kitchen and found a jar for them. The window overlooked a plot of ground with trees, long grass, deck chairs. You couldn't see the sky for the backs of apartment buildings in the next street.

"What's a girl like you doing in a place like this?" I asked Triss when I came back.

"Oh." She looked vague. "I just live here, you know."

Half an hour later, the liquor and Perry Pierce arrived. He was certainly a beautiful fellow, skin the color of polished cinnamon, eyes like two stars twinkling in the sky at night, and the least movement he made you'd think he was going into a dance. "Five six seven eight!" he said as he glided into the room.

"Who do *we* appreciate?" Myrna spotted him from her crib by the window, gasped, and made a chortling sound. "Hi, there, Clover baby," he said.

"Perry Pierce and babies always have a thing about each other," Triss said. "I sort of hate them actually."

"I like most things." Perry Pierce stood looking down at me. "I even like life. But way above all I am insane about the talent of this person here. I know pretty much everything about her. From the first moment I saw her on the screen, there was Rapport."

At first you might have the impression that Perry Pierce came on like "Gangbusters," and for a minute I wondered if I'd have to start looking for a new apartment tomorrow, but then I realized he was a genuine Force of Nature and I was impressed. He took it for granted that we were going to be extremely close friends, and by the end of the evening I certainly asked myself where he'd been all my life. Both of us were lit, but I also knew I'd wake up sober and still like him. In fact I liked everybody in the room—there were at least thirty characters sitting around by midnight—and I remember suddenly thinking this was the first big party I'd ever given, all the guests were people I'd never met before, and it was a Smasheroo. Triss fetched her record player and Perry Pierce's collection of my albums, all the way back to *Four Leaf Clover*, and they never stopped playing them. I carried on a good deal about Hollywood, etc., and Perry Pierce talked so much I couldn't absorb or even hear all that he said, it came floating above everyone talking and my own voice singing and a comfortable warm feeling that Myrna and I had somehow made port—

"You mean you never saw *Footlight Parade*? I'll take you tomorrow afternoon, they're showing it at the Museum of Modern Art. One truly great thing about this town, honey, is that there's always an old Keeler or Rogers or Alice Faye playing at some old movie house with a yellow stain on the screen—

"And in a thousand years from now, I mean it, an old Keeler movie will look like a Lascaux cave painting. They'll dig it up and see her tapping, and it'll strike them as a genuine primitive of its era, just like those animals scrawled on walls. So will you, of course—

"Garland? A great talent, but she doesn't have your honesty. She fell for her own tragic mask and now she's a clown playing Hamlet. In this world, if you *are* Hamlet, never let on. Be a clown. But you know that, don't you?

"When you took this apartment, it was an act of extra-sensory perception. I mean it. Everyone who lives in this house, everyone who drops around—they're all exiles. It's the Exiles' Club, I christened it that two years ago. And if anyone who moves in shows signs of belonging, we hound them out!

"Did Triss tell you she comes from a very fine English family? Her mother's lady-in-waiting to the Queen, her father's descended from a Cecil and pees in the fireplace. Triss came here on a wild love affair which ended badly, now she's finding herself—

"Where did I come from, honey? That's a long story. To make it short, I was *discovered*—in a filling station in Bridgetown, Barbados—by a fairly distinguished author on vacation—

"And everything's the way the wind blows. I was once an exploited colonial nigger and now one of my best friends is a girl who ran away from her nigger-exploiting family—

"You did the right thing when you left Hollywood. I've a pretty good idea what they did to you there. I may not be the best person to discuss success and all that, because I can't honestly claim I've had very much—but I've watched them come and watched them go. They only get thrown when they expect life to *stand still*. Which it never does! What's universal today is terribly affected tomorrow—

"So what is the answer? Well, better to ask with Gertrude Stein, what is the question?

"So what is the question? Personally, honey, I don't have one. I mean, I accept. *Everything*—

"Everyone in this room tonight is a wonderful person, but I hope a boy called Clinton Harris comes in later. He's starring in an off-Broadway show, and I have the strangest hunch you're each other's type—"

I woke up extremely late next morning with a definite feeling of having lived through a key experience in my life. My only trouble was not being able to remember it. I noticed Triss's yellow tulips in a jar by the window through which you couldn't see the sky. Glasses and Dixie Cups and empty bottles lay all over the room. I remembered that I had to get up immediately, wheel Myrna to the bookstore that Triss worked in and leave her there, then go to see *Footlight Parade* with Perry Pierce. And I realized what had happened to me. I accepted. I accepted the tulips and the party remains and my program for the day. In fact I accepted just about *everything*, including Clinton Harris, who was still asleep.

It's amazing how much there is to do in a new place, when you've really nothing to do. A year passed and I couldn't believe it. What had I achieved? Well, as Perry Pierce says, half the trouble in the world comes from asking a question like that. If you must ask anything at all, just say—what have I enjoyed? I had some pretty good answers, like—

Sitting out in the garden in a deck chair among the uncut grass, with Myrna in her buggy and *La Mer* by Debussy stealing through the open window from Perry Pierce's record player.

Seeing at least thirty American musicals. I never thought of myself as part of a tradition before, but Perry Pierce said that's maybe because it died with me.

Being able to accept the fact that Clinton Harris was just one of those Bells that now and then rings.

Watching Perry Pierce walk on his hands and turn cartwheels for Myrna. Last month she suddenly stretched out her little arms to him and said, "Dada!" I decided to go along with the situation for the moment, until Myrna could really talk.

A week on Fire Island—with P.P., Triss, and a few others—staying in a house that one of P.P.'s friends lent him, and showing the ocean and the beach to Myrna.

Finding my first gray hairs on both temples, and deciding to let them grow—which they did, into two streaks, getting me looks from smart women who thought it was some new fashion.

On the morning of January 1st, 1957, in the middle of my second real winter with Snow, Perry Pierce came up and said to me, "Happy New Year, honey. How are you feeling?"

"Well, Happy New Year, P.P. That's a pretty strange question."

"When we came out of *Follow the Fleet* last night, you didn't say a word for at least fifteen minutes."

"It was a disappointing picture."

"That wasn't the reason."

I stared at him. "P.P., I've no idea what you are trying to prove."

"When we go to the old musicals, when you see Keeler and Powell and Ginger carrying on up there—do you ever get a twinge?"

I was taken aback, he'd never brought up this kind of thing before. "Even if I did, what's the use? My career is over, everyone says so."

"Big balls. Do you agree with everyone?"

"And I've got to think of Myrna. The kid's growing roots, I'd hate to tear them up now. She needs a few more years at least of the kind of stable life she's been getting."

P.P. sighed. "You really are giving me plenty of crap this morning."

"I'll admit I get my twinges, if that's what you want. Who wouldn't? Frankly, P.P., it's pretty tough, considering my situation, to go with you to musical after musical."

He looked pleased. "So you *have* thought of going back?"

"I never said that. And I'd never go back *There*, anyway. Not to that place." Then I shrugged. "I'm not even sure I want to sing again. I think about it sometimes, but it doesn't worry me too much."

"Don't expect me to believe that. No real artist throws it all away without a struggle, and I don't think you're a Rimbaud."

"Who dat?"

"Some other time, honey. I'm trying to say that the greatest human sin is waste."

"But I don't know if I want to go through all that again. It drove me pretty crazy. It wasn't until I stopped, and came out here, and started to mature, that I realized I'd never had time to *think*, I mean *think*, P.P., about what I wanted out of life—"

"What is it you think you want?"

"Oh . . ." I guess I hadn't really thought about it. "I like things the way they are. I have an extremely good time on the whole. There's no pressure, and I've stopped waking up with my fists clenched."

"There's a time to rest and a time to start up again." Perry Pierce looked out of the window at the falling snow. "And you certainly have been resting."

"I was tired."

"If I had one-twentieth of your talent, I'd go out of my mind."

"Exactly."

"Big balls again. I am a frantic person!" He stood close to me. "You know I'm practically hysterical. But I don't have the ridiculous notion that it's because I'm talented. I'm one-twentieth as talented and fifty times as nuts as you are."

"P.P., I still had an awful time out there."

"Because you're a perverted idiot. You never believe that people admire you or care about you. You never let anyone help you. I have very strong feelings about talent, honey, and to be in the *presence* of it for more than a year, and not to see a sign, a flicker, that it's aware of itself—"

"Oh, I'm aware of it. Honestly. I know I was pretty good."

"You said that as if you were talking about somebody else."

"I was. It gave me a bad time, P.P., I definitely got fed up with it, and I'd rather live without it. I'm accepting that. You put me on to this whole accepting deal, so you ought to appreciate how I feel."

Perry Pierce suddenly beat his forehead and closed his eyes, as if in pain. "Accepting isn't just doing nothing at all. It's a state of mind which prepares you to be *ready for anything*. In your case, the legitimate theater—including night clubs."

"You really believe I should try singing in those places?"

"They're made for you. Just prop yourself against a piano or grab a mike somewhere, informal as hell, and sing till you drop."

"Yes," I said, "I remember I thought that's what I should be doing the day I made my test. But it was so long ago, P.P. I don't really feel I want to sing again. Which probably means I *do*. Which is very likely the story of my life. Which is certainly depressing."

Perry Pierce shook his head. "It just means you're an old flirt, and should have been born in the Orient. In certain parts of the Orient, entertainers are expected to be prostitutes, like night follows day. Show-business life out there would make your problems look pretty silly, honey. In fact, the way you've been carrying on reminds me of a story by Maupassant—you wouldn't know it, you're always reading pretentious trash—about a Madam who takes her girls out to the country for her niece's confirmation. Well, at the sight of a white dress and the simple life, the most popular whore in the whorehouse starts weeping over her shame. That's the story of Daisy Clover in New York."

"Okay. You're a pretty smart fellow, P.P., so you must realize you can't make me a whore again without making yourself a Madam."

The rented piano arrived next afternoon, and we placed it near the window. Perry Pierce sat down and started to tinkle "Love Is Sweeping the Country." Outside, it had stopped snowing. The garden was frozen. I closed my eyes, and for a second the darkness turned into a sound stage, with most of the lights switched out and silhouettes moving silently around. Then I looked at my living room in the flat winter light, in the freckled mirror over the mantel I caught a glimpse of myself with a gray curl dangling over my forehead. Perry Pierce went on strumming, a bright expectant look on his face.

Since I hadn't sung a note in two years, I expected a sound to come out like a warped door creaking open. That didn't worry me. What I waited for was *something to come alive*. The room felt so cold and dead. For some reason I pushed the two leather armchairs and the black Oriental coffee table against the wall.

"That's fine," Perry Pierce said. "You need to move around. Just get warmed up now. Take it easy." He tapped a foot to the music.

Now I was standing alone on the slightly faded green carpet, snapping a finger in time to P.P.'s tapping foot. After a moment, I began to giggle.

"I don't know why we're doing this," I said. "It feels ridiculous."

"Take it easy, honey. Don't force anything."

I snapped my fingers again. "P.P., would you try another song? I don't think I want that one."

As he went into "It All Depends on You," I lit a cigarette. My hands were steady, but they felt somehow stiff.

"No, that one's no good," I said.

Perry Pierce looked surprised. "No one ever did that one as well as you."

"Thank you, P.P. But try another one."

"I've Got Plenty of Nothing."

I flopped down in a chair and stared at the floor.

"Now take it easy," Perry Pierce said.

I closed my eyes. Blankness. I got up and put out my cigarette. "Okay, this is it. Daisy sings again." Then I said, "Not yet she doesn't. Try something I never sang in my life. I don't want any of the old ones."

"If you never sang it in your life, honey, you won't be able to sing it now."

"You can give me the words. I memorize very quickly."

So he sang "Bye Bye Blackbird" all the way through. I stared out at the garden.

"That was great, P.P. Much better than I could do."

I remembered Carolyn talking about a flame that burns very bright but not very long, and thought, What the hell, she's probably right. I've gone out. When I shut my eyes, not a single image came. What I'd really hoped for was to get back to Twitcher's booth and the pier, etc., and then it would come

[220]

belting out, rusty but strong. Now I couldn't think what to do, the blankness was making me dizzy.

"Let's try it again tomorrow. Don't worry, P.P."

I went into my bedroom and picked up the shell. As I put it to my ear, I could hear Perry Pierce singing "By Bye Blackbird" again softly to himself. Then, three thousand miles away from where I found this shell, the darned waves were breaking as loudly as ever. But *where?*

The middle of that night I woke up sleepless and jittery. Getting out of bed very quietly so as not to disturb Myrna, I put on my duffel coat over my pajamas, slipped up the hood, and padded into the dark freezing living room. On the piano I picked out a few notes of "Let's Do It," tapped a big furry slipper against the floor, and started to sing.

By the end of the first verse I knew I could still carry a tune and keep a beat. Frankly, that was all. Otherwise it sounded like amateur night on TV, blank and empty as the darkness when I closed my eyes. I stood there feeling stupid, staring at my breath as it floated in the air.

Next day I had the piano taken out.

Perry Pierce wasn't pleased with me, and I made a bad scene. "I should never have listened to you," I told him. "You made me try and sing when I didn't want to. Now I find I can't, and I'm really bugged." And I supposed that now he knew my talent was gone, he wouldn't care about me as a person any more. He denied it, called me a pain in the ass, we both cried a little and made up. However, I decided to stop going to musicals with him.

In June he went off for a three months' tour with the primitive dancers, who were taking their leaps and drums on a summer circuit. Triss and I threw him a farewell party, most of the company bounded around my living room for hours. In the morning when he'd gone, I felt extremely depressed.

I really liked New York, though, except on certain days when it made me feel closed in, the buildings much too tall, and I

[221]

needed space. I put the shell to my ear and wished I was in Tahiti. On these days too I wondered if something in my life hadn't gone completely wrong, and yet I couldn't see what I'd have done differently if I started it all over again. Still, after all that had happened to me, it struck me as mildly unexpected to be sitting in a ragged old garden on a sweltering afternoon, with a postcard on my lap from P.P. in Buffalo—"Niagara Falls steals most of our business, but guess what's playing in a downtown fleabag—*Little Annie Rooney!*"

16

<hr>

They say everything takes time, but after more than four years of trying to figure out where those darned waves were breaking, and what someone in my position should be getting ready for, I really gave up and wondered if time didn't take everything—including the Trust Fund, which was definitely low. However, my one triumph during an uncertain period was Myrna. A kid certainly takes a lot out of you, always hungry, waking up at the wrong time, interrupting conversations, and almost swallowing nickels, and at first I wondered why The Dealer didn't throw me out very early, then I grew to like it. One of the greatest satisfactions in life for me has been something turning out well against all the odds. Myrna as she entered her sixth year was beautiful enough to make people stare at her in the street. She's tall for her age, which I guess is Ridge's influence, and by the time she's ten I'd say she'll stand higher than me. She'll make a marvelous model one day, if she's interested. Although she doesn't say much—always chooses her words carefully, as the principal of her school remarks—she's a real sharpie and has picked up a lot of cute expressions. I was extremely anxious for us to like each other, I mean as people, not just a mother-daughter act, so it was a great relief when Triss asked her how she enjoyed her new school and Myrna said, "I like it okay, but I like Daisy and P.P. better than the other kids." Also, she's given me no real trouble over this father business. I had to explain that Perry Pierce definitely wasn't her father, so naturally she asked, "Then who is?" "Well, dear," I said, "he went away quite a while ago, in fact before you were born, and I don't think

[223]

he'll be back. He doesn't seem to dig either of us. But if that's his attitude, who needs him?"

After a moment Myrna said, "Okay."

"Is that all, Myrna? Just okay? Are you satisfied?"

"I'll buy it."

Much of the credit goes to this progressive school, which I heard about completely by chance when I ran into Christy Williams at Macy's. She said all her friends sent their kids there and swore by it, so I went to see the principal, gave him a general idea of the circumstances of Myrna's birth, and he was definitely interested. "Send her over at once, we'd love to handle her," he told me. After her first week he said she was an exciting personality, everyone was fascinated by her, and she wanted to learn the guitar. I remembered reading somewhere that bastards often turned out the most intelligent.

Just for the hell of it I sent a photograph to Gloria and Harry, thinking they might like to know what their little niece looked like, but they never answered. California seemed to have given me up. Not a word from the Swans, nothing from Ridge, Carolyn sent a Christmas card my first year in New York, Perry Pierce heard a rumor that Wade Lewis and Malcolm had opened a hotel in Tangier. Julie Forbes said, "A light has gone out," when I left Hollywood, but she'd never been in touch although I read in the papers she'd visited New York a few times. Also a friend of P.P.'s in Laguna Beach sent him a cutting from a Los Angeles paper which said my reputation was zero, I hung around with the tackiest crowd you could imagine and had let my hair go gray.

As I explained, my one link with the past was meeting Christy Williams at Macy's. She looked as if she hadn't changed her clothes in five years, but was buying a sweater. We went off to have a cup of coffee together, she told me she was looking for a play and was going to classes at the Actors Studio. She said something had happened to Hollywood, it wasn't the same, Magnagram Studios weren't doing so well although they'd struck oil right outside that church on the back lot, and were pulling down the small-town square to drill for more. Also, Mr. Swan addressed the stockholders and told them all the Studio needed was one good picture. Then she said she still hadn't found a strong man and talked about anxiety in the American male, etc. Although she couldn't conceive of a life without acting, she envied me my courage, also Myrna, and wanted to know about the crazy rumor that Ridge Banner was the father. I said it was true and she cooled off.

I gave her my number and she promised a little reluctantly to call me, but she didn't. Next thing I heard, she was winging back to the coast to appear in a new movie.

4th of October 1961 was the day after my twenty-fourth birthday, when Perry Pierce and Triss took me on the town, we had an Italian dinner, heard a sick comic, and ended up at a party for an off-Broadway show, with several of our friends in it, that had just closed after one week. I woke up with a slight hangover and took Myrna to school in the rain. "Well, dear," I said, "plant you now and dig you later." "Be good, Daisy." And she ran up the steps. I didn't want to go back home, it promised to be one of those long empty days when I couldn't really think of anything to do, Perry Pierce was at dancing practice, Triss at her new job as secretary to a publisher, and none of us were the least bit in love. I dropped into a coffee shop and read several newspapers until it was time for lunch and still raining. In the afternoon I took a bus to Times Square and went to see an old Cary Grant movie that was playing at one of those Pick-up Palaces on 42nd Street. When I came out, it had stopped raining, so I took a walk to a nowhere special, got caught in a downpour and rushed into a bookshop. I read *Dr. Spock Talks to Mothers* and *A History of Erotica* until the sky cleared. Outside, dusk was falling and lights came on. I thought what a rotten day it had been, but at least it was over, P.P. would have picked Myrna up from school and she'd be wanting to watch "Superman" on TV, so I'd better be heading home.

Then I passed this music shop with a radio blasting out a number I'd never heard before. Something about the words made me pull up, and I had an extremely curious sensation, listening to this song called "I Wonder What Became of Me," staring at my reflection in the window kaleidoscoped with rain and lights, not minding that the sky had started to weep again, but *goose-pimpled* and *duck-bumped* by this voice above the scurrying crowds,

> *"Oh I've had my Fling,*
> *I've been around and seen 'most everything,*
> *Yet I can't be gay, for along the way*
> *Something went astray . . ."*

I pressed my face against the cold wet glass, closed my eyes, and the images came! They were certainly different from any I'd ever experienced, but clear and spooky, like—

> thin trees waving their arms in the desert
> Alex Conrad naked with a brandy snifter
> The Dealer lying in a roomful of cards—

and for a moment I thought I was going to pass out. The orchestration was marvelous too, violins under the melody getting lost along quiet nostalgic trails of their own. I opened my eyes, my reflection looked all blurred and streaky now. I went into the store, bought the album, stood on the sidewalk impatiently hailing cabs and singing to myself, *Life's as sweet as honey, and yet it's funny, I get a feeling that I can't analyze,* after about fifteen minutes a cab stopped, I told the driver to take me to East 9th, stared out at people sheltering in bright doorways as we headed down Broadway, *It's like well, maybe, like when a baby sees a bubble burst before his eyes,* and ran breathlessly up the stairs crying, "P.P., you've got to listen to this!" Myrna told me to shut up because she was watching "Superman," so I ran downstairs again to play the number in Perry Pierce's apartment. He listened very carefully and at the end said, "It is *you!*" My palms were sweating. Perry Pierce switched off the record player and looked at me. "You're tuned in again," he said, and explained that of course there had to be a *new* Daisy Clover, the old one had nothing more to say, all those years I'd been waiting for signals from another wavelength, and did I know Rembrandt's painting of a "Young Girl at a Window"?

"Hell, no," I said, "but it sounds like a good idea for a number. This girl looking out, I mean, and what has she seen? I could do a number like that."

"The portrait is also *you*," and Perry Pierce described this girl in a wide-brimmed bonnet, long hair falling to her shoulders, soft grave eyes, enigmatic lips, and you felt she was half a child and half an old lady, in front of your eyes she seemed to change from fifteen to forty and back again.

"Honestly, P.P., if I ever make another album, you'll have to write the jacket notes."

" 'Yesterdays,' " Perry Pierce said. "That's another number the Rembrandt suggests to me."

The rented piano came back next afternoon. I could hardly sleep, did a hundred breathing exercises, saying *Lights are bright, Pianos making music all the night* on one note, etc., and thinking that it's extraordinary how little we know. All this time I'd been fairly resigned to never hearing the call again, and not caring much anyway, I had Myrna and my friends and a kind of new life. Now I felt as helpless and pigheaded and ready to move heaven and earth as on that day, years ago, when I sat it out in Venice waiting for Mr. Swan to call and give me a chance to square my shoulders and give it to them.

After a month I felt I'd driven the moths out of my voice and collected a really great new repertoire. "I Wonder What Became of Me" set the mood, and a friend of Perry Pierce's, who'd written an off-Broadway musical, composed this "Young Girl at a Window" number for me. Perry Pierce also knew this manager who booked acts in night clubs and theaters, he'd sent the primitive troupe on its summer tour, and since I had no one else to turn to I agreed to an interview. His name was Holbrook Masters Productions, he had an office on the 12th floor of an old Broadway block with a photograph of Miss Portugal behind his desk. He was younger than I expected, pushing forty, skinny and elegant in a black silk suit with very white protruding cuffs. He took both my hands in his and said it was fantastic that I'd been away so long, he'd feel privileged to help bring me back. I liked the idea of running myself in at some little supper club on Long Island, but he shook his head. "You're Theater, Daisy.

You're Carnegie Hall. I don't see you wearing a sheath dress and carrying a mike around to the half-stoned expense-account set." It sounded convincing, so I asked what he had in mind, and he said he'd get back to me very soon. In the meantime he thought I should sign with him, which I didn't like, I told him I never wanted to go under exclusive contract again. He got quite angry and said that if I didn't have faith in him, as he did in me, he wasn't interested. "I firmly believe you're one of the great singers of our time, Daisy, but don't forget you've been away. I also firmly believe all those stories about you were exaggerated— but I'm in a pretty exclusive minority." Then he advised me to try one of the big agencies and see how they reacted. Finally I agreed to make him my personal manager for a year, but he insisted on options.

Another month went by and I didn't hear a word. So I called up Holbrook Masters Productions and asked how things were coming along. He told me he'd had several nibbles, and was sleeping on them. This made me feel slightly better, but after another month and not another word I was depressed and impatient. I went to his office this time, and he said, "Look, this is a tough business. I could book you somewhere tomorrow, but it'd be cheap, not right, and the right things take longer. I'll be frank with you, Daisy. You're harder to sell than I expected, a lot of people thought you were in a nuthouse or something, and they hear you've let your hair go gray, and they ask what is this?"

"Well, the sons of bitches."

"I hope I haven't hurt your feelings. But if we respect each other, isn't it best to tell the truth? It doesn't affect what I feel, and I know in the end they'll come to you on their hands and knees. Right now I have to go out, Daisy, but I'll be talking to you very soon."

"Okay." Almost before I knew it, I was left alone in the office, staring at Miss Portugal and wondering what had happened to *her*.

When I got home I asked Perry Pierce if he thought Holbrook Masters Productions was really on the level. "I know he believes in you, honey, and I'm sure he's doing everything he can." Then, in a low voice, "did you know that a famous star of the forties is at this moment broke and ill and working in a cocktail lounge uptown? In the middle of serving a martini she glances up at the TV over the bar and sees her old glamorous self on the Late Show. It's a tough business."

"P.P., I'd rather be encouraged if you don't mind."

"Well, she never had your talent."

At last Holbrook Masters Productions got back to me with the news that we had an offer for me to open the season in Atlantic City. He explained about this theater near the pier, which was mainly a tryout place for shows on their way to Broadway, so I'd draw a crowd from New York as well. "It's only five hundred a week, Daisy, but it's right. Frankly I think you should jump at it."

"Well, it sounds possible." I didn't wish to appear desperate. "I'd like to follow your example and sleep on it."

Perry Pierce said he'd never played in that particular theater, but Holbrook's description of it didn't exactly match some others he'd heard.

"Then it's a dump?"

"I wouldn't say that. I just don't think anyone tries out anything in Atlantic City."

"Would you say I'm being relegated to the Sticks?"

He shook his head. "Faceless urban types, honey. Solid family audiences. Conventioneers."

"You mean Elks?"

"Yes, there might be Elks."

"You think I should go down there and sing to them?"

Perry Pierce frowned. "Rule Number One in the theater, Daisy—never despise your audience and never be scared of it."

"Oh. What should I feel about it?"

"Well, my personal solution is to think of an audience as someone I want to go to bed with. I have to seduce it."

"Isn't there ever a night when you don't feel like having sex?"

"Sometimes. Then I just tease."

"You're a real old pro, P.P., I can see that."

The idea was beginning to appeal to me. My earliest audience had been the ocean and the fog, when you make movies you don't have any audience anyway, and the time I sang at Julie Forbes's party I cared more about that plane flying overhead than all the smiling people on the terrace. But who were all those strangers in the dark applauding my previews? Maybe when I crept in to watch *Song and Dance* from General Admission, I sat next to an Elk without knowing it.

"Holbrook, I've thought it over," I said on the phone next morning. "This is a simple little nut who's supposed to express universal emotions, and Atlantic City sounds like a good place to find out whether or not she still has a message for anybody."

He liked my attitude and we signed contracts. It was a quick little ceremony, I went up to his office, he was extremely friendly, held my hands for longer than usual, and thrust all these papers at me.

"My sister Gloria tied me up last time," I said. "Seven years at Magnagram Studios. Two weeks at Atlantic City ought to be a lot less complicated."

"You don't have to read them." Holbrook Masters Productions spoke rather quickly. "It's a standard form."

"Shall I just sign myself away, then? Okay." I gave him a bright smile, and scribbled. "Now I'm all yours. Or all theirs. What's the difference, anyway?"

He gave me a shifty look. "Before I have to go out, tell me exactly what kind of act you have in mind, Daisy."

"Oh, something informal as hell. I'm just getting together enough songs to keep Atlantic City between tears and laughter for a couple of hours."

"Now don't kill yourself." He paused. "Twenty-five minutes is all they want. They've got a few other acts on the bill, you know."

"How could I? It's the first time you've mentioned it." He didn't answer. "Who else have they got?"

Not looking at me, he said he wasn't sure of all the details yet, but it was settled that I should close the first half of the evening, coming on after some joker with a magic-bird act.

"Holbrook," I said, "you're my Personal Manager, and I guess we'll be in business together quite a while, but I have to say you're a fairly sordid type. You were waiting for me to sign that contract before letting on I'd just be part of some circus deal."

"You know you don't believe that. I took it for granted you knew something about vaudeville."

"No, I'm quite an ignorant person. I never learn about anything until it's happened. But I'm making no scene!" And I smiled at him again. "I'm throwing no fit, Holbrook. I know I have to begin again."

He seized my hands gratefully. "To me you're still a great star, and if there weren't a lot of idiots—"

"Bullshit," I said. "I don't care. But don't kid yourself I'm acting this way out of humility. No sir, my strong suit is pride. I know I'm fantabulous, it doesn't matter if I come on after performing poodles."

He looked at me as if he wasn't sure what to make of this, then gave a loud forced laugh. "They'll never break your spirit, will they?"

"They certainly try."

"If you're not happy with that contract, I'll be happy to tear it up."

"I'm afraid," I said, "you'll have to. I signed every copy *Sarah Bernhardt*."

He picked up the sheaf of papers. "My God, you *are* crazy. What the hell was the point of that?"

"I'll sign my real name if I can close the second half of the bill, not the first."

"They won't buy it."

"Who do they want to put above me?"

He mentioned the name of some comedian. I said I'd never heard of him, and Holbrook told me in a knowing voice, "he's pretty good, Daisy."

"Well," I said grandly, "I don't mind who I'm billed with, but I want my name at the top. That's how much dignity I've got left. So you go out and give them a little of that faith you talk about, otherwise you'll be left with Sarah Bernhardt on your hands."

Although I ruined my exit by sweeping through the wrong door and finding myself in a closet, it turned out they hadn't even booked *anyone* as the main attraction, all they had was a vague suspicion I wasn't it. Holbrook finally convinced them I could be. This made me realize just how little people believed in me, which was fine. When they do, I've usually found myself in trouble.

✳

Now here I am, outside this theater which faces the entrance to a pier. It's a more elaborate deal than the one at Venice, with a carousel and miniature golf course and a broken one-handed clock over a billboard. It's still raining, and the Ferris wheel doesn't move. The ocean looks dull, about a hundred gulls swoop over the empty beach. In my oldest pair of jeans, a sweater, and a scarf around my gray head, I stare at a photograph of myself singing "Between You and Me" from *Little Annie Rooney*. And the boardwalk stretches away for at least a mile, up to another pier, which the gulls are flying over now.

Inside the large old-fashioned theater with mosaics on the walls and marble pillars holding up the balcony, there's an odor of disinfectant and the house lights are switched on very low. The orchestra runs through "I Can't Give You Anything but Love, Baby." A side door stands open, I can see the rain pelting down the alley. And then a man in top hat and tails rushes down the center aisle and coos like a pigeon at a Magic Bird that's escaped and beats its wings on the balcony ledge. By the time the orchestra finishes it's captured, the man carries it away with a cloth over its head, I hear the sound of rain plopping on the roof and even a faint roar from the ocean.

The musicians smile at me, I shake hands with the conductor, we say Hello, Fine, That'll Be Great, it's all vacant warm well-what-do-you-knows? because they're like people on the other side of a scrim curtain and secretly I'm getting ready to give Love, etc. I go on the stage, the opening bars of "I Wonder What Became of Me" drown out the rain and surf, an electrician shifts his spotlight and traps me neatly in the center. A small crowd huddles alertly in the wings, Perry Pierce and Myrna are sitting down near the front. I close my eyes, and would you believe it, there's Twitcher! I can see a tiny wax disk turning on his machine, I think I smell tar and seaweeed. I take the scarf off my head, shake out my hair, give a nod to the conductor, rub my sticky palms against my sweater—and, like an instant electric shock, because the mike was more powerful than I thought, my voice tingles back at me from all sides of the empty theater. With the passing of years, and a hundred thousand breathing exercises, and maybe more than a few vermouths on the rocks, it has a darker sound, which Perry Pierce calls a new dimension but I'd just describe as slightly frantic. Anyway, I went from number to number without a break, in the middle of a shuffle almost lost my balance and fell into the orchestra pit, and at the end of "Yesterdays" the spotlight went away, someone in the wings said "Bravo!" and it had stopped raining.

Myrna turned to Perry Pierce and asked calmly, "Shall we go on the pier now?"

Then I heard a very soft descending scale of laughter, a woman's laughter, it sounded disembodied at first and might have been coming from the sky, which definitely fazed me. I looked around, and traced it to somewhere nearer the earth—the balcony, in fact. Three people were getting to their feet up there, in a moment they'd disappeared, it was too far away and dark to know who they were.

For some reason I felt quite nervous. "Who was that? Who was that up there?" People came up to me looking shaken but thrilled, murmuring "Greater than ever," etc., I kissed them all and said to Perry Pierce, "Why don't you put Myrna on the Big Wheel or something? I'm going to rest up until the performance."

Daylight almost blinded me as I left the theater, clouds had sailed away on a breeze, it was like curtain going up on a clear bright sky. Extras poured onto the boardwalk wearing bright colors, as if they'd been waiting a whole winter for sun, I really felt I'd stepped into a production number that was about to begin. As I walked back to my hotel I glanced at faces that maybe I'd see again at my opening tonight, tried to look through them *into their lives*, as you might say, and find something I could recognize and touch—but it didn't work. There was nothing at all between us, and with a sudden ache of fatigue I thought maybe there never will be, except when I sing, and in the end that's why I have to.

The first thing I saw when I got back to my room was a huge bouquet of flowers on the table. A white envelope was stuck between two yellow lilies. I didn't open it at first, but made myself a drink. Then it occurred to me there might be a connection between the flowers and the people in the balcony at the theater, and the same little shiver ran through me again. I opened the envolep and found a note—

Welcome Back! Ray and Melora.

As I stared at it, the phone rang. I knew at once who it had to be, and was disgusted at the commotion inside myself. You'd think more than enough water had flowed over the dam, and yet, as some people never get over a fear of heights or break out in a rash if they eat onions, etc., the thought of Mr. Swan still brought back the idea of a thumb pressing on my neck. I decided not to answer, and poured myself another drink.

Two minutes later the phone rang again. "What the hell," I said out loud now, "they'll get you anyway," and picked up the receiver.

"Daisy?"

"Hello, Melora. Thank you for the flowers."

"I hope I'm not disturbing you, honey, but I couldn't wait to hear your voice." She explained very smoothly about happening to be in New York this week and reading in the papers that I had this engagement in Atlantic City. "It was quite mean of you not to let us know. But now I've heard your voice, I just have to see you right away. Come over, won't you, and have a drink with us?"

She always had this knack, I thought, of making me feel as if nothing had ever happened. If I met Melora by genuine coincidence for the first time in thirty years, having lunch on top of Mount Everest, she'd look up and say, "Hello, honey, I was just going down to call you."

"Okay. Just a quick one though, because I want to go to sleep."

"We're in Suite 306."

"My God, you're right next door."

She laughed.

It wasn't until I pressed the bell that I remembered I'd taken off my shoes, and was standing barefoot as the door opened. Melora was hugging me before I could even get a real look at her, then as she stepped back I saw she was wearing tight green pants and hadn't aged a day. I recognized a chunky bracelet on her wrist.

Mr. Swan wasn't there. The suite looked exactly like mine, and yet different. Melora had filled it with flowers—lilies, stocks, blue asters, all the kinds that made me think of California—and had turned the top of a chest into a bar. At least a dozen bottles stood there, including the Scotch with the gold stopper. A copy of *Variety* lay on the couch, also some scripts, and book matches with MAGNAGRAM printed on them.

"Your hair's cute," Melora said. "It looks so natural."

"It is."

She seemed surprised. "That's what I heard, but I never believed it. What's your drink, honey? Still vermouth on the rocks?"

"What a memory, Melora."

She swept up *Variety* and the scripts—"We've hardly unpacked, I'm sorry it's such a slum"—and went to the bar. The bedroom door opened and Mr. Swan came in. My first reaction was that King Stag looked as if he'd lost a battle or two, not to mention about 15 lbs. His face was less tanned and his eyes had a kind of deadness, unless he was just sleepy.

"Well, Daisy." He sounded dry. "How does it feel?" Then, before I could answer, "If they tell you the house doesn't look sold out when the curtain goes up tonight, it'll be on account of people not wanting to sit through two hours of lousy vaudeville before you come on."

I shook my head. "Down here it's a local crowd, Mr. Swan. Faceless urban types, you know. I'm being very sneaky till I get the feel of things again."

"You've learned nothing." Maybe he'd lost those battles, but

[235]

King Stag was still ready to lock a mean old antler. "I think you'll recognize quite a few faces out there. The real pros in this business don't forget."

"I had the impression from my Personal Manager that almost everyone had forgotten."

Mr. Swan poured himself a shot of his favorite Scotch. "You've signed yourself up with some horse dealer? Is that what you've done?"

"Now shut up," Melora said quite rudely. I'd never heard her speak that way to him in the past. "But apologize first."

"I'm pretty sore about it." He grinned, a hint of light showed in his eyes. "This little genius I spent a great deal of money to introduce to the world—I hope you'll agree I did that, Daisy—goes off and leaves me, not a peep out of her for more than five years, then she turns up out here with jugglers and animal acts. No taste at all."

"He's got a point, honey, it's always risky to downgrade yourself." Melora put her hand on my shoulder. "But you're going to be so great, it doesn't matter. We both know you'll be up there again."

"You were in the theater this afternoon," I said. "Who else was with you?"

"No one." She stared at me. "Just the two of us."

"I'm not ashamed to admit there were tears in my eyes," Mr. Swan said. "But only partly on account of the way you sang. I also wept to see you in such vulgar surroundings. Then Melora reminded me that the first time I ever heard your voice was on a twenty-five-cent record, and I cried then, and made you a star, and it could happen again." He turned away. "I'm going to lie down for a while."

"That's a good idea," Melora said.

He went back to the bedroom.

"Ray has to take it easy." Melora stood by the window, gazing out at the ocean. Her arms gave that birdlike stretch. "He had two heart attacks last year, and after the second one, honey, he literally hovered between life and death. Did you know that when death might be going to take you, it's the time you ask yourself questions?"

"I honestly hadn't thought about it. What kind of questions?"

She shrugged. *"Have I lived for the right things? Were my values worth anything at all? Will I go out with meaning?"*

"Mr. Swan asked himself all that? What did he decide?"

"I watched him," Melora said. "He didn't speak, but I knew he was on the rack. Afterwards he told me he felt like a man drowning, his whole life passed in front of his eyes. He weighed himself in the balance, without tilting the scales, and he found himself not wanting. For two days he wrestled with the inner man, and came to the conclusion he had a great deal to be proud of. Especially what he did for *you.*"

"Well, that's great. Listen, Melora, I'm going to lie down for a while too, but before I do, are you sure there wasn't someone else with you in the balcony?"

She didn't answer at once, but looked quickly away from me, glanced at the bedroom door, which was closed, then sat on the couch and leaned her head back, as if she felt exhausted. "It was Ridge Banner. I wish you hadn't seen us."

"Why?"

She got up again suddenly and went back to the window.

"What's going on?" I said. "I don't understand why Ridge should come."

Melora turned and looked at me for the first time since she'd mentioned his name. She had a peculiar crooked smile, the tip of her tongue crept between her teeth.

"Oh," I said finally. "Maybe now I do. Yes, I guess I definitely do. So how's he making out, Melora?"

"Honey, you know that story."

"Yes. I hear you also struck oil."

She nodded. "It's tided us over difficult days, but the place looks awful. Half our back lot's razed to the ground. It's like a desert. Like a ghost town. Especially when the TV cowboys walk through. So you're not the only one ending up where you started. Which reminds me—here's to you. Here's to a wonderful marvelous night." She raised her glass, found it empty, and went to the bar. "All the luck in the world, anyway. One more for you too?"

"Not a drop. I really have to go and lie down, but before I do, is Ridge also staying in this hotel?"

"Suite 302." She was putting ice in her glass. "Right the other side of you."

"He'd better remain incognito as far as Myrna's concerned." I was starting to feel weak. "She's gotten along very well without a father, and right now she'd find this particular situation extremely confusing, even though she's a bright kid. It's not simple for me, either."

"I really am sorry about it," Melora told me. "Ridge wants to see *you*, of course, but I'd planned for you not to know he was here until you'd sung. I hoped to keep you clear of personal problems."

"Melora, you are truly amazing. You come here with Ridge and plan to keep me clear of personal problems. That's pretty deep."

"But I need him," she said in a low astonished voice. "I won't go anywhere without him now. These last two years with Ray, they've been the hardest of my life, and I couldn't have borne them alone. When things start to fall away, you know, I mean really *solid* things just seem to break up, it's . . . Oh, honey! I just can't be alone with Ray any more, you know what I mean? I won't leave him, there's still too much going for us, so you see all I'm doing is trying to *hang* on. That's all I'm doing—" Her voice went up rather wildly, she checked herself and gave another glance at the bedroom door. I stared at her with a kind of stupid amazement, but she didn't seem to notice. In fact, her poise came back as if she'd pressed a secret button, and she flashed me a smile. "Fancy boring you with all that. Ray never mentioned that script, did he? I guess he was tired." She rummaged in the pile and thrust something with a red binder in my hands. "We're sadder and wiser people, aren't we, but not too sad and wise enough to know a cute thing when we see it."

And she kissed me.

I couldn't think of anything to say. I just left the script on a table and went to the door. As I opened it, I turned back and looked at her. She was gazing calmly out of the window again.

"Melora, I'm going to lie down, but before I do there's one

[238]

last thing I have to ask you. For some reason it's slipped my mind until now. At the time I married Wade Lewis by your pool in Beverly Hills, was your father still alive in Stumpville?"

Her face went blank. "I haven't the faintest idea. I certainly hope not."

Back in my room I drew the blinds, took off everything, got into bed, and had instant insomnia. Worse than that, a kind of nausea seemed to be wriggling its way like a cold snake from my stomach toward my throat. It reminded me of the day I had to do that number I didn't like in *Song and Dance*. I lay twitching in the dark for a while, then decided to have a drink, got up and took three, which made five counting the one after rehearsal and the other with the Swans. This may sound extreme, but remember that what always throws me is the idea I'm surrounded by people waiting to Take Over. Right now *I wished to God the people on both sides of me would go away*. There are certain days, like the time I took a flask of martinis on the beach, when I shouldn't drink. It gets me in a really black mood and I can only imagine the worst happening, like Ridge meeting Myrna in the elevator, the Taking Over crowd grinning at me from the orchestra, Mr. Swan having a heart attack in the middle of "Yesterdays," etc. Morbid? Okay, but what do you do when after more than five years you've come to the point of getting yourself on the road again, feeling emotions you can put across, ready to experience what Perry Pierce calls the substitute orgasm—when the hearts out there are beating in time with your own, which is the next best thing to perfect sex, which for some reason doesn't come often—what do you do, that's my question, when the moment you've been waiting for starts to *fall away* like Melora's world?

The answer is, you take another drink, and tell yourself to be rational. What are you afraid of? That's where the trouble starts again, because it's like licking your finger, holding it up to the wind, and learning that a storm is on the way. A sky that looked blue is already clouding over, light's turning gray, nasty dark stuff piling up on the horizon. That's how I felt sitting in this hotel room with the Swans to the left of me and Ridge to the right, and being expected to go out and give love, be poignant, or laugh in spite of it all. An old pro would give you the show-must-go-on line, but it doesn't work if you stop and ask why. A couple more drinks and I definitely wouldn't be *able* to go on, so I took them and felt almost calm in a desperate way.

When the phone rang I didn't answer it. There was no one I felt like talking to, not even Perry Pierce or Myrna. It rang again, and I picked up the receiver with the intention of saying Stick It, but it was the clerk at the desk downstairs telling me the hairdresser was ready to come up. With a shock I discovered it was past five o'clock, time to start getting into shape, and I was so confused that I forgot I'd decided not to go on, I said, "Tell her to wait, I'll call you back," pulled up the blinds, and took a look at myself in the mirror. I'd also forgotten I was naked, which was another shock. I couldn't walk straight, my eyes were on fire, anything I touched I somehow couldn't hold on to, so I sat on the bed and imagined a headline—CLOVER CROCKED!—and the phone rang again. With an idea of making coffee I stumbled to the kitchenette, put the grounds in the percolator and the percolator on the stove, but turned the wrong dial and an awful smell began to give out. I stood sniffing the gas, then turned off the dial and opened the oven door for a look-see. It was a rotten little place, not built for a head at all, but it could do the trick. I realized now I didn't want anyone coming up and finding me a stupid panicked mess but alive, it had happened before and could get monotonous. Better Clover gassed than Clover crocked, I thought, and actually started to laugh in a very unhealthy way at the whole idea.

I should explain that I wasn't thinking of suicide primarily as a way of killing myself. That's *banal*, honey, you need a more positive reason, and mine was, Better the hell you don't know than the one you do. I once heard a joke about this famous movie producer who dies and goes to heaven, St. Peter welcomes him at the gate and says, God wants you to produce a movie. The producer complains that he's tired, in fact he just died from overwork, and St. Peter says I know, but God really does need *you* for this movie, please do Him a favor, and tempts the producer with the names of all the wonderful dead directors, writers, and movie stars at his disposal. Now the producer gets interested, he realizes it could be the chance of a lifetime. Okay, he says, he'd like to set up a few meetings. St. Peter tells him the productions can be absolutely independent, no front office, but there's just one thing he should know about—God has this little Angel. . . . Well, of course, a joke like this is really saying Heaven is Hell, so what the Hell, and more than likely it has a grain of truth. So if there's any way of letting the folks I leave behind know what the pressures are like up there, I'll certainly get back to them. Don't call me, though, I'll call *you*.

As for boring practical details, I wondered whether to leave a note for anybody, I was slightly worried at the idea of sending Myrna out on her own a couple of years earlier than I'd planned —but I couldn't think of anything to say. Besides, when they find my Theme Books, they'll realize I've already written the longest suicide note in the world.

I drew the blinds again, switched on the radio and the gas, then made my way cautiously, as they say, into the oven. The smell was disgusting, I wasn't sure if I could stand it, but even worse was having so little space in this darned kitchenette, I got a crick in my neck and the floor ground into my bare knees. I backed out, switched off, zigzagged into the bedroom, tried another station on the radio because a number I never particularly cared for, "Try a Little Tenderness," was coming out, found a cushion for my knees, folded my jeans to make a little pillow for my head, switched on, got back inside and started to relax. I closed my eyes and quite distinctly heard Wade's voice saying, "The hounds *are* after you, dear heart, you know," then the phone rang again.

My first reaction of course was not to answer, but I was afraid it might be Perry Pierce saying he'd got back from the pier with Myrna, and he'd probably come up anyway, and naturally I didn't want either of them to find me like this. I felt shaky now but my mind was ticking over surprisingly well, I got back to the phone and picked up the receiver. However, it was the desk clerk again, to tell me the hairdresser was still waiting. "I'm sorry I need another five minutes," I said, "then she can come straight up and I'll be ready for her." It seemed a long time before I was making myself comfortable again, resting my head on my blue twill pillow, and even longer before I realized that although I was weak and dozy, I didn't seem to be getting any worse. Would you believe it, with all the constant interruptions I'd forgotten to switch on the gas this time. As I groped for the dial, I began to sniff another element in the air, stronger and more appealing. It fazed me for a moment, then I remembered I'd left the coffee percolator on top of the stove. Now it was boiling and spilled out a rich burnt-coffee aroma, something I've never been able to resist, it's exactly like life, because I always fall for the wonderful smell even though I know the taste will be ghastly and bitter.

Okle-dokle. I opened all the windows and found it was raining again in the hell I knew. Deep breathing helped, but I was afraid my energy was definitely low, so I called Perry Pierce and said he had to find me a pill. While the hairdresser went to work, I drank all the coffee and promised her I couldn't smell anything odd. Then I filtered myself into this dress which was designed for me by another of Perry Pierce's friends, and if you want the truth it's a shocking-pink afternoon-length outfit, I'm not exactly sure what it does for me. However, considering that I was full of liquor, gas, burnt coffee, and doped to the gills, I'd say I never looked better. I'd brought my shell with me, and picked it up just to hear if the waves had anything special to say. They sounded rather tired at first, but when I closed my eyes the murmur came a little nearer, and you could almost mistake it for applause.

The real applause that night you could have mistaken for ten thousand oceans pounding on the shore. The first wave broke as I walked to the center of the stage, and the spotlight, which was apparently expecting me to enter from the other side, caught up and held me there. There were gasps and murmurs like the tide being sucked back, then the whole place thundered. Somehow I'd managed to radiate even before I went into my opening number. The last wave, after I'd sung half an hour longer than

I was supposed to, was definitely tidal. I swept out to the wings on its backwash, blowing kisses all the way, then collapsed halfway up the narrow iron stairway leading to my dressing room. I lay against the cold metal balustrade, perspiration drenched my shocking pink, and one of my shoes fell off, clattering between the rungs to the floor below. I let the other one go as well. I guess I took forty winks, because the next thing I remember is a cat's concert of voices, and Perry Pierce saying excitedly, "Now just a moment, everybody, please! She *seems* to be asleep up there, no of course she's not dead or sick or anything, she's just getting her breath back, wouldn't *you?*" I looked down and saw a crowd of people at the foot of the stairway, with Perry Pierce gallantly barring the way up. It was fairly dark, I couldn't make out faces.

"The whole world's waiting to see you!" P.P. called. "Are you ready?"

"Oh, send it up," I said. "I'm too tired not to see anyone."

Now I'd been warned by Mr. Swan that the Taking Over crowd had sent representatives tonight, and it knocked me for a row of Chinese pagodas, but if I'd known *before* the performance exactly who was out there, I honestly believe that not even the smell of coffee would have stopped me turning on the gas again. I didn't get up, but let them come to me. "Do you have a cigarette?" I asked as the first figure stepped out of shadow—and, would you believe it, my ex-husband Mr. Wade Lewis took a pack from his pocket and offered it to me.

He looked better than I'd ever seen him, not quite sober, but a kind of new brightness in those dark warm fatal eyes. Right behind him, a cute fellow with curly reddish hair held out a lighter.

"This is Malcolm," said my ex-husband, and kissed me.

"I adored you in the movies, but tonight was greater than all of them." Malcolm gave my hand a strong, you might say brotherly squeeze. "And it's wonderful to meet you at last, Wade told me so much about you."

Before I could answer, my ex-husband was saying he was proud of me, then Malcolm explained how they'd been in New York for a month and planned to go back to Tangier yesterday, but stayed over to catch my show. Also, if I ever found myself in Tangier, I could be a guest at their hotel for as long as I liked.

There was no time to do anything except stare at their faces and realize they weren't kidding—because a large false mouth suddenly brushed my cheek, a voice cried "Baby, for God's sake give your sister a big hello!" and there was Gloria in bottle-green linen.

"I can't bear it!" I said.

She stepped right over me, then squatted on the stair above and gave me a hug from behind. "Did you think we could keep away? We'd never have forgiven ourselves if we'd missed the greatest moment of your life!" And up came bony Harry, "Kid, it's so good to see you back on the track," and now the iron stair was chilling my ass, and I had to get up anyway to take stock of this entire situation. It was certainly a busy flight of steps, with Gloria and Harry above me like king and queen of the mountain, Wade, Malcolm, and P.P. all laughing together, the Swans and Holbrook Masters Productions deep in conversation, you could tell they'd sniffed each other out like dogs that hunt in the same pack and were already talking business—and finally, elbowing his way through, very tall and broad-shouldered in an expensive suit, Ridge Banner at my side, looking into my eyes just as if they were a mirror, his hand with a silver bracelet tilting my chin. I smiled, turned away to avoid being kissed, but couldn't escape his happy crack about Daisy Clover being the girl who once told him she'd never go back to work because bringing up a child was a full-time occupation.

It wasn't funny, but it made me laugh. I laughed so much that everyone stopped talking and became quite nervous. Even after coming all this way and congratulating me on my triumph, etc., they were still frightened I might flip my lid. "Oh, it's nothing!" I told them. "Emotional release, that's all. It's been quite a night." They agreed, and began exclaiming all over again how they'd never forget it. "My dearest darlings," I said, "I would love to go out and have a drink with you all, and talk about old times until dawn comes up, but I'm afraid I have a previous engagement in Sleepville. You'll forgive, won't you? You'll

understand, won't you? You always did, didn't you?" I blew
kisses, Ridge suggested we all get together for breakfast, I
thought that sounded fantabulous but warned them I might
sleep till they had to catch their trains, and escaped to my
dressing room.

A few minutes later, Perry Pierce called through the door,
"They've all gone, honey! Shall I wait for you?"

"Not tonight, P.P. You go on home too. I'll see you in the
morning."

I heard his feet echo down the iron stairway. A door slammed,
and I was snugly alone in my dressing room, which suddenly
reminded me of the trailer in Playa del Rey, it was just as small
and crummy. This made me think about The Dealer, and wonder why I'd always felt she was a kind of genius. I realized it was
because she had the best answer in the world to bad dreams and
craziness and the nerve of practically everybody. She shook her
head when she meant yes, nodded when she meant no, and
laughed when she wanted everybody to go to hell. So I laughed
now, harder and harder, until I was completely exhausted and
had a pain in my belly. Then I hummed a snatch of "I've Got
the World on a String," walked through the big dark empty
theater, and came out on the boardwalk. Beautiful silence, except for the ocean. I decided to walk home along the beach and
maybe laugh some more, loud enough for the sound to break
(like those waves) on the other side of the world.